Justice Served

A novel of the Embellish saga

By

R. L. Sloan

Justice Served[rvs]

A novel of the Embellish saga

R. L. Sloan

Harrison House Publishing
San Antonio, Texas

This is a work of fiction. The events and characters described herein are imaginary and are not intended to refer to
specific places or living persons. The opinions expressed in this manuscript are solely the opinions of the author
in addition, do not represent the opinions or thoughts of the publisher. The author has represented and warranted full ownership and/or legal right to publish all the materials in this book.

Justice Served: A novel of the Embellish Saga

v2.0

Edited by J Halley Alexander, Genesis Productions©

Cover Art designed by Javan Alexander

PUBLISHER'S NOTE

Harrison House Publishing
HarrisonHousepublishing@hotmail.com
Paperback ISBN: 978-0-578-06314-0
Library of Congress Control Number: 2010910728
Harrison House Publishing and the "HHP" logo are trademarks belonging to Harrison House Publishing.
PRINTED IN THE UNITED STATES OF AMERICA

For Bear…who now hibernates until the home-going spring comes.

ACKNOWLEDGEMENTS

This book dedication is to my family and all those who have loved me through its process. A very special Thank You to our Father and Savior: Thank You, Lord, for being my savior. I would also like to give a special Thank You to all the folks that have now become fans of the Embellish Saga. Thank you so much. May God bless and keep you all.

GLOSSARY

The decedents:

Basira (Ba'seer'a) Caraway --- deceased vampire twin to Basrick Caraway. Basira was poisoned with Colloidal Silver by Justice Treemount

Mathis Bouvier (Boo'vee' ay) --- deceased detective of the San Antonio Police Department; hexed love interest of Childress Treemount.

Olvignia (Ol'veen'ia) Henderson --- deceased grandmother to Solis Burkes. Olvignia was killed in an explosion at her home, initiated by Childress, Klein, and Erland Treemount

Leonine Henderson --- deceased grandfather to Solis Burkes; husband to Olvignia Henderson

Lisa Henderson --- deceased mother to Solis Burkes; death occurred for Lindsey at the age of 29 years old, with mysterious circumstances surrounding her death

Frances Treemount --- deceased mother to Childress, Klein, Justice, and Erland Treemount

The living:

Bureau (Bu'row)Treemount La Deaux (La'Doe) --- Mambo of Dogwater Swamp; Aunt to Childress, Klein, Justice, and Erland Treemount; Sister to Frances Treemount

Urgata (Ur'gata) --- daughter of Bureau

Solis (So'leesz) Burkes --- raped by Klein Treemount as a child; survivor; mortal enemy of the Treemount Clan

Nacio (Na'see'o) Puente aka Nacio Galvazio De Puente --- vampire, ex-slave from the Middle Passage, Canary Islander; Owner of Puente Masonry

Bose (Bosz pronounced with a long "O") Puente --- Vampire kinship brother to Nacio; caretaker of the Puente Mansion

Armando Caraway --- European vampire, friend to Nacio and Solis; lives within the Puente Mansion; husband to Patience Caraway, father to Basrick and Barsira

Patience Caraway --- European vampire, friend to Nacio and Solis; wife to Armando Caraway; mother to Basrick and Basira

Basrick (Baz'rick) Caraway --- surviving vampire twin to Basira

Nayphous (Nay'fuss) Aljeneau (Al'jen'o) --- Fiancé to Urgata; eye candy to Childress Treemount

Chase Henderson --- uncle to Solis Burkes; victim of the Treemounts

Priestess Auldicia (All'dee'see'a) --- Powerful African Voodoo Priestess Vampire; whereabouts Unknown; believed to be dead; ancestor to the Treemounts; demon possessed.

Tahiti --- Daughter of Bureau; tramp, gold digger

Nuke Henderson --- Owner of the Laurence Funeral Home and Sunset Services and other conglomerate assets.

1

Thick and Thirsty

The ground seemed to shake Justice from a coma like slumber. Confusion cloaked his mind, as he fought internally for an explanation for the painful itch that irritated his nerve impulses. Blue veins squirmed beneath his paper-thin skin.

Why is my body so sore? He thought. *I don't understand what all the pain is from. I have come down from being high before, but my flesh is missing and my head feels like worms are crawling around inside. It hurts. It hurts. This is intense. I've tried rubbing my arms, but nothing I do seems to help the pain go away.*

If I could just stop shaking maybe that would help, but I can't control my muscles. Hell, I don't even have muscles anymore from the looks of it. I wish I had a joint or some alcohol --- it would help me get my head together. Damn, I don't know what time it is or where I am.

I want to see Basira. I need to find her. I've never met or felt this way about anyone until I laid eyes on her. I'm going to go find my sweetheart and when I do, we're going to make love again", he secretly thought, becoming aroused remembering the moment when he first entered her.

Holding her is like holding an angel. He tried to rationalize through mangled thoughts, but found it difficult.

Her eyes are turquoise blue, and her hips are full and round. Her lips taste like strawberry wine—satisfying my thirst. I'm aching to feel that pleasure once more.

"I'm going to get my lady now," he uttered as he jumped to his bare feet, still confused. Not knowing which direction to travel in to find the object of his heart's desire, and not caring which direction he chose, he began his quest. Nothing mattered, because he knew he would find her.

Every step he took in anticipation of finding her was faster than the other, in hopes of finding her soon --- he called her name.

"Basira...I have to find you."

Anxiety soon settled in, slowing him instantly. Answers to questions he did not want to ask himself forced him to acknowledge the reality that came crashing down on him. If there was ever a time he wished to undo the past, that time was upon him now. The final kiss of their last encounter came rushing back to him with the force of a tidal wave --- deception sealed his beloved's fate.

"Dammit, what did I do? Why did I do it? How could I have ended her life?" Justice assumed the worst and knew that he would never see the beautiful young vampire that he fell in love with at first sight.

"I mixed Colloidal Silver in a bottle of wine that I had tricked Basira into drinking after we made love. That shit killed her I know it did, it must have because she would have been here with me now. Now I'm all alone. I'm aching and in pain.

I'm thirsty, so very thirsty."

Wallowing in sorrow, Justice continued to shout his regret to the stars above.

"Baby, I'm sorry. I'm so very, very sorry, Basira. I loved you, oh how I loved you."

Recalling his last visit with her, he remembered spiking the wine he gave Basira with Colloidal Silver upon the request of his hateful sister, Childress. For vampires Colloidal Silver is a destructive poison, bringing the vampires return from the dead to an end. Having enough sense to figure out how to kill vampires from her book of spells, Childress threatened everlasting harm to Justice if he did not kill Basira.

Gnashing his teeth in rage, he came to his own conclusion about what to do about his deceitful sister.

"Childress, you BITCH. You knew I loved her, but you hated that I might take advice from someone besides you. You could not stand the fact that some other woman might love me and that I might listen to her rather than you."

It was nightfall, and he continued to huddle underneath a bridge. A drainage pipe near the San Antonio River had become his only sanctuary from the elements as his body continued to slough the flesh from his extremities. Having shelter was necessary, but it would have to be a second priority for what currently ailed him.

The dry ache that lingered in his throat was a painful reminder of what he had become, and how his existence had drastically changed.

"I can't stand the dry burning in my throat. It's driving me insane."

He checked his pockets and found he had a few dollars

in them. Allowing his thirst to lead him, he started a quickened pace across a trail in a meadow that led to a convenience store at a busy intersection.

Coming down the trail up ahead, he took notice of an inebriated young woman. A set of dilapidated apartments stood on the opposite side of the meadow. Missing grass indicated a frequently used path by apartment residents. Staggering and off balance, the woman clutched a forty ounce malt liquor bottle. His eyes held strong to the bottle, while he made a futile effort to moisten his chafed, pasty lips.

At a glimpse, the young woman looked to be a tender 21 years old, clad in a miniskirt that barely covered her hips, accented with a tissue thin halter-top. The arid inflammation in his throat reminded him just how long it had been since he had anything to drink; and his arousal was not too far off from earlier thoughts of Basira.

"Hey, sweetheart, what's your name?"

Startled, the young woman stopped in her tracks and squinted at Justice. She extended her arms towards him.

"You want a sip of my beer?"

Careful not to make any sudden moves as his eyes studied her, she glared at him and contemplated a hasty retreat from the danger she felt. A wispy-looking blonde mustache attached to pale white skin, hung stretched across porous bones. Crusty eyes sat in the sockets of a skull that was absent of his curly blondish locks --- leaving him completely bald. Justice whispered a confirmation in a heavy seductive voice he did not recognize as his own.

"Yes, please, I would like a taste of beer if you don't mind?"

Slowly raising her arm, she motioned for him to take the bottle. Acknowledging her gesture, he walked toward the young woman and secured the bottle in his grasp. Catching her off guard, Justice embraced the young woman. Following his mind splitting thirst, he lowered his fangs -- plunging them into a warm spot on her neck that beckoned him. Overcome with gluttony, he drank savagely as the thirst-quenching blood plasma revived him.

Drinking deeply, the pain began to stop.

Licking and slurping were the only sounds that echoed across the meadow, as the young woman lay limp across his chest. Screaming was not an option. Breath left her lungs as her eyes bulged --- expressing horror as death mounted her face. As with any new vampire, Justice did not fully understand what was happening to him.

"Oh father, what did I just do? I just murdered a young woman who had no idea that this was her last night on earth."

Completely drained of her life force, Justice dropped the young unidentified woman on the ground with a dull thud. His appetite was completely satiated, and he was once again on the rocket high he had first experienced with Basira. This feeding was ecstasy and exhilaration all at the same time. His fangs hung in full view, as he wiped his mouth with the back of his hand. Having just fed, he looked as if he had just come out of a microwave.

Flesh was beginning to return to his arms to cover the blue veins that hung like cobwebs on him. Creole heritage gave him very fair skin. Realizing he was a vampire, he was accustomed to a fair complexion. His mustache seemed to have shortened in the last few moments. Perhaps he would get some of his great looks back that he remembered having. Although he hadn't seen himself since the changes took place, he knew having flesh fall from his arms and the rest of his body was a bad thing.

Most vampires have the allure of seduction, making it easy to entice their victims to their death. In his case, Justice was evil prior to his change, and therefore his inner soul was finally showing its true evil outwardly. The young woman whom he'd just murdered was not the first life he had taken, nor would it be the last. Spawned from an evil bloodline, for years he had lured women with his looks. Now he would repulse them as soon as they laid eyes on him. The blood he took from his unidentified victim somehow regenerated his body, giving him a little more strength as his mind continued to race.

My eyesight is sharp now. Wow, all that from a little blood? Damn! Justice thought to himself. *Is that a bird's nest down the street? I can actually see a bird's nest and the birds sleeping. Aw, look at their little heads. I can see them breathing. I wonder what it would be like to squeeze their necks. I bet it would sound like stapling papers with a stapler. Is that a...a train whistle blowing? Hot damn, I can hear at least a quarter of a mile away!*

Realizing this made him remember his train of thought. He knew he had to return home. Stepping over the young woman's body in the grassy meadow, he put one foot in front of the other faster and faster until he was running. As the wind whipped all around his thin flesh, he ran faster and faster until he blurred within the night shadows. Running helped him clear the brain fog coalescing in his head. His sense of smell allowed him to remember where he lived, and he headed there with all speed. Even though he was a mile away, the closer he came to his neighborhood, his nostrils filled with the familiar scent of his home environment.

Familiar street signs came into view while passing through the neighborhood where Childress's old crime hustling friend Believa Beaushanks lived. She and Childress pulled a purse theft heist, stealing purses at every mall outlet in the San Antonio and Austin area.

There's Believa's house. Childress thought Believa had snitched on her, sending her to the state Penitentiary. I don't know what the true story was, but I've always had a crush on Believa since we were kids. Oh, I can smell her, she smells so sweet to me.

The scent of her spicy blood slows him to a mere jog. He positioned himself to spy outside her bathroom window, as she rose from the bathtub -- curtained in a veil of transparent bubbles. Continuing his reconnaissance, Justice took note of how supple her breasts appeared. Believa's curvaceous cocoa figure sent shock-waves of arousal through him.

"Damn, I sure want to taste those," he said as his eyes glanced at her breasts. "I am thirsty again. I know Believa will help me."

Her curly hair was stacked in a heavy loosely cascading bun on her head. His physical needs were once again controlling his actions. Within the blink of an eye, Justice had found his way inside her house through the back door that was unlocked. Being a thief herself, she was never a fan of home security, and never locked her doors. Even as a kid, her house was always as busy as a bus depot with folks coming and going. He made his way into the bathroom, as steam poured out. Slithering up behind her as she stepped out of the tub to dry her wet body he, whispered her name.

"Believa, I need you, don't be afraid."

Believa screamed, jumping at the sight and sound of her uninvited guest. He prowled towards her slowly at first, and then more desperately.

"Who are you? Please don't hurt me!" The baldhead and long wispy mustache was enough to send anyone who saw him screaming into the night.

"It's me baby, it's Justice!" He tried to comfort the beautiful young woman, but nothing he did could put her fears at ease.

Unsuccessfully, she attempted a dash for the door, but when she turned to run in the opposite direction, there he stood before her once more.

"Please don't hurt me!"

Pleading for her life as her towel fell away from her body, she held up her hands and surrendered to her unannounced acquaintance.

"What happened to you?"

"I won't hurt you, I promise."

The towel that shrouded the young woman's body fell to the floor, allowing his eyes to take in her beautifully proportioned petite frame.

For someone who knew no boundaries, nor self-control, he reached out and took her naked wetness in his arms. Running his tongue down the warm pulsating vein in her neck, he sniffed her. Opening his mouth wide, he began to feed greedily. Believa cooed with each touch, as her muscles became flaccid. Justice rushed her to the nearest surface, which happen to be the bathroom vanity. He placed her beneath him, and she obliged him by submitting, completely. When their bodies connected, she experienced a level of intimacy unlike any other, nor with any other.

"That feels so good, please don't stop."

Initially there was pain, but she soon found herself placing her hand on the back of his neck, holding it in place. Responding to his movement, catching every wave of his passion; their desire filled the night air with a melodic cacophony of moans and whispers.

***

After satisfying his desire, Justice lay motionless next to Believa and watched her as she slept.

"You are so sexy, and you have satisfied me."

Passion lingered, as he flicked his tongue along her lips. Her deep brown skin had taken on a gray ash looking pallor after he fed from her. Using his finger, he held it just underneath her nose to make certain that she was breathing. After confirming that she was still alive, he rolled over on his back and stared up at the ceiling.

Being in this room brings back so many memories, he thought. *I, Childress, Klein, and Erland would play kickball here with Believa.*

Justice had been the youngest of Frances Treemount's children for a very long time; until Erland was born, taking away his rightful place as the youngest child in the home.

Dammit, I hated my childhood and my mama. I

shouldn't say that. I loved my mama, but I hated that bitch too.

As an infant, Justice remembered his mother Frances never held or kissed him. He remembered lying in his crib some days with hunger pangs so strong, that it felt as if his stomach were a wet towel --- twisting to wring out the water.

She hated me too. I remember crying myself to sleep from being scared from all the damn screaming and fighting that she and whatever asshole she was with would do. I hated childhood. Whenever I reached for mama to pick me up, she would push my little arms away from her, ignoring me — leaving me to take care of myself.

"Move you little bastard!" she would say to me. "You look and act just like your sorry nothing-ass daddy, you hear me?"

Man, as I grew up, I tried to steer clear of mama's hatefulness and mean ways. Even though it was four of us kids, I was always by myself, and lonely. Days would come and go, and I'd find myself playing with animals. They made me feel like I had some control over them. I liked playing with cats. I liked the feel of a little kitten's fur. Cats were soft and warm, and felt good to touch.

"Come here little kitty, kitty, kitty," I would say to the cat.

When it came to me, it would curl up in my arms. I would stroke the cat's tail slowly, steadily, slowly...and then yank the cat's tail. Man, that cat would hunch his back. That was too funny to see.

Then the bastard would scratch me. I'd catch his ass later and punish him good. Oh yes, I would. Killing cats was a sportsman game of choice. I liked this because I could control them -- hell someone had been controlling me all through childhood.

Justice continued to reminisce about one hot summer day when his mother had just finished cleaning scales off some catfish that Childress had caught outback in a swamp. His Aunt Bureau, his mother's sister, lived at the edge of Dog water Swamp. The phone rang and his mother went to answer it in the living room, leaving a skillet full of hot fish grease on the stove. A mangy looking brown cat walked up on the back porch, and meowed from the smell of the fresh fish on the counter.

"Meow, meow, meow," the cat pleaded to Justice to be let in the house to eat the fish.

Angry and annoyed, Justice looked at the cat through the screen door. He then grabbed the handle of the hot skillet and flung the hot fish grease out the back door on the cat. Scalded to a crisp, the cat looked like a wet brown Ping Pong ball, bouncing from rock, to ground, and finally to treetop in pain and in search of shelter. Justice let out a sidesplitting laugh, causing a furious Frances Treemount to come in and backhand him across his jaw; this sent him flying sideways into the kitchen pantry door.

"Why the hell did you waste my damn grease? Clean this mess up now!"

Justice gathered his wits about him, and did just as his mother said --- even physical punishment from his mother for misbehaving was better than not having any attention from her at all.

I hated when she would hit me like that, hell, she would never hit Childress like that, he thought to himself.

After she would hit me, hell, I'd go out and kick a cat or any other animal I could find. I didn't care what it was. I just wanted to punish the thing — it felt good to do that. What was even better was setting the dead animal on fire. Whoosh is the sound that fire would make. That's better than sex. Warmth near my skin feels good to me. I love me some matches. That's what I would play with as a little kid to start fires. I'd find matches lying around from when mama would smoke her cigarettes.

After reminiscing about the past, Justice jumped up and headed out the door a few blocks down to his house.

"I hate thinking about this shit. I need to get out of here for a minute."

He moved with ease and grace through the night like a gentle breeze. Only a few brief seconds had passed and he was at the front door of the home he and his siblings shared.

"I wonder what the hell happened in this house."

Crime scene tape stretched across the mauled screen door. He tore past the barrier and entered the house in astonishment at what he saw. A tornado could have been to blame, but he had good sense enough to know that his siblings had left in a hurry. The couch was overturned; the arm to the recliner chair broken, hanging helplessly by a mere piece of cloth. The air in the home had a rancid smell of rotting food in the refrigerator with an underlying hint of bleach. There was no electricity on in the home, but he could see just fine in the dark. He took a moment to piece together the situation at hand.

"Whatever went down was not good. I wonder, did they get busted? If they are on the run, I know they will probably head east to Aunt Bureau's house. I'll catch up to them later."

Childress and her brothers had obviously left, and more than likely were hiding out; the crime scene tape indicated that. No matter, he would track them down and catch them.

"I miss my sister. When I see her again, I am going to show her just how much. I have special plans for Childress. Her ways remind me so much of mama's hatefulness towards me."

Taking a few minutes to reflect upon his life was all he needed to sow the seed of vengeance towards his sister.

"Just the thought of how she would slap me around whenever she felt like it makes me resent her just as much as I did our mother."

With anger beginning to course through his veins, he found his way into the kitchen. Reaching for some oil on the stove, he doused it over the trashed furniture in the house. Circling for a moment to locate what he needed, he raced down the hall to the tiny bathroom. There underneath the sink in a cabinet, he found an aerosol air freshener.

"I'm going to burn this bastard to the ground."

With his sickened love for destruction, he lit the match --- making a flamethrower out of the air freshener, setting their home on fire. A few brief seconds past, then the entire frame of the house was set ablaze.

He walked through the kitchen and out the back door. Looking to take cover, he found a clearing in some bushes in the backyard and crouched down on the ground. Anxiously watching, he felt a sense of pride as the flames illuminated the night sky.

"Fire is so beautiful. It feels so warm to my cold

skin," he said watching hypnotically. Orange flames whipped wildly up towards the sky sending white smoke through the neighborhood. Entranced, he sat with the smile of a lunatic splashed across his face.

2
Piece It Together

I can't believe how out of control I feel. My emotions are raw. The loss of my grandparents is devastating. Waves of crying spells catch me off guard, and I have to try to deal with them when they do. No matter if I hide the tears; Nacio can still feel me when I drown in my sorrows. He's been so loving and patient with me, even when I don't feel I can return his affections. His love for me has been the highlight of my life for a while now. So many things have transpired since we met.

My childhood enemies have come back into my life to wreak havoc. Childress, Klein, Justice, and Erland Treemount held my Uncle Chase hostage and nearly blinded him. After that, they blew up my house and killed my grandparents. They also stood accused for several murders that had occurred during Fiesta at the Texas Taste Tease.

Childress and her hellion brothers were on the run now, trying to escape the impending doom that would someday catch up with them all. I keep thinking back to the night that earsplitting explosion rocked our quiet little neighborhood. The Treemounts blew up my house because they had figured out that they were being hunted and eliminated by Nacio and his friend Armando and his family.

Armando's daughter, Basira had fallen victim to Treemount treachery. Deliberately poisoned to death with Colloidal Silver --- somehow the stooge-like Treemounts had figured out that Silver was deadly to vampires.

More than likely, it was Childress who had figured out how to poison Basira. Childress resented her brother falling in love with Basira, because she had more control over Justice. I guess she felt that Basira would have been competition for her. She had tight control over her brothers, and Basira was interference.

The Treemounts were descendants of the evil Voodoo Priestess Auldicia. I finally had a taste of vengeance as Childress and I battled before the explosion. Her physical appearance had changed drastically since I had seen her at the Taste Tease. She looked as if she had taken a turn for the worst --- practicing evil black magic in hopes of punishing her enemies. She is truly twisted and psychotic.

She has jade green eyes, but the night we fought, her eyes were the color of crimson embers. Nacio explained that in the wrong hands black magic transforms a person into whatever the essence of their inner being happens to be. Childress had power and control over Voodoo magic, allowing her to cast spells. She was becoming stronger --- taking on the likeness of her ancestor Auldicia, making her more dangerous.

My own supernatural ability made me a formidable opponent for Childress. I discovered my gift of Telekinesis, allowing me to move objects at will. With this discovery, I also realized that I was still spiritually linked to my deceased mother. She had come to me in a dream, telling me how to defeat Childress, by using my own abilities and spiritual chants to subdue her. This was only temporary, because I went to care for the vampires and that's when she and her brothers got away.

After the explosion killed my grandparents, the Treemounts went on the run. Nacio vowed to continue the work we started to annihilate the damned family.

My mother's surviving siblings and I buried my grandparents. They helped square things away with the destroyed house, and helped relocate Uncle Chase. Aunt Etienne has Chase staying with her until he makes a full recovery. I've asked Chase not to say too much to her, in case the Treemounts make any more attempts on their lives.

As for me, I have been staying at the mansion with Nacio. Luckily, when he and I met, my classes were ending. What a way to end another semester in college; I planned to take the summer off, and return in the fall. At least that is what I had planned. It's too bad you never know what is coming around the corner for you.

Law enforcement agents made it known witnesses in the case would have to be available to give statements - the investigation is ongoing. The cops wanted the Treemounts as badly as I did, and they would not be satisfied until the criminals were caught. The night my grandparents died, three no-nonsense homicide detectives took charge of the investigation.

San Antonio Detectives Menlo Kildare, Prestwick Tausch, and Kerrville Detective Sergio Ortiz were leading the investigation, and they were gunning to bring the Treemounts down. I had two separate interviews with the detectives; both were emotionally draining, leaving me anxious to find Childress as well.

The first interview was with Detective Sergio Ortiz from Kerrville, Texas. He stood 5'2 inches tall, with a boiler on him that gave him the appearance of an expecting mother-to-be. San Antonio and its surrounding area didn't get the title of the fattest city in the nation for nothing---calling it Fat Antonio. Wearing a sport coat, his boiler made the thread in his coat buttons scream in agony from the tension around a too thick waist. One button hung free from misery, as it dangled from a torn string.

The Texas sun slowly simmered his scalp, as parted in the middle cropped black hair lay slicked to his head. A short nose bridge made it difficult for the sweat-drenched sunshades to remain settled on his nose, as his brown eyes squinted behind them.

Detective Ortiz informed me that his partner Detective Mathis Bouvier's body had been found on a cavernous mountain range in Kerrville. Allegations of murder linked the Treemounts to his partner's death. Although there was no neighborhood watch, out of fear, the residents kept surveillance of the Treemount home from a distance. They identified a man fitting the detective's description at the Treemounts home, just before he went missing. Reports of a car fitting Detective Bouvier's left the Treemount residence in the middle of the night. My Uncle Chase had been held hostage, during this same night.

Detective Bouvier was the original detective assigned to investigate the Treemounts involvement for the shooting and stabbing deaths at the Texas Taste Tease. He had an immaculate law enforcement career, with intermittent bouts of depression that had made him vulnerable and easy prey for a woman like Childress to manipulate.

The Coroner's office completed an autopsy, yielding a large dose of a hallucinogen in his system. A large bullet to his right temporal lobe was the cause of death. Postmortem incineration made it difficult to determine the sequence of events leading up to his death. Pieces of skin tissue and hair identified as belonging to Klein and Erland Treemount was the evidence used to open a case, and charge the savage brothers. The question remaining was the whereabouts of the murderous family.

"Ms. Burkes, can you tell me if you recall ever having seen Detective Bouvier?" Detective Ortiz asked, as he smacked heartily on a piece of spearmint gum. He wadded up the wrapper and placed it in his coat pocket, and took out a photo of the deceased detective. I responded with care, and ease.

"Well, I've never seen him face-to-face. I came home one night and I remember seeing a Ford Mustang parked outside the cul-de-sac. It sat there for at least thirty minutes, and then drove away. Other than that, I have never seen him. Could it have been him parked outside of my house that night?"

"Possibly, right now I'm trying to piece together how old Bouv' got involved with the slick Treemount clan," Detective Ortiz said, making his spearmint chewing gum pop like a skillet of frying bacon. "It just doesn't add up."

"Why is that Detective?"

"Well, you see, Detective Bouvier's service revolver was found inside his vehicle along with his remains. With the Treemounts history of gunrunning it just seems that they would have taken the pistol with them. Then again they never were

too bright."

As he reached in his coat pocket and offered me a peppermint, the Detective's gum flew out of his mouth landing on the asphalt, narrowly missing my windblown toes.

Reflexively, I moved to the left of the pasty masticated adhesion that was glistening with saliva as the detective scrawled my statement across his pocket pad --- piecing together his investigation. Right when I thought I was good to be dismissed from the perplexed law enforcement unit, along came Detective Kildare and Detective Tausch. Great, just what my shattered wits needed.

Detectives Kildare and Tausch were rather extraordinary looking cops. Detective Menlo Kildare, a female officer with caramel colored skin that stood an estimated 5'9, with brown shoulder-length wavy hair. I couldn't make out her ethnicity, but the closer she came to me, I heard her dialect — definitely a southerner — possibly African American or Creole. Her sunshades nestled atop her head gave her aqua-colored eyes full view of her surroundings. She had an air to her that commanded attention. It was obvious she was not from here, but the way she presented herself let you know she was someone that knew a thing or two about street life and survival skills.

Detective Prestwick Tausch was definitely eye candy. He was a tall Anglo male, standing 6'6 inches tall, wearing jeans that looked as if his muscular physique poured into them. Curly red locks crowned his head, as his eyes hid behind blackout shades.

As the duo approached, they were engaged in a heated conversation. They also brought along someone I hadn't met, but I knew that I soon would. I couldn't make out what caused the intensity of their discussion, but beyond any doubt I knew it was Treemount related. Detective Kildare sashayed up to greet me.

"Hello, Ms. Burkes, it's good to see you again, and thank you for speaking with us today. We wanted to follow up with you to see how you are holding up"

"Just fine, thank you." Detective Tausch stood next to his partner and stated his intentions.

"Ma'am, we wanted to give you the listing of an area bereavement support group for…" I interrupted him, clearly irritated with my patience exhausted --- shaking with anger.

"That's a nice gesture but please tell me what you have found out about the Treemounts"

Detective Kildare cut a sharp look with her eyes at her partner, then back at me.

"We've just been notified that a 1964 Chevy Impala was found on the Southside near Mission park, not too far from where the body of an unidentified female body was found. The victim's cause of death was exsanguination from two small puncture wounds to her left jugular vein."

"The vehicle was registered to Erland Treemount, but there was no sign of Erland," Detective Tausch said.

The news really shook me then. I knew things were going to hit the fan at that moment. I started to lose it --- I gasped sharp rapid breaths.

"Oh father, oh father."

My worst fear was confirmed. There is another vampire on the loose. That vampire can be none other than Justice Treemount. Gracious. I knew I couldn't let the detectives in on the San Antonio vampires who consisted of Nacio, Bose, and the Caraways. Instead of a pamphlet on bereavement, they would be giving me the admission packet to the Villa Rosa Mental Sanitarium if I told them about the vampires. I knew I had to keep it together. The detectives did their job, noting all of my reactions. Detective Tausch made his concerns for my emotional state known.

"Ms. Burkes, are you alright?"

Faintly, I clutched my chest for breath.

"I'm fine, I'll be okay. Do you have any idea where they are?"

Detective Kildare attempted to give me a little hope that their investigation was making some headway.

"Well ma'am, we believe they are headed to New Orleans and there is an all-points bulletin between here and the Louisiana border and other bordering states."

"Ma'am we are also linking the open cases of the other missing Treemounts," Detective Tausch said. "Missing are cousins Dukane and Montclair Treemount. Missing but presumed dead are Hastings and Duboc Treemount. It is presumed these two are dead, because of suspected foul play. There were minimal traces of blood at each resident crime scene, but there are no bodies to confirm this."

"On the other hand," Detective Kildare said, "Judd Treemount is confirmed dead, but there are no suspects and no witnesses."

Detective Tausch tried to tie things together.

"That's where you come in Ms. Burkes. Do you know of anyone that would want to execute the Treemounts?"

"Well, sir, I know that they had rubbed lots of people

the wrong way. The Treemount men are gang bangers."

"Right, right, we know that," Detective Kildare chimed.

I tried to lead them in the opposite direction away from Nacio and the Caraways.

"But I also know that Childress had several enemies as well, starting with myself. Childress has always hated me without cause. She taunted me all throughout elementary school. She even had her brother Klein..." I paused and searched for breath. "She had her brother Klein rape me when I was six-years old."

The two detectives turned to each other and shared an astonishing glance. I took the defensive, because I hadn't shared that with anyone, until my now deceased Grandmother Olvignia had figured it out.

"Hell, yes, I hated the Treemounts, but I didn't kill those Treemounts," I said to the two law enforcement agents, but I was thinking to myself 'those aren't the Treemounts I want dead. You two haven't told me the whereabouts of the ones I want put in the ground'.

"Oh no, we understand that," Detective Tausch said.

"Our next lead was to Dr. Kross Malveaux here," Detective Kildare explained, introducing the gray streaked haired man quietly standing beside them.

"Hello, ma'am, my condolences" Dr. Malveaux said, extending his hand to shake mine.

"He was the psychiatrist that Childress had while serving her time in the Texas State Penitentiary," Detective Kildare explained. "He'll give us an in depth profile of what we are dealing with."

"Yes, well, I can tell you that I have aged at least ten

years since my last encounter with the seductive Childress Treemount," Dr. Malveaux slurred his words as he wiped blazing sweat from his forehead onto his handkerchief.

"Oh, I'm sure the good doctor will give you an earful," I said, trying to keep from exploding. "I know that I met a girl named Believa Beaushanks whose boyfriend came up dead a few weeks ago. His name was Katalo Nickelson. He had his wake the same time my deceased friend Affinity Johnson had hers."

"Affinity Johnson. That's right!" Detective Kildare said. "She was one of the victims at the Texas Taste Tease correct?"

I hung my head sadly, confirming what the detectives already knew.

"Yes, she was. Anyway, Believa said that Katalo's body looked as if an animal had attacked him. When I went to look at his body during the viewing, I saw there was a green boa feather left across his chest. On the night of the Taste Tease, Childress had on the same green boa that was used to strangle Affinity. I feel that Believa might have had a motive to want the Treemounts dead."

Okay, now I have just lied to the police, which made me a criminal for aiding and abetting. Oh well, I'm not going to lead the police to Nacio.

"Uh, Ms. Burkes, if I may," Dr. Malveaux interjected. "What you are dealing with here is possibly something far worse than our minds might be able to comprehend. I'm saying that Childress Treemount is no ordinary inmate by any means."

Rather than Dr. Malveaux shedding light on the situation, this only formulated more questions for Detective

Tausch.

"How is that, Dr. Malveaux?"

"What I'm saying is that you will need to consider the supernatural in dealing with Childress, more specifically Voodoo," Dr. Malveaux hummed in a slow and heavy southern drawl that left a listener impatient as he dragged out his words.

Detective Tausch was amused at Dr. Malveaux's hunch of what was going on. Little did he know, the good Dr. knew best. "Voodoo? That is truly crazy. I'm afraid you are going to have to come up with one better than that doc."

Dr. Malveaux balked at the Detective's non-belief in the world of Voodoo.

"I'm telling you the truth Detective Tausch. Childress put some Ju Ju on me and I haven't been able to satisfy my wife since that day she was released from prison, I'm telling you. I have been led to believe that Childress Roarquel Treemount is one of the most deadly females I have treated in all my 35 years of psychiatric practice. Her mind holds within it the most unyielding evil that seems to have no beginning or end. Sadism and psychosis are the core foundations of her personality, and she knows no remorse which profiles her as a homicidal sociopath."

Unconvinced of what transpired during the conversation, both Detectives each grabbed one of Dr. Malveaux's arms and led him away as if he needed placement in an asylum. Detective Kildare ended the interview with a nod.

"We'll be in touch. Take care of yourself, Ms. Burkes."

I was still defensive and on edge, especially after their manhandling of Dr. Malveaux.

"Well, unlike the Treemount criminals, you can reach me right here in town."

Well, I knew then I would have to get an apartment of some type to keep up the appearance of my own place. I don't want the authorities nosing around the mansion.

Yes, I remembered that awful night; and draining interviews that followed. All I wanted to do was protect Nacio and the grieving Caraways. So many lives had changed from the negative impact Childress and her family had on everyone.

I can't let my newfound happiness be destroyed by this ongoing investigation mess, nor do I want to interrupt the vampires and the plan they have righting the wrongs of the evil family.

My cell phone rang, interrupting my thoughts. It's Uncle Chase. He's still a little shaky, but nonetheless he was alive. Thanks to Basrick Caraway, Armando Caraway's surviving offspring, Chase had his mind wiped clean and reset. Freeze-framing a glimpse of time was one of the wild supernatural vampire abilities that Basrick and his deceased twin Basira possessed, after they became vampires. Basira knew how to capture a moment in time, and Basrick could rewind events that had just occurred. The night we freed Chase, Basrick needed to feed to get some of his strength back after so much exertion.

After Basrick worked his magic on Chase, he thought he had been in a fight and lost. He had no recollection of the vampires he had encountered. Chase really hadn't gotten a good look at the vampires the night he was rescued from the Treemount home, because Childress had blinded him with ground crushed glass and black pepper. We are still not clear on the severity of damage to his eyesight. Having my uncle back safe and sound is all that matters. The narcotics had him lit up, coasting, and very groggy.

"What's up, Solis?"

"Oh, nothing much; how're you feeling Chase?" We were all hoping that Chase would be able to get his visual acuity back somewhat, considering he had lacerated corneas after Childress threw crushed glass and pepper in his eyes --- temporarily blinding him.

"I'm alright; I just wanted to check on you. When are you coming over here?"

"I'll be over to see you again soon Chase, just take care of yourself alright? Make sure that you take your medicine."

"I know, I know," he said. "Damn, my head keeps hurting. It feels like a bass drum beating inside my head. I could sleep for a year."

"Have you had your follow-up?" I knew he probably hadn't.

"No, not yet, but I will." At times, he sounded like a young boy who had just been caught with his hand in the cookie jar.

"Well, make sure you do. I'll be over this weekend, I promise. I just need to tie up a few loose ends."

"Alright, I won't keep you. I just wanted to hear your voice to make sure you were okay," he said. Then he broke down into the most heart wrenching sob my ears had ever heard coming from a grown man.

"Solis, I just miss mom and dad so much. I just don't know what to do."

His deep sorrow only reminded me of my own sadness

as I wept softly. "I know Chase, I miss them too, but they live on in us. Don't forget that."

"I know they do, it's just so strange that they both died of natural causes at the same time." Chase was perplexed, with only half-truths to keep him from unraveling the calm put in place.

You see, I knew exactly what was going on with Chase. Basrick had done such a precise job in resetting Chase's memory, that he was actually having trouble recalling details, and there were fact omissions for his safety.

A lie replaced the truth about the death of Leonine and Olvignia Henderson. Well, it was somewhat a lie, in truth there had been a house fire. Chase did not know that his captors actually blew up the house. While being held hostage by the Treemounts, he overheard them speak of their plans to blow the house up, but Basrick erased this memory. Chase had difficulty controlling his anger at times, and giving him too much information could have further put our surviving family in danger. The more Chase tried to recall his memories about that tragic night, the more pain would pound the back of his head. Hastily, I closed the call.

"Alright, Chase, be careful, and I will talk to you soon. I love you."

"Love you too," he said hanging up. Little comfort found its way to my uncle or to the Caraways at the Puente mansion. Grief had seized everyone, making it nearly impossible to carry on. Basrick seemed to be unreachable.

His ability to manipulate time was amazing and frightening. He still blamed himself for his twin Basira's death. Putting a ripple in time to stop the moment she ingested Colloidal Silver would have been nothing for him to accomplish. I caught glimpses of Basrick's bereavement, or more so his rage, while at the mansion.

As I left Nacio's suite one evening, Basrick went passed me in the corridor, his eyes were empty. It was terrifying to feel the dark and desolate presence of this individual who at first glance appeared as a handsome young man. No one would suspect him to be a human killing machine. Basrick could make unsuspecting victims forget to acknowledge their natural instinct to sense danger just before he took them to his mouth, allowing his fangs to clamp shut while drawing blood to their death.

"Hello, Basrick," I attempted a subtle greeting, but there was no response from him. A thick and heavy aura of regret lingered in the air.

His beautiful sky-blue eyes had become dark and murky, and his mood was irritable. Any attempt to communicate with him was futile. Basrick would not speak with me or anyone else in the Puente mansion.

Armando and Patience, Basick's parents, acted in the same manner. Patience wailed painfully over the last few nights when she and Armando were together. During the day, she stayed well hidden within the comfort the walls of their suite provided. No one needed to speak words, their grief emanated from their gestures.

Nacio and the Caraways were still eliminating the remaining Treemounts. They had gone over to the Puente Masonry factory. I could only guess what was going on there. Nacio was determined to keep me out of as many of the gory details as possible. He had Bose working around the clock to find research to support other ways of getting rid of the family by starting their work on eliminating the female Treemounts.

If our plans succeeded, the curse would end once all the females stopped conceiving children. Nacio had Bose researching two congenital birth defect causing drugs. Diethylstilbestrol or Dieth for short, will twist the reproductive organs and cause disease in the children should they be born. The other drug Mifeprex or Mife, will lower the pregnancy-stabilizing hormone, and then cause a spontaneous miscarriage. Nacio wants to give a dose to the female Treemounts in hopes of contaminating their reproductive organs to stop the curse. As long as reproduction was possible for the female Treemounts, there was no end to the curse.

With his methodical approach to research, Bose amazed me at how thorough and expedient he was. What would take weeks to do with organizing and cataloging information, he could do in a few hours. It was fascinating to watch him at work. He moved so quickly, he looked like a white cloud moving across the room as stacks of periodicals neatly aligned themselves along a huge table in the library.

Lately, Bose had been finding genealogical information on the Treemounts that had spanned continents. The slave information that he uncovered was extraordinary. Nacio had wanted him to search the African and American continents and all of the Caribbean islands for history on Priestess Auldicia and the children born from liaisons she had. From the information I glanced at revealed she had several children who were left here and there, later sold into slavery.

Bose had the talent and organizational skill to find any information needed. We all had our trust and faith in him to take care of everyone in the home. Having the extended family he had always hoped for in the home brought him joy. Basira's death had taken its toll on everyone in the mansion. Bose loved Basira as if she were his daughter.

As a loyal keeper, Bose ran the house and was the backbone of Nacio's well-being. Running the Puente Masonry Company and all the other business affairs, Bose proved he was more than a servant. He had come to love Nacio like a brother, making certain that he and Nacio continued their comfortable life style. I have never known a more loyal friend in my lifetime, other than Affinity.

When I made my way into the living room, I had only been there for a moment when I felt that cool and dewy mist that had courted me so lovingly a short time ago. It captivated me effortlessly. As usual, the mist encircled me, tantalized me, and traveled up the length of my body crowning my lips. A tall figure materialized right before my eyes.

First, the image of long midnight black wavy hair formed that sat atop broad shoulders. A long torso covered in a white linen short-sleeved shirt blew lightly in the breeze that came with the teleportation process.

Rippling muscle lay underneath the shirt --- followed by firm and beautifully tanned thighs sheathed by linen pants. The rest of this broad estimated 6'7 figure followed, as a pearly white smile accented with deadly fangs greeted me, as they sat behind succulently full lips. Seeing the height of this figure is often overwhelming, but my eyes enjoy seeing it nonetheless. Strong arms caressed me, welcoming me, and as usual igniting my desire - leaving me weak and drenched with arousal. I knew he could smell my desire as my body continued to respond to his welcoming affections.

Nacio, the vampire, love of my life, was home.

3

Hours of Ours

Standing before me was the most devastatingly handsome being my eyes had ever fallen on, Nacio Galvazio De Puente, my vampire soul mate. Any normal female would have probably been afraid to witness such shape shifting. After all, it defies the modern science of the living. Although it defies the laws of the living, it is one of many standard laws of the undead.

To think I could have lost him the night my grandparents were killed. He and the Caraways took stab wounds to the back with silver knives, and had Colloidal Silver thrown on them in an attempt to destroy them as well.

I quickly pulled the knives from each of their wounds that night. All it took was a little rest, and the vampires healed as if the whole incident had never occurred. The thought of living forever is a bit overwhelming. I have thought about what it would mean to leave forever. Some days I wonder how I would adjust to my new life as a vampire. I love cookies, and eating, and I have always wanted children. All of these things would cease to exist for me the minute I become a vampire. None of the vampires eat anything --- they only survive on blood and plasma. Everything about blood is gross to me, and it smells awful. I'll be the first to admit that I question my own strength.

Although these thoughts crossed my mind, I had been living at Nacio's mansion with other vampires and yet no harm had come to me at all. I could have well been a meal to any one of them, but that was not to be my fate.

When night fell and my body became tired, I slept in Nacio's suite. His tender caress was my nighttime lullaby that would send me into a peaceful slumber. This proved to be increasingly difficult for me --- for my desire for him was unbearable at times. Often led by lust, I would make physical advances toward him --- yet he would not surrender to me, imagine that. Never have I been involved with a male that actually wanted to hold off on consummating our love as much as Nacio had.

He actually had it worse. Vampire blood lust is not an easy feat to overcome. Certainly adding sexual desire would make for an explosive situation for any human or any immortal alike. After silently adoring each other for several moments, Nacio spoke leaving me slack-jawed — hanging on his every word.

"Hello, Mistress. I've missed you." His lacquered smile held my gaze, as he kissed me once more.

"You've been missed as well. Tell me, what strategies have you and the Caraways decided as our next plan of action?"

"I will tell you all you need to know soon enough. Just know that we will leave for Louisiana within the next day or so."

"I'm ready to continue our pursuit of Childress. I feel that she will soon drop out of sight and I don't want that."

"I understand sweetheart, and that won't happen. In the meantime, we have to track down Justice. The Caraways and I have been trying to find out more about our weakness to Colloidal Silver."

"What have you discovered?"

"Basically to stay away from it, it is as deadly as swallowing acid would be to any living creature. Although, perhaps the physical make up of a vampire actually gives it some delay time before it turns the vampire corpse to silt."

"So then, Basira fed on Justice more than once, turning him into a vampire," I said. "Detectives Kildare and Tausch found the body of a young girl near where they discovered Erland's Chevy."

"This is true," another sultry voice said from the shadowy corner of the room. With that said, Bose Puente walked into our midst.

Bose possesses a certain charisma about himself just as Nacio does. Exhibiting his Creole descent, he had jade green eyes that dazzled any admirer from near or far. With his curly blonde hair now worn at his shoulders, he too made women swoon just from raising his eyebrow. His voice was often the voice of reason in any conversation.

"I have a feeling that we have a youngling vampire on our hands. If this is true, we must use all the resources we have necessary to capture Justice and destroy him before anymore can be made…if we aren't too late already."

Tension slowly crept into my beloved's face as he began a slow pace across the room, contemplating our next move.

"We will soon hunt again, Bose. Continue identifying the other Treemounts as you have. Childress and her brothers are predictable as they are hapless and stupid. The strong arm of the law just might get to them before we do."

"Yes, Hefe, I understand. Actually you have other matters to attend to as well…a ceremony, I understand?"

"Oh yes, thank you for reminding me, Bose. Have you prepared everything?"

"Indeed, I have. I am only waiting for you to give me the confirmation and the event will begin. I will leave you now, Hefe."

Feeling like "C" in an "A-B" conversation for about ten minutes or so, I stood there between these two gorgeous creatures in confusion.

"What confirmation?" I asked, feeling like I had totally been left out of a big secret. Nacio grabbed my hand and led me with him.

"Let's go into the garden out back."

My body responds to him so willingly that I know he feels my physical arousal to him as my loins moisten. I also know he enjoys my response as much as I do.

Out in the backyard was a tropical paradise. There was a very beautiful and intelligent red, yellow, and blue Scarlet Macaw that flew straight to Nacio's right shoulder. Stunning and gentle, the bird perched himself next to his master.

"Solis, honey, meet Manolo."

He stood before me beaming with pride as he fed the bird a piece of bread he'd noticed on the way out of the kitchen. "He answers to Manny as well."

With me not being an animal person, this was somewhat of an awkward moment. Looking at the beautiful bird, I waved a timid greeting.

"Hi, Manolo." I really do not have any kind of relationship with animals, and this confirmed it.

Nacio laughed as I couldn't decide to pet the beautiful bird or retreat to safety. Nacio gave his pet a command.

"Go on, Manny. She's afraid right now, but we'll get her used to you."

Upon Nacio's last word, Manolo took to the wind and found himself a nice branch to occupy near the second story of the mansion.

Nacio let his eyes fall on me with a seriousness that left me anxious. The silence that followed his expression made me brace myself for the unknown. I sat on a magnificently constructed wooden bench that sat in the middle of the garden as I allowed him time to find words to express himself. The carved bench masterpiece had paisleys and roses meticulously etched into the frame, with the legs of the shaped like that of a porcelain bathtub. Nacio shrugged his shoulders, and slowly revealed his sentiments.

"Solis, you know I have been in love with you for a long time… longer than you'd realized, right?"

"Yes, honey, I know that," I slowly melted as he spoke. "Why do you ask?"

"Well, I know you have been living here with me, and I don't feel right about that."

I allowed the impact of his words to settle in heavily --- instantly making me defensive.

"Well, I can leave, that's no problem…I don't have to

stay here."

My heart jumped causing an emotional avalanche. I stood up and headed back into the house when his hand grabbed me and put me in a vice hold. Nacio's voice rose as he realized how tightly he held me as I tried to flee before he saw tears streaming down my face.

"Wait, sweetheart you misunderstand what I'm trying to say to you."

If he was breaking up with me, I certainly wanted to leave with some dignity. Hell, I had survived breakups and being dumped before. It was nothing new for me. Easy come and easy go. Just move on. I knew how to do that well. Surely getting dumped by a vampire was no different. The only thing was that the pain I was feeling in my chest from my heart breaking was devastating. At this moment, a kick in the chest would have been better than how I was feeling now. Nacio stood firm, not allowing a retreat.

"Solis, calm down. Listen to me, please."

"Hey, look, no problem, alright? I'll get my junk and go. I know when to make a move when I'm not wanted. Don't worry, I'm gone."

"Will you listen, please?"

Nacio pleaded, now with tears of mist coming from his eyes. That stopped me in my tracks. His misty tears seeped from the corners of his hazel eyes. Never had I witnessed a man express sorrow over anything I had done or said. He continued to reason with me.

"What I don't feel right about is the fact that you and I are not bound to each other, Solis. I want to bind with you forever…will you do that for me?"

He slowly began his descent to his knees.

"I have waited for you for so long and I have been in love with you just the same…I don't want to wait another day for you to be with me. I watch you sleeping and want to fulfill our desires but I can't do that if we are not one with each other. Do you understand that? I will not lay with you, if you are not mine and mine alone. Mistreating your body like that is something I will not do. No man should ever ask any woman to do such a thing…if he loves her…I'm in love with you. All that you see before you is what I am, and I want you."

My face was so hot with tears of joy, that the bench caught me before I went crashing to the earth. My dream had come true. Nacio asked to take ownership of my heart. He had literally loved me all my lifetime --- I froze. I sat stunned with my eyes closed, only to hear him ask again.

"Will you be one with me?"

I opened my eyes to find in his hand a thick gold banned ring with a pink stone that had what looked to be one drop of red deep within the stone — blood perhaps. The stone was at least three carats in weight. As he held it up for me to see, his smile turned me into a puddle.

"Yes, Yes, Yes, I will bind with you. Thank you, yes, I will. I am so in love with you and have been since the day our lips first met."

Nacio took the beautiful ring and mounted it on my finger. He then kissed my hand, and I could have sworn light sparkled in the air around us as he did. He wiped a tear that had freshly fallen from my face.

"This is a pink and red diamond that I sent Bose to retrieve for you from a diamond mine in Australia. I guess it was when you were about 15 years old. You knew nothing of me then. I have been saving it for you, because I knew I was going to ask you to be with me forever someday."

I facetiously grinned at this beautiful creature, completely overjoyed.

"And you just knew I would say yes, huh?"

"Well, I was hoping so."

We kissed desperately as he swept me off my feet.

"Now that you have agreed to be mine, it's time for you to take your rightful place as Mistress of our home, and as the head of your family."

"Okay, I guess that's easy enough."

I was agreeing to anything at that moment. Captivated by the beautiful stone, I kept lifting my hand to measure its weight. The stone was gorgeous.

I looked up and found all three of the Caraways, Armando, Patience, and Basrick looking at us as we stood arm in arm. Nacio had to explain things a little more clearly for me, because he knew I did not fully understand what he meant.

"What I'm telling you sweetheart, is that it's time for your induction ceremony ---your Kanzo. I know your Grandma Olvignia would be pleased to know that you are ready to take her authority, and carry on your family's namesake."

My eyebrows furrowed at the weight of his words.

"You mean me as the new Mistress?"

"Yes."

"Nacio, I don't know about that, I mean I am not as strong as Grandma Olvignia."

"You're right Solis, you're not as strong as she was,"

Armando spoke, taking a step towards me, and stopping just breathing distance from me. "You are stronger than she was, and you know it, she knew it, we all know it."

Armando's vote of confidence made Patience step out from the shadows to cast her ballot as well, as she chimed in softly and barely audible. It had been a while since she had spoken. She stopped speaking after Basira's death.

"It's true, Mistress. You are the chosen one to carry your family's knowledge."

"To complete the transition to Mistress you must have a Kanzo, an induction ceremony," Nacio said. "Our binding ceremony is for me. I want you for myself, and I don't want to wait any longer."

Having heard Nacio say those words to me, I knew exactly what he meant. We all did. His desire to consummate our love would allow him to wait no longer. We stood staring into each other's eyes. His physical response to me became obvious. Flushed and clammy, desire had rendered me useless. His words matched his actions as we held each other.

"Is tonight too soon to take you as my own?"

Closing the short distance between us, I answered by kissing him deeply. His response to my affirmation was an erection that had as much strength behind it as the aged Oak tree we stood under. He wanted to give in to his desire, as his eyes never left me.

"Go with Patience, she will dress you in your garments for the ceremony. Armando and Basrick will assist me in my dressing garments for the ceremony. We will bind with each other under the stars, sweetheart."

"Tonight is our night."

"Yes, my love it is. Bose is a Houngan, a voodoo priest that will conduct the Kanzo and Ason ceremonies. The two ceremonies represent your transition into the highest level of practice of Rada Voodoo, which is peaceful and family oriented. The taking of the Ason is the last step completing your transition to your rightful power. The art of this religion was something that was part of Bose's Creole heritage. He will mark you when it is time for you to cross over into the authority of the mambo mistress. At that time, your transition will be complete. You will feel different down to your very soul. The magic that is rightfully yours will be at its highest intensity. This magic comes with great knowledge and a commitment to conquer evil."

"I don't know what to say."

"Just know that you have made your ancestors very proud."

Again, tears of joy ran down my face, as the wind blew softly. I felt the presence of my mother and grandparents near. Somewhere in that light breeze, I felt the warm presence and smile of my dear deceased friend Affinity. I knew they felt my joy as well.

***

Patience escorted me to the suite she and Armando occupied. This was also one of my favorite places in the mansion. Queen Nefertiti's portrait hung high on the wall. It was accentuated by artifacts that belonged to the beautiful Queen herself. Nacio had traveled the world and acquired these things. They weren't from a museum. He was actually able to lead his own expedition to excavate from deep within one of the pyramids to acquire gold bracelets and rings.

In the middle of the room was a huge California King bed that cradled the most intricately woven red and white ceremonial dress I had ever seen. A sleeveless bodice connected to shards of material that hung feathered and loosely over the side of the bed. Patience acted as my maid of honor.

"This is the gown you must wear as you take your place into the authority and power that is rightfully yours. You must cleanse yourself, and I will return to dress you."

I was far from being a virgin. Klein Treemount ripped that from me years ago. I could only guess that when Patience meant I needed to cleanse myself. It meant to wash away the pawing hands of other men that I had so readily given myself to over the years - after Klein had marked his territory, while Childress laughed.

Patience waved her arm towards the bathroom. A gentle stream of water ran in the tub decorated with floating Gardenias that tickled my senses and invited me closer. Soft lilac, sage, and lavender stirred in the air as my clothing dropped to the floor and I dipped my foot to bottom of the tub.

A mound of soft body wash cream lay in a soap bowl with a body sponge for me to cleanse with. I'd never dreamed this would be the night — the biggest one of my life. I could hardly contain myself. It was as if magnetic electrical sparks were sizzling under my skin. I was finally going to consummate my love for Nacio — I couldn't wait. I continued to let the water soothe me, as I entertained images of his gorgeous body.

I stood and looked at my own figure under the dim

track lighting in the bathroom and hoped that he would want me as much I wanted him. My hair was swept up in a cascading ponytail, as water dripped down the small of my back. Patience knocked at the door.

"It's time, Solis."

"I'll be right out."

I opened the door—greeting Patience. I let my towel fall to the floor as she held the gown for me to step into. The imaginary sparks under my skin sizzled more strongly now—faster, hurting almost.

With a quick draw, Patience tied the sash of my gown---cinching my waist. A beautiful gold nugget necklace accessorized the ensemble. The weight of the necklace seemed to attract all the energy that was radiating from my skin. Patience looked on in excitement.

"Bow your head, Solis."

She began crowning my head with what looked to be a white royal head wrap. When completed, the headdress sat high above my shoulders commanding attention.

When I was fully dressed, I could not believe my eyes. I looked like a Queen, waiting to be escorted to her court. Patience stood proud admiring her work. She too, was misty-eyed.

"You look so beautiful, Mistress."

"Please, you will make me cry again,"

We hugged each other. "Thank you for everything, Patience. This means so much to me."

"Let's go. Your love awaits you."

"I'm ready."

Patience opened the door to the suite. Surprisingly,

dimly lit candles lined the hallway. Ceremonial drums beat outside in the garden. A trail of white rose petals comforted my bare feet as they took steps closer and closer to my beloved. Looking over my shoulder at Patience, I discovered she had changed from her two-piece linen pant set, to a beautiful white linen skirt set. Her outfit was complete with a headdress that was much smaller than mine, not as towering. I could have questioned and wondered how it was that she had changed so quickly, but superhuman speed was definitely an advantage of being a vampire.

As I began my entrance march slowly and steadily, a single drumbeat became louder until I reached the kitchen—the cadence of several drums exploded in rhythm. Drums ordered my steps as I began to pulsate in movement. Never having been involved in a ceremony such as this, by body responded to the command of the sound. Each beat worked in unison with the electrical charge that conducted itself underneath my skin.

Louder and louder the joyful music sounded, while my bare feet tapped their way outside to the garden. Nacio, Armando, Basrick, and Bose stood around a stone altar adorned with what looked to be small white bones that lay underneath a small blue bowl. Bose stood behind the altar as the maestro leading the beat that Armando and Basrick mimicked on their instruments.

Bose was dressed in a white loincloth, with a mesh robe to cover him. His painted face displayed intricate patterns of gold and white warrior-style make up. A top hat styled headdress made of spectacular gold and white feathers crowned his head. As I made my way towards the altar, Nacio materialized just in front of me, pulsating to the hypnotic lead of the music that shook the ground below our feet. His footsteps fell in line with my own, making us one in our ceremonial march with the altar as our destination.

Captivated, my eyes took in a full view of his muscled body. His virile physique was dressed in a golden loincloth matched by a full-length golden mesh Maxi cape. Conch shells strung together by leather straps graced his ankles as his bare feet danced among white rose petals with my own. A large golden crown, enhanced by white peacock feathers were fanned out and positioned on his head, as his shiny wavy locks lay across his back—my king at last.

With our bodies in perpetual motion, it felt as if Basrick was being naughty once again by making time pause and allowing us to enjoy each other in this moment. Nacio placed his hands on my waist and guided me towards my destiny. The closer we came to the altar, the more I felt Nacio close in behind me gyrating—inviting my hips into his nonstop motion. Throwing my arms high over my head was all I could do to keep the electrical charge underneath my skin from bringing me to a hypnotically induced moan. Arriving at the altar, we continued to dance. Bose reveled in his role as maestro and master of ceremony as he chanted the sacred call to the gods.

"Voudoun al cooroo, sefwey, ilama, mezu koo reek, Legba, Legba, Legba, oh Dumballah."

Drumbeats echoed off the brick walls of the mansion, while our small audience looked on. Tadada, Tadada, bump, bump, bump, Tadada, Tadada, bump, bump, bump. The beat quickened, then all sound ceased upon the last spoken word. Our rhythm came to an abrupt halt. Nacio soothed me through all the excitement.

Do not be afraid, my love, Nacio telepathically whispered to me. *Bose is only chanting to call the gods. One god guards the spiritual crossroad, and the other is peaceful and brings protection. Bose will summon your mother, Grandma Olvignia, and Affinity to the spiritual crossroads to witness our binding ceremony, and give us their blessing.*

Nacio's words gently blew through the corridors of my mind, intertwining his thoughts with my own feelings--putting my fears at ease. Accessing my thoughts and feelings was something he did so easily; assessing my every need, and filling my every void.

Bose raised his hands beckoning for Nacio and me to step forward. My skin felt as if it were going to rip to shreds from the charge that was underneath it. In one eye-blinking movement, Bose reached underneath the altar and brought back an Albino Ball Python. I was trying to remain continent and not ruin my wedding night, but at that moment I wished I could have teleported to the other corner of the city, or at least to the nearest bathroom in the mansion. Approximately eight feet in length, and a minimum of six inches in diameter, with beaming red eyes, this snake dared to raise its colorless head and look directly at me. I was beginning to lose it.

Easy sweetheart, again Nacio intervened during my fight or flight decision. *Be at ease, I'm here. No harm will come to you...ever.* He knew to quickly plant some seeds of encouragement in my thoughts, fore he knew I was not a winged or four-legged animal loving person—surely a limbless serpent would send me screaming into the night. I thought them all to be crazy, if he expected me to remain calm.

My own limbs betrayed me as they held me as a lustful

captive at my own matrimonial altar. Nacio reassuringly grabbed my hand, and stepped in as support, substituting for my failing legs. Bose picked up the blue bowl and stretched his hand forth, while the lazy reptile became bored with its view of me, and slithered up Bose's other arm and around his neck, stopping to rest.

Nacio took the bowl from Bose. Using his other hand along with his thumbnail he sliced a wound into his wrist — spilling blood into the bowl. My eyes felt as big as beverage coasters. The blood ran like a faucet with no spigot to turn it off. Bose chanted again. He reached behind his back and pulled forth a chicken by its feet. In a futile effort to escape, the chicken flapped its wings sending loose feathers into the air covering the altar. Bose continued to lead the ceremony, while pulling the chicken apart.

"Amama funde Dumballah."

Bose was quick with his hands as he dismembered the chicken---splashing blood over the altar and across our ceremonial garments as we stood there. A bloody mess, Nacio continued his grip on the bowl, unflinching in any way. I, on the other hand, was trying to keep it together.

Bose did what I knew somehow was going to eventually take place. The python had made its way down the arm of its host, and was now lifting its head to place its eyes on me once again. Armando and Basrick began the wild drumbeating again. My heart raced again, faster, faster, faster. This serpent began to extend its entire body down the length of Bose's arm, making its way over to me.

Reach out and touch the serpent, Solis. You must make contact with the serpent god Dumballah.

I can't…I don't know if I can. I don't want to touch that damned thing.

BELIEVE IT, SOLIS, YOU CAN DO IT, YOU MUST.

His telepathy rattled my brain into making my arm respond to this slithering reptile as it lingered dangerously close to my face. Bose began throwing white crystallized powder over us both just as the python stopped just in front of my face.

Protection powder will keep us safe. Touch it, Solis. He is offering you power and authority now.

With its eyes as red as arterial blood, and its head the size of a tea saucer, the serpent continued its stare. I blinked my coaster-sized eyes once, just as the python slammed its head down on top of my forehead---zapping me with a jolt so violent and powerful that thunder and lightning rolled across the clear night sky, sending aftershocks through the ground beneath our feet.

Dazed from the zap the crimson-eyed reptile had given, I realized that I was not harmed --- being bitten was my main concern. I looked up to see Nacio's Scarlet Macaw; Manolo perched on a branch in a tree. It was done. My transition to Mistress was complete. A powerful manifestation transferred to me from this reptile, fulfilling my destiny. I am now able to carry on the knowledge that was bequeathed to me from Grandma Olvignia. I heard the voices of my deceased loved ones speak through Manolo.

"We are with you, Solis. Bind with your mate, and find all the happiness that is meant for you," Grandma Olvignia, my mother, and Affinity spoke in unison through the beautiful bird. My only response was shock and a heartfelt smile at the beautiful bird who conveyed a message to me from beyond.

Since Bose had made his sacrificial gesture to summon Dumballah, he marked Nacio and me once with the chicken blood that was spilled. A strong wind gust blew as Nacio dipped his thumb in his blood that was in the bowl, marking my forehead where the python had just planted his mark. As soon as his thumb met the surface of my skin, a flash of lightening blazed in the night air around us. We noticed that our garments had been cleansed of all sacrificial fluid, and it removed the color red from the garment turning it to a gleaming white. In fact, we all had a luminescence that glowed under the moonlight. Bose thanked Legba and sent him away, as the spirit of Dumballah possessing the serpent slithered back underneath the altar.

It is done, sweetheart, you are mine. We are each one, Nacio conveyed his thoughts to me. In doing so, he simply raised his left eyebrow, and smiled with his eyes. My legs found their loyalty, and allowed me to step into his arms and deliver a savage and lustful kiss to his lips.

Another explosion of drumbeating, and celebration shouts from the Caraways filled the night air. Manolo cawed and flapped his wings wildly, letting me know that a celebration was taking place at the spiritual crossroads where my departed loved ones chanted hymnals of their own making.

Taking the lead, I released my beloved's hand, slowly walking back through the garden making my way to the mansion. This time I was dressed in all white. My headdress sat high upon head, confirming my newly acquired status as Mistress. My skin was no longer in pain from the tingling. Now it was sizzling with lust for my soul mate. I stopped my pace just a few steps short of entering the mansion, when I turned and looked over my right shoulder at Nacio, I stepped into submission.

I can wait no longer... I need you. Come to me now, I teased. My desire flowed between my thighs and down my legs onto the ground underneath my feet—leaving drops like breadcrumbs for my king to follow into our suite. With urgency, he responded to my needs as usual.

I can barely contain my hunger for you. Every drop you leave behind for me leaves a scent that will cover every inch of my body in a few moments...lead the way, Mistress... lead me to our home...into our bed.

I began my pace once more towards our home. Yes, finally 'our' home. The celebration continued as I walked up the stairs in the garden that led to the second story straight to our loft in the east wing. Each step of the staircase had beautiful white rose petals that came from our garden. I raised my arms over my head allowing Nacio, while in mist form, to seduce me agonizingly up the stairwell. The ache was unbearable.

Opening the door to our private paradise allowed the sweet smell of Gardenias to lure me in. Already inside the suite, Nacio met my footsteps and led me by my waist over to the bed. His unblinking eyes assessed the curve of my hips. He then slowly began to unravel my headdress, allowing the garment to fall to the floor, as my hair cascaded over my shoulders. I watched his lips speak, as the humid copious fluid between my thighs continued to inch downward, engorging my organs, with heat hot enough to melt candle wax.

"My happiness is now complete…you are perfect in

every way…you are mine now. I belong to you, and will love no other as long as you are in existence."

"You've redeemed me from my nightmares and from grief. I've never been so in love with anyone, nor have I ever loved so deeply."

Nacio took two steps back from me and held up his hand for me to continue to undress, as he watched with lips parted and turned up in a satisfied smile. I began to slow my haste, as he dropped his cape to the floor. With only a loincloth remaining between us, we anxiously anticipated our soon to be unforgettable consummation. Nacio waved his right arm, summoning the smooth jazz to pour from the surround sound stereo system. I teasingly took steps back towards our bed.

He pulled at the loincloth sending it to the floor, along with my eyes as they settled on his manhood. Letting out a subtle moan, knowing from this night forward I would be a very satisfied bride each time my groom would touch me. Pleasuring him would allow me to pleasure myself. Impatiently, he waited for me to become acquainted with his body as I took a handful of him to my lips—throwing his head back as whispers of desire escaped him.

Finally releasing him, Nacio gathered me in his arms and gently placed me on our bed. Ripples of golden satin sheets were turned down to receive us both. Lovingly, he entered the foot of the bed, crawling underneath the covers, burying his head in the saturated mound between my legs. His hair tickled my bare hips, while his hands roamed freely. Acknowledging the source of the scent he has been longing for all evening, he kissed the intimate folds of skin—bringing forth more of the copious fluid that now pooled beneath my hips.

Pulling my body closer and entering with a slippery thrust meant no boundaries would hold us from each other. Our passion was endless throughout the night, as the smooth jazz song "Sure Thing" by St. Germain rekindled our desire repeatedly. Moonbeams graced his face in the shadows, as I caught a glimpse of his fangs as they flashed through his lips. Whispers of adoration slipped filled the room, deepening his erotic thrusts as we melted into each other. He softly pricked his lower lip, sending a drop of blood to the corner of his mouth as I moved in to kiss him once more. Tasting his blood and in doing so strengthening our connection, Nacio marked my soul.

"Do you trust me?"

"You know I do."

Affirming our trust, he reached a milky climax that sent tremors throughout his body that ricocheted off the bed's surface---filling me up and leaving me wanting more. Before the next wave of his desire met mine, sharp fangs met the artery in my neck---relieving my erotic agony, making me ready to receive him again.

Childress Treemount

4

The Grifters

"We're just about out of Texas Childress," Klein said looking in the rearview mirror at his sister in the back seat of the Black Beetle.

"This little car is good on gas. We made it all the way from San Antonio to Orange with no problems," he continued. "We were lucky to be able to stop in all these little towns to lay low, until the media alerts for us die down some. We need to get some gas now, though."

"How the hell are we going to do that, damn fool, when you know SWAT, CHIPS, US Marshals, and the FBI are hot on our tails?" Childress slurred from two chipped front teeth. "You are so basic; it makes my head hurt just talking to you. This only aggravated Klein.

"Well, take your ass back to sleep then. I know why your head hurts. It's because Solis whooped your ass up and down and up and down, and back up the street again, that's why. You look a frightful mess, Childress. Your teeth are missing, your skin looks somewhat greenish, your head looks flat, and finally yet importantly, your hair looks like a nest of snakes. What the hell is wrong with you?"

Without warning, Childress hissed and grabbed a handful of Klein's curly mane pulling his head back towards the headrest and slamming it forward onto the steering wheel—bloodying his nose. Failing an attempt to recover from a swerve, Klein sideswiped a guardrail ripping the driver's side view mirror from the door. Enraged, Childress was ready to strike once more.

"Say something else, Klein, I dare you. I'll twist your nose off your face like a damn doorknob and hand it to you. Just keep talking and I'll make good on my promise."

Her youngest sibling, Erland, eerily began a cackling laugh as he rocked back and forth in his seat, slapping his hand on the dashboard in humorous hysterics. Instantly escalating to agitation, Erland began to flail his arms wildly as he began to weep. Gurgling screams began to fill the interior of the little vehicle. This prompted Childress to send her right arm whipping through the air to slap Erland's face, his head, and lastly cracking him across his back as if he had been choking on a marble. She continued her verbal assault.

"Close your mouth, damn fool! You want us to get busted now?"

Out of control and sniveling, Erland flinched from anticipated pain.

"I need a joint or something. My nerves are bad." His childlike weeping was the direct result of substance abuse detoxification. "I need my medicine."

Although she and her brothers were prone to deviant behavior, Childress had no patience for her brothers off kilter antics.

"Well, too bad, dumbass. I bet next time you get some

of your medicine, you'll eat a few of those pills like you are supposed to instead of using other kinds of dope to calm your nerves."

A few moments passed, settling the unruly Treemounts for the duration of their ride. Childress had become defensive because she knew what her eldest brother said was true. She knew she looked like road kill connected to the undercarriage of a bus, and dragged across the state. Ever since the night she swallowed her mother's blood and that of her ancestor Priestess Auldicia, she had the strangest sensations circulating through her veins—like needles pinning her organs.

Weakness and fatigue had washed over her in the past few days as they rode in and out of little towns between San Antonio and the Louisiana state border. When she tussled with Klein earlier during their small skirmish in the little car, she knew her life was about to take a sharp turn. It was hard to accept the eyes staring back at her were those of pure evil.

"I hate Solis Burkes so much," Childress thought. "I should have just let Klein kill her after he popped her cherry when we were kids. Who would have missed the little fat thing? I could have had Klein stab her in the neck with one of his number two pencils after school. Then we could have escaped and blamed that homeless bastard that lingered there every night in that old house. Yeah, that's what I should have done. Hmm, I'll get another chance, and this time I won't make any mistakes, Cher."

Erland composed himself just in time as the little Beetle began to sputter and jerk before finally dying out. Out of gas and out of luck, the little car coasted off the freeway onto the access road just inside the Orange City limit, just a fraction of a mile away from a gas station. Night had fallen, and this would have made the Treemounts navigation a little easier to cross into Louisiana. The car finally came to a quiet stop. Erland became lucid, and proved he had a thimble full of common sense.

"Hey, man, there's a filling station just up the road there. Let's get the gas and some cash too."

"Man, we can't just go walking in that place," Klein squealed. "I'm telling you that we are wanted."

"How do you know, fool? We just need some gas; and I want to eat. I want a joint too. Yeah, I want eat and smoke at the same time."

Erland's last reply earned him a crisp slap from a still irritated Childress. Her patience with her youngest sibling had run out after traveling through the past fifteen county lines with his emotionally imbalanced hysterics.

"Listen up, goons. We're going to hit this store, and get us another ride so we won't be detected as we pass through the Texas-Louisiana state line, you hear me?" Childress had mapped out the plan for their freedom.

"Now, Klein, you see that gas lane closest to the edge of the asphalt near the field?"

"Yeah, I see it, so?" he implied.

"I want you to watch for female customers that pull up with at least three females in the car with one paying for the gas. They'll be easier to rob. Once they gas up, we are going to snatch their money, their clothes, and their car, you got it?"

"Well, hell, Childress, that's good for you, but what are Erland and I going to wear? I am not wearing women's clothes, and any way…" Klein attempted his last words before she quickly drew back her fist mimicking Baseball Great Walter Johnson pitching a ferocious side-winding right hook to his left jaw.

"Look bastard, do what I say, you understand? Unless you want to stay here and be caught, just know I won't be coming to see your sex-sick ass when they lock you up, nor will I be sending commissary money. I refuse to go back to the pen, you hear me?"

Klein chose his words carefully before conveying his thoughts to his sister. His nose was still too tender to experience another round with her. Knowing he had no choice, he gave his seething sister his full attention as she put her plan in action.

"When you see some females pull up at the last gas lane, go up to the window and sweet talk them and hold their attention. While Erland and I are out here, we will take care of the rest, you got it?"

"Yeah, I got it, but what about this shirt? It's all bloody and stuff from you slamming my head into the steering wheel."

"Take the bastard off. I just told you to sweet talk the female when you see her. Leave that bloody shirt in this car," Childress said, taking the bloody shirt from Klein and tossing it on the floor of Beetle.

Erland knew to keep doing what he was told if he didn't want to have another round with his sibling in command.

"There come some females now."

A carload of females pulled up in the last gas lane as Childress had anticipated.

"Alright, fools, here we go," Childress said. "Get yourself together, Klein, and get us that car."

Shirtless and seductive, Klein started up the road to the rest stop that was a gas station. Tall and stout, his powerful chest held his posture upright with every step he took. Using his hands, Klein ran his fingers through the blonde-reddish curly tresses to further attract and lure the unsuspecting females into his grasp. His eyes became fixated on a young brunette that sat in the front seat of a navy blue Cadillac sedan. The closer he came, the more he could hear the fragments of conversation as the brunette spoke to a brown-skinned female in the back seat.

"I can't wait to get to Coushatta Casino. My mama and daddy always win big bucks when they go there. I know I'm going to hit the progressive jackpot as soon as I pull down on a slot machine handle."

Coushatta Casino in Kinder Louisiana is the hottest gambling spot in the southern region. Many travelers make it a point to indulge a little at the beautiful Coushatta Casino Resort.

"Well, I'll be right behind you getting the progressive jackpot on the Double Diamond machine," the brown skinned female said. She was about to respond again when she noticed a bare-chested Klein coming into view behind her friend. Klein stuck his head in the window just breathing distance from the female.

"Hey, there, Cher, where 'bouts ya'll headed from here?" he said, with his green eyes blazing directly into the beautiful brunette's blue eyes. Klein had begun to smack his lips as if anticipating a meal.

His sexual sickness began to arouse him in the usual disgusting way—first brutally pornographic images of the young brunette paraded through his mind. Klein entertained thoughts of inserting objects into the young woman. The images of the woman screaming and begging for mercy only heightened his feelings, making him give notice to a bulge forming in his jeans. The brunette noticed as well.

Instead of her modestly turning away, she continued to encourage Klein's response by putting her mouth dangerously close to his as she answered his question---knowingly finalizing her doom.

"We're headed to Coushatta Casino; you want to ride with us?"

Her brown-skinned friend sat in the back seat and watched in awe as her friend flirted and acted like a student floozy. Klein continued his pursuit. Childress was not too far behind him, lurking in the dark and clocking his every move---timing her strike perfectly.

"Look, here Cher, is your friend inside paying for the gas? If so, I'll pump it so we can be on our way."

With his face in the young woman's personal space, Klein traced the shape of her lips with his tongue. She responded by slamming her legs shut, as orgasmic shivers raced through her. He knew he had accomplished his goal. As Klein pumped the gas, the brown-skinned female responded to her friend's behavior.

"Layla, you are acting hoe-ish,"

"You're just jealous, Axley".

"How the hell am I jealous? You don't see me kissing a half naked stranger."

"Like I said, jealous."

The two traveling friends continued their argument,

just as the third red headed female and owner of the vehicle returned.

"Alright, are you two ready to go?"

"Yeah, I'm ready to go, Dayden. Your buddy here picked us up a stray," Axley stated just as Klein finished pumping the gas and put his face back in the window---sharing a breath with Layla.

"Looks like that filled the tank. Ya'll ready to make a move?" Klein stretched to kiss her once more the moment Childress walked up to the driver's side window and delivered a deadly warning to the females.

"Don't get too cozy. He bites."

Childress jumped in the car shoving the red head over towards her friend in the middle of the seat. Klein immediately got in the backseat of the car. Axley looked on in horror as she knew they were being abducted.

"Where are you taking us?"

"To hell, if you don't shut up," Childress barked.

Knowing that they had to act fast, Childress drove a ways down the road to where the stalled Beetle had been before. Erland had pushed the little car off the road, and into a pond to sink it to the bottom---never to be discovered. He waited in the shadows a few yards from where it had stalled out. When he saw the Cadillac approach him, he started jumping up and down while flapping his arms. He looked like a hatchling attempting to take flight. Childress admonished him immediately.

"Fool, are you landing or taking off? Stop flapping your arms; you are drawing attention to yourself. You never know who is watching."

"I'm just happy, because I know once we get back on the road, I can score a joint."

Childress rolled her eyes at her loony baby brother. Just then, she took notice of how the red head next to her had been staring at the On-Star button just above the rearview mirror. Knowing if the woman pushed the button to notify the On-Star online operators of the abduction, they would be located and caught. Childress warned what would become of her should she make any sudden moves. She encouraged an escape attempt from Dayden.

"Is there something you want to try to do, tramp? Go ahead. If you reach for that button, you will draw back three less fingers on the hand you touch it with. Make your move, and I'll promise you that."

Dayden quickly took her eyes off the On-Star button, and looked down at her hands as she clenched them together in frustration.

Confident, after making her point with a threat, Childress drove to a country road off the main highway. Once she made it to an open field, she stopped the car. Caught off guard out of nowhere, Dayden took a swing with her fist at Childress in an attempt to escape, hitting her right jaw.

Surprised by her audacity, Childress turned towards Dayden and grabbed a handful of her hair. In a fury, yet with an evil grimace, Childress dragged the young woman out to the open field and beat her like a drum. Klein and Erland pulled the other two women out of the car as well.

"That's the last mistake you will ever make, bitch!"

Reaching in her pouch, Childress brought out her little gray canister. Pinching some black crystallized dust between her fingers, she drew in a huge breath and blew it into the faces of the hostages, bewitching them---leaving them paralyzed. Childress granted her brothers their wishes.

"Klein, you and Erland can have your way with them," Childress said as she turned and walked back towards the car. Each step she took proved to be difficult, as she began to feel weak once more. This had happened a few days ago. She noticed her leathery hands trembling, as she wiped her forehead. Her skin looked as if it is beginning to decompose. Childress continued to ignore her symptoms, instead, she diverted her attention back to her all too enthusiastic brothers.

Prisoners in suspended animation, all three women met their twist of fate in a nearby open field. Childress knew what Klein would do once he was alone with the brunette. Erland followed suit behind his brother, and soon grunts of pleasure and release permeated the air---echoing off the corn stalks in the distance. No cries for help, no screams of terror, or futile escape attempts by the captives.

After half an hour went by, footsteps in the grass were the only sounds left in the abandoned field, as Klein and Erland made their way back to the car. The sound of Erland's zipper sliding back into place notified Childress that both brothers were finished amusing themselves.

"Let's roll," Childress said.

"What are we going to do with them?" Klein asked, motioning his chin in the direction of the half naked women that lay still in the field.

Realizing that the women were loose ends needing to be tied up, she once again got out of the car, and slowly walked over to the edge of the field. Knowing her spell from the black dust was still in place, she mumbled these words to them.

"Dig and lay yourself in the earth…dig and lay yourself in the earth…forget us…forget us."

Without a moment to spare, the women that lay zombie like out in the field began to reanimate and started digging up the ground using their hands. Faster and faster, the three women who had been mere happy-go-lucky friends a few hours ago had fallen victim to the Treemount treachery. With skin peeling away from their hands, and acrylic nails flying off into the soil, the victims began to see blood come from their delicate fingertips. Lower and lower they dug into the dirt. Childress could not help being proud of her handiwork.

"By the time somebody finds those tramps, we'll be long gone and home free. Here, take the keys, Erland, you drive."

Once again, Klein chimed in giving his unsolicited opinion about his sister's physical appearance. He playfully threw his arms up to block a punch from her.

"What's wrong with you now? You look awful, Childress."

Instead of playfully throwing a reflexive punch of her own, Childress barely made it back to the car. When she completed her staggered sway, her last step caused her to collapse in Erland's arms. Klein freaked.

"Hey, girl, you're scaring me, what's wrong?"

"What are we going to do now?" Erland said beginning to come unglued himself.

"Keep it together, man; I can't have you flipping out now."

Childress pulled herself together long enough to realize

her problems were coming faster.

"I'm alright, let me go. Just do what I say so we can get across the state line."

Steadying herself back on her feet, Childress went into the trunk and found the luggage the women had packed away. Bottles of makeup, eyeglasses and several different billfolds with loads of cash lay at the bottom of the trunk. There were t-shirts and blue jeans that were fresh clothing. Goodness knows they needed a change of clothing. Childress gathered her bearings and pressed forward.

"Alright, listen. We are going to head down the road to the other little pond we saw. We can wash up and change there. When we do, we will put on this makeup foundation the backseat tramp had, and we will darken our skin so that we can roll through the roadblock at the state line, you got it?"

Klein and Erland both protested with fierce tenacity. Erland shook his head back and forth without speaking hard enough to cause the onset of a seizure. Klein bellyached.

"Nuh uh, I am not wearing makeup, Childress, I told you. That's nasty."

"Do you want me to make your peter draw up to the size of your big toe? You know I can and will do it, just keep on acting stupid."

The dumbfounded brothers had no more rebuttals for their sister. Erland stood alongside the road, quiet as a rock. He provided no input into the discussion.

Childress opened the small bottle of liquid makeup foundation and applied a capful of it to her pale face and hands. Instantly, her leathery skin soaked up the liquid and her appearance took on a dramatic change. Her pale complexion went from pale high yellow to a well-cooked pound cake color.

Klein was pissed because he didn't want to wear the rouge, but dared not go against his sister's orders. His appearance took on the same appearance as Childress' and so did Erland's. Childress completed her disguise with a crooked pair of horn-rimmed glasses that sat out on the bridge of her keen nose.

"I'm putting my hair in a bun, along with these."

Her green eyes stood out like sapphires now in contrast to her complexion, as did her brothers. She looked like a Sunday school teacher. The only thing she was missing was a bible. She rushed her brothers to complete their transformations.

"Take this comb, and comb your curls out, both of you."

No longer on mute, Erland whined, and he combed through his curls.

"Damn, I hate doing this."

He combed his hair out and parted it down the middle of his head, making him look like a professor seeking tenure with the glasses shoved up the bridge of his nose.

Klein slicked his hair back with some gel, and instantly became a nerdy social outcast. With the new clothing and Childress' chipped teeth, they looked nothing like the wanted Treemount clan that every law enforcement agency was looking for. They were looking for four high yellow black folks; three men and a woman, not three brown- skinned black folks. They were, minus Justice. Klein couldn't help but express his concern for their wayside sibling.

"I hope Justice will catch up to us soon. I'm starting to

worry about him."

"Don't worry about him," Childress barked. "He'll find us soon enough. We have to keep moving. No one told that damn fool to go off with that vampire. All I know is he better have taken care of her like I told him. Now, let's roll through to Aunt Bureau's."

Erland took the wheel and drove toward the last four miles to the Texas-Louisiana county line.

***

The city of Orange was the last city just before the Texas-Louisiana border perforated the two states. As expected, a roadblock was waiting on all visitors leaving Texas. Tension instantly seized the car of criminals as they tried to remain composed. Erland's anxiety started to buzz.

"Aw, hell, there it is. The roadblock is stacking the traffic up. I need a joint or some mouthwash, or something, dammit."

"Keep it down, fool, don't lose it," Klein whispered, beginning to tremble himself.

Erland rolled the big sedan right up to the roadblock that had Texas State Troopers on the IH 10 East bound lane. Again, the Treemounts had the whim of chance on their side. Traveling at night made it easy for them and for their disguises to be more genuine. Erland desperately tried not to give away their disguises as he eased up to the checkpoint and rolled down the window. A big burly Texas State Trooper shined his flashlight in the vehicle.

"Hello, folks, where you headed?"

"We're headed to Hammond, Louisiana, officer," Childress hummed, batting her thick eyelashes behind the thick frame --- lying to the trooper knowing her goon brother wouldn't pass the strenuous interrogation. Klein pretended to be asleep as the officer shined his foot long flashlight on his twitching face. Tensed muscle and short breaths in the car made getting through the checkpoint seemed to take hours, although it was only a mere few seconds. Satisfied these three harmless traveling misfits were not the wanted homicidal fugitives, he gave them clearance.

"Alright, you folks have a safe trip," the trooper said, waving them through to the state of Louisiana, convinced of the Treemounts masquerade.

Klein hooped and hollered in relief that he wouldn't be booked into custody this night. For he knew leaving the state as a convicted sex offender, and being around his convicted siblings, would prove to get him a life sentence if he were caught.

"Hot damn, we made it!"

Childress licked the jagged edges of her chipped front teeth as she shouted.

"Freedom, oh, freedom!"

***

Erland drove until sun up to Dog Water Swamp, on the other side of Jefferson Parrish. Childress was fast asleep on the passenger side --- restless from time to time as she fought for a peaceful slumber. The blue sedan turned down a muddy dirt road just off the main Parrish thoroughfare.

Fog hung low over the road, cutting driving visibility in half. Humidity pressed the air, making it difficult to breathe. Moss-covered trees stood with long wispy vines that led a visitor to believe that the trees were the true historians of the area, as they stood towering over the murky wetland. Erland was relieved to know they had arrived at their destination. Aunt Bureau's home stood off in the distance, in a basin at the foot of a hill.

"We're here. I can't wait to wrap my lips around a cold one."

Rolling to a stop just in front of the house, the grifting Treemounts sat in awe at what would be their new home. Although Aunt Bureau's house sat in a basin, at the edge of the swamp, it sloped backward at a 45 degree angle, giving an illusion of standing at least 50 feet tall.

The structure met the horizon just below the trees. With a sinister presence comparable to that of Amityville, Bureau's house was one you didn't want to wander around in at night without a flashlight. Tall columns supported the structure and disclosed its history as being a plantation house, and if you stood still in the front yard, restless spirits would give any visitor an earful.

Erland and Klein stepped out of the car, just as the sound of an alligator's tail went splashing into the swamp. Toads and crickets joined in the early morning symphony of sounds as the Treemounts reacquainted themselves with childhood memories. Klein became ill at ease, as he and his brother stood still for a moment.

"Damn, I forgot about the gators. I'm already home sick just smelling this place."

"You think I could get high if I rolled up some of that moss off that tree?"

"Man you need rehab."

"Hell, don't act like you don't smoke too, Klein."

A hoarse and scratchy reply came from behind the screened in porch. All three Treemounts turned in the direction of a long since forgotten voice that was only second in command to their late mother Frances.

"What the hell you two fools arguing 'bout?"

The raspy voice called from within the house. A shadowy corner of the screened in porch revealed a short round-as-she-is-tall, fair-skinned woman with the same green eyes as their own. Folds of reddish blonde hair fell beyond the short woman's waist, which wasn't too far from the floorboards of the porch.

Ms. Short and stout held open the screen door and bid them permission to enter the house. Standing in the doorway with a brown Virginia Slim clamped between her fingers in her right hand---with ash dangling dangerously on edge, was Bureau Equel Treemount La Deaux, the local mambo that all the swamp dwellers revered. Childress woke up at the sound of her aunt's raspy tone and greeted her properly.

"Hey, Aunt Bureau."

Bureau did not blink, twitch, or even breathe. Suspicion held them in her gaze, freezing out the greeting her long lost niece extended to her.

"All four of ya'll come on in here out of this heat."

"Four? Aunt Bureau it's only me, Klein, and Erland. Justice will be here later," Childress quickly lied to her aunt, hoping not to further fuel her rising suspicion about her wayward brother's whereabouts.

"I said four, and I meant four. Justice would make it five."

"Auntie, I think you must be seeing a gator or something."

Bureau finally let out a slow stingy breath --- hating to let the taste of the delicious Virginia Slim escape her nostrils. Posturing while releasing the smoke from her lips, she simultaneously raised her left hand on her hip.

"Are you that damn dumb, girl?"

Her niece's delayed response time confirmed her suspicions.

"I guess you are then," Bureau murmured, lifting the ultra slim cigarette back into the right corner of her mouth.

Furrowing her own eyebrows, Childress did little to hide her irritation at her Aunt's obvious blindness.

"Auntie it's just us. Justice is not here."

Bureau stood on her porch cool as ice --- holding firmly to her belief and her instinct. Her cigarette burned, dropping ash onto the wooden floor.

"You have Auldicia's curse veiled across your face, heifer," Bureau said, fanning her arm in a circular motion as she addressed Childress.

"Curse, what curse? Nothing curses me, Bureau." Childress said, clutching her pouch, contemplating putting a curse on her aunt.

"You are with child, Childress."

5

Blind, But Now I See

"Sister Childress, sister Childress. Oh how I can't wait to see you. It won't be long now. I do plan to open your eyes as mine have been opened. Oh boy, you have so much to see. Just wait until I catch up to you, sister dearest."

Justice now had vengeance running through his stagnated blood --- escalating his rage as he continued to dwell on past treachery that Childress had inflicted upon him.

Seeing his home collapse after torching it, he left the burning structure behind, as he listened in on a neighbor down the street calling 911. His body still ached from his need. There was no understanding of the new changes his body was going through.

"Ouch! Damn, I just bit my lip. These fangs are sharp as hell. I guess I need to figure out what to do with them until I need them. Oh…here it comes again…that burning in my throat. I'm going back to Believa's house. I hope that she has a few drops left in her. Before I go and get her last drop, I have a taste for something new, and that's just what I'm going to do."

Stalking down the street in the direction he heard the

neighbor call 911 for the fire department; he suddenly realized this was Ms. Amelia Sterling's home. Ms. Sterling had just hung up the phone and walked to her front door to go on the porch to watch as the Treemount home continued to burn. When she opened the door, she found a demonic looking figure that appeared as if it had just come up from the gates of hell. Cataract colored eyes, a long mustache, and missing flesh that reeked of a buried carcass, Justice started his advance inside Ms. Sterling's home.

"Yes, indeed Ms. Sterling, I'm glad you called the fire department, like your smell called me to come to you."

Ms. Sterling was a woman about 42 years old. A widow, and still very attractive for her age, she had lived alone for years after the death of her husband. Mr. Sterling was a prison guard, and while on duty, he was shanked to death in a prison riot during the time Klein was serving a sentence for rape. Speculation surrounded the allegations of whether or not Klein had been involved with his death. Klein had been lusting after Ms. Sterling for years, so upon release he would be free to ravage her for himself—making him the number one suspect for Mr. Sterling's demise. Justice was about to beat Klein to that opportunity of fulfilling his pleasure. Living a lonely and celibate life since her husband's death could be the only rational explanation as to why she found that she was terrified and aroused.

Rich cocoa-bean-skin covered Ms. Sterling's 5'8 frame. High cheekbones and long muscular athletic legs made her a particularly interesting neighbor to spy on, when Justice was a young boy while playing in the neighborhood. Watching this demon walk right into her home, Ms. Sterling had no breath in her lungs to scream for help.

"Ms. Sterling, I've been waiting a long time to put a little of my cream in your rich coffee colored body. Oh yeah, I want to put something in you, my dear. Here's my chance. I know you are going to like it as much as I am," Justice said, taking a handful of his manhood, heightening his arousal as Ms. Sterling began to withdraw from him. Turning to run, she found Justice directly in front of her.

"Please, don't hurt me. Take whatever you want. Just don't hurt me."

"You are what I want. Don't you know that?" Still pleasuring himself, he found it hard to keep his hands off her beautiful skin.

"Let me give you what I've wanted to give you for all these years," he said, as his crusty lips spoke sloughing off pieces of skin in doing so.

With nowhere to run, Ms. Sterling stood impinged against an antique chiffonier. As she stood in a satin robe covering a lace camisole, Justice tore away her clothing while he kept his eyes on her firm breasts. He squeezed her left breast as it made contact with the wet fluid that oozed on the surface of his skinless chest.

Although petrified with fear, Ms. Sterling moaned as she surrendered to him. Justice loved every minute of it, as he lifted her hips and wrapped her legs around him ---joining their bodies with his enhanced endowment. Forgotten sounds of erotic bliss startled her, as sweet moans of pleasure left her lips. Soon shame joined her fear as she continued to enjoy the disgusting situation she found herself in, yet she could not stop her actions.

"I know you're lonely, Ms. Sterling, but I'm going to help you and me out. Do you feel how good our bodies are together? It has been a while since a man filled you up, hasn't it? Let me dust you off, and loosen you up a bit."

Continuing his superhuman lovemaking by driving his sex deep into Ms. Sterling and answering her longing for intimacy, she looked as if she were sitting on top of a washing machine riding the spin cycle. Tilting her head back --- her pulse beat wildly under the skin in her neck. With his natural instinct running loose, he opened his jaws as wide as he could. Taking a bite so savagely, he heard the sounds of her lower back break, as he continued to pound her spine up against the chiffonier.

He released his pleasure with a moan that vibrated off the hollow walls of the small home, as sweet warm plasma washed the dryness from the back of his throat. Slipping into unconsciousness, Ms. Sterling's limbs fell flaccidly to her sides as Justice continued to ride her to death, literally.

"Hey, what's wrong baby? You can't handle it?"

Speaking through sprays of blood as he released his jaws from her neck, he finally discovered she was unresponsive --- with eyes rolled to the back of her head. Allowing himself to slide out of her, he smudged his sticky seed on the insides of her thighs. Her broken spine weighted her limp body to the floor. Without an intact spine, her torso was hyper-flexed, making her appear as if she had been in a magician's trick gone terribly wrong --- leaving behind a torso split from its bottom half.

"Dammit, it happened again. I killed another female. This time I got a little extra pleasure out of it though," he said smiling, as he repositioned his manhood in his jeans, fastened up, and stepped over another dead woman's body.

Heading for the tiny kitchen in Ms. Sterling's house, Justice reached for some bacon grease that was in a tin coffee can on the stove. Dousing the grease over the entire kitchen, he created a trail of the oily liquid that lead back to the surface burners on the stove. A small box of matches sat above a cupboard near the ventilator.

"Time to light it up, baby."

Deciding to leave the scene of the crime, he dropped the match, setting the kitchen ablaze. A stream of flames trailed back to the stove, causing an explosion of blue and orange flames --- instantly engulfing the home.

"I might as well make the fire department earn their money tonight. Hell, I'm feeling good now, buddy," he said to himself, slipping out of the backyard avoiding the hullabaloo with all the neighbors out on their front lawns.

Watching the fire department from a distance trying to keep his burning home from igniting the others around it; the explosion at Ms. Sterling's home caused mayhem and panic, alarming the already preoccupied firefighters to send in a warning to dispatch more firefighting units.

"I never knew blood could make me feel this good. No wonder Childress wanted to become a vampire. She was truly jealous, and that was the one thing she knew she couldn't have," he said. "Ouch, damn, now what? My flesh is hurting again. The pain is too much."

With a little more blood in his system, Justice took notice of his arms. Skin reanimated across the bony finger digits of his hands, as it washed over the ligaments and tendons that lay strewn over porous bones. His mustache began to recess into layers of skin above and below his lips as they continued to thicken, bringing him to human form.

It was back. The sex appeal that previously led unsuspecting females to their doom, once again found its way to this male Treemount. With every step taken, his veins inflated with stagnated blood that sat thick and sludge-like, plumping his newly formed skin. Highly defined jade green eyes with reflective hints of hazel, adjusted his night vision as he ran through backyards avoiding the frightened gatherers.

Minus the beautiful blonde-red curls that once crowned his head, Justice sported a newly bald perfectly round head. High thickly arched blonde-brown eyebrows held a sinister gaze if anyone stood in his line of sight.

"Yes, I'm feeling mighty fine. I think I want to do a little more devilment before I head back to Believa's crib. I think I'm going to go and pay a visit to my third grade teacher Ms. Valmeen Olin. She took my squirrel's paw from me, that bitch did…I had just cut it off fresh that morning when she did, too. Valmeen, Valmeen, how'd you get so mean?" Justice hummed — as he plotted his next move to punish a soon to expire Valmeen Olin.

***

Sister Valmeen Olin sat on her couch and reminisced about her career while looking through her old memorabilia from her days as young teacher. She had long since retired from St. Benjamin's Catholic School on San Antonio's eastside. Known throughout the community as a sweet and gentle woman, Sister Olin had devoted her life to worship and education. Each of her students had a special place in her heart and she kept in touch with them as adults.

She loved educating but suffered a nervous breakdown, which ended her career. Events leading up to the termination of her career still played as a slideshow in her mind daily. Her mental decline forced her into retirement after watching a psychotic little boy viciously kill a helpless squirrel. The furry creature was stoned to death at the hands of Justice Treemount. Sister Olin allowed her mind to drift back in time to that dreadful day.

The scene of blood and fur staining the beautiful school lawn was a gory sight that was too much to take in. Sister Olin admonished Justice for his inhumane actions. Being the hateful scoundrel he was, Justice balked at the idea that Sister Olin could punish him.

"Shut up, bitch! You can't talk to me like that!"

Astounded at the explosive remark from such a small mouth with an adorable face, Sister Olin continued to stand her ground, "You will not talk to adults like that, young man!"

"I said, shut…up! That wig on your head looks like a crooked baseball cap!"

Fed up and close to blasphemy, Sister Olin made one last attempt to salvage his 'going straight to hell' soul, "Come with me, young man. You are going straight to the principal's office!"

"And my mama's foot is going straight to your a—" Justice tried to purse his lips to finish his curse, but dry wrinkled hands of Sister Olin clamped them shut, as Justice Treemount made what would be his last march to the St.

Benjamin's school office.

She snatched a bloody paw that Justice held in his grip. His actions resulted in a swift school expulsion and a call to his mother. A conversation with Frances Treemount was not something Sister Olin was looking forward to, but she knew it had to be done for the disciplinary action to be upheld. She dialed the Treemount home.

The phone rang once, twice, three times, with no answer. As soon as Sister Olin thought she was about to get a well-deserved sigh of relief, an irritated Frances Treemount picked up the receiver on the other end.

"Who the hell is this calling me when you know I'm watching my damn stories?"

Sister Olin had so wished that she had lost her nerve on the third ring. Frances Treemount answered the call, making Sister Olin obligated to receive the verbal assault that waited on the other end of the receiver.

"Hello, Ms. Treemount, this is Sister Valmeen Olin at St. Benjamin's," she greeted. "I regret to inform you that your boy Justice has killed another animal on the premises and is being expelled permanently. I am calling you to come and withdraw him from school. He will no longer be able to attend school here." Sister Olin heard slow deep breathing on the other end of the phone, just before Frances let out a curse that would change the remaining days of her life.

"You are a slow rolling hoe on a low slope, if you think I am leaving my house to come to that school and pick that damn fool up!" Frances bellowed. "This is his seventh school this year and I'm not going to withdraw him. You deal with his flat-headed ass, Cher. I don't have time for that," Frances set

the phone down in its cradle with a loud crack.

Hating the fact that she was held responsible to deal with the negative behavior of this psychotic child, who was clearly in an aggravated state of mania, Sister Olin slowly looked over at a smug Justice.

"I told you!" Justice sniped at Sister Olin. "All you did was piss her off. She was looking at her soap opera 'All my Children'. You probably called her when Erica Kane was on. Now she's going to put a curse on you --- make your hair fall out or something, you damn dummy!"

Sister Olin was about to respond to the threat made on his mother's behalf, when she quickly reconsidered after hearing from the rat-turd faced child.

"Nobody takes an animal foot from me. I'll make sure you are dead before the bell rings tomorrow."

School dismissal was at 2:45 pm, and Sister Olin had taken the threat Justice made to end her life seriously. Before the ink from her signature was dry on the forms, Valmeen Olin hung up her habit, swung her purse on her shoulder and retired at 1:02 pm.

Sister Olin shuddered uncontrollably as she realized how reclusive she had become. Hoarding stuffed animals started out slowly, but soon turned into a shrine to a dead squirrel. Several furry little toys stare with black button eyes at Sister Olin --- at times telling her she must feed them. Clearly, dementia had found a home in her emotional imbalance.

Taking hallucinatory auditory queues from her stuffed friends, she left pieces of bologna and lunchmeat in front of them on the floor, chairs, counters, and other parts of the living room. Ants, gnats, and flies took up residence in her little home. With the foul smell of rotting food, and insect decay, the scent from the wafting wind turned the air into a zoo animals den.

Living in fear is not how the savior would want her to live her life. In knowing that, she still hid from the ever-evil Treemounts. The news had just finished reporting a four-alarm fire a few miles away from her residence.

"Gracious," Sister Olin whispered. "These children are absolutely awful today. They lack such self discipline."

Sister Olin's stroll down memory lane had made her oblivious to the cool breeze that circulated through her small living room. A small picture framed with her last faculty photo crashed to the floor. A jolt of fear seized her attention to the back door ---ajar with a lurking shadow. Standing in the threshold was a grinning Justice Treemount, with his fangs fully drawn.

"Valmeen, Valmeen," he repeatedly sang her name out of key. "Oh, how I dream of Valmeen.

Stiffening with fear, she froze as no scream left her body. Overcome with terror, she had forgotten how to breathe. Finally, her worst fear had come true. The Treemount boy had found her. It was obvious he planned to fulfill his mother's threat.

"You know I've been dreaming about you, Sister Olin? How could that be? Oh yes, no one takes from me. You took my squirrel's foot, and now I'm here for your foot."

"You are going straight to hell, Justice Treemount."

"And I'm taking your foot with me. You're not so tough now, are you witch?"

Sister Olin began to cough uncontrollably, in efforts

to spit phlegm from her last breath in her intruder's face but found the attempt unsuccessful. Justice grabbed her right leg and suspended her in mid air. Sister Olin screamed in hopes of getting the attention of a passerby.

"Put me down, you little turd."

Justice brought the woman's foot to his mouth, as she dangled helplessly from his grip. His eyes instantly located a vein that surfaced so boldly underneath the peeling skin on top of her bunion-covered foot. A parched thirst rippled down his throat --- making the gum line around his fangs throb.

Agility and strength made feeding time for Justice a joy each time he did it. Upon contact, he nearly snapped the petite woman's foot off her leg. Rich and nutrient blood plasma washed over his tongue sending him into a feeding frenzy. He fed so hard he sucked the skin, ligament, and tendon from Sister Olin's foot.

Now satiated, Justice released his grip on the woman. Sister Olin fell from her mid air prison, crashing through the glass coffee table top dislocating her neck upon impact. Her wounds did not bleed, as Justice drained every drop.

***

Believa thought she only dreamt being in the throes of multiple orgasms, until she felt a searing pain of irritation in her groin. Pain throbbed throughout her body, as if she had taken a beating with a mallet. When she finally came to terms with the fact that what she thought was a dream was reality. Justice Treemount had shown up in her home, he had rocked her world, and he had bitten her. She had been in fights before with other females and lost, but never had she felt like this. She was weak and could barely sit up.

In an attempt to get to her feet, aching perineum muscles made moving her legs a strenuous effort. Believa slowly stood up from the bed --- nearly falling as her legs started to wobble immediately. She staggered into the bathroom to splash some water on her tepid face. Washing her face sent daggers of pain to her sensitive neck area.

Remnants of early morning passion slowly leaked down her thigh as she stood before the mirror. Looking on in horror, she glared at the bite mark Justice had given her. The two wounds were inflamed at the openings and surrounded by squirming blue veins that rooted just beneath the skins surface. His fangs were lethal, and Believa knew without a doubt, Justice Treemount was now a monstrous killer --- giving a new level of dread to his family name.

An empty feeling and nausea indicated to her that she needed to eat. Her body had fed Justice and now she needed to replenish her strength. Shuffling helplessly, she made her way to the kitchen fruit bowl, and devoured an apple and banana at the same time. The hunger left little time for her to peel the banana before biting it.

Confusion and fear clouded her mind. The ecstasy she shared with Justice was one thing, but she also came to grips with the fact that he was a killer in the rarest form. He had no regard for anyone or anything if they were an obstacle for him---he would kill in cold blood.

Nourishment filled her reserves of strength, clearing her brain fog.

If I pack a few things, I could make it to my sisters

across town, and hide from him, and hopefully from there I could just leave town---yeah, that's it.

Without a moment to spare, Believa jumped to her feet and grabbed three days worth of clothing. Hastily rummaging through the house reminded her of her days running from the law with Childress as they robbed high-end retail stores of their loot.

Stuffing bras, panties, girdles, and other personal items into an overnight bag, Believa reached for the door handle, just as her blood iced over from the low hum of a bass filled voice that resonated behind her. Out of nowhere, Justice had entered the room and sat perched on the edge of her dog-gnawed sofa.

"Where you going Believa…? You are not planning on leaving me are you, Cher?

Too terrified to move, Believa felt the little breath she had slowly leave her lungs. Any courage she previously had as she backed her things to leave had left long before she had. Closing her eyes, violent tremors started from her toes to her knees. A beaded sheen of sweat glazed her upper lip and forehead as she searched for words to answer her monster houseguest.

"Hey, baby," Believa whispered. "I was getting rid of some old clothes. There is a sale tomorrow and I wanted to get some new," she tried to finish but was unable to. Blinking her eyes once was all it took. Justice closed the distance between them in that moment.

"Don't lie to me, girl," he said grabbing her and pinning her arms behind her back. "I can smell the fear in your sweat. Do not fool yourself into thinking you can run from me, girl. I will hunt you down and mount you on this wall, if I have to.

You got that?"

Changing his expression from anger to lust in a matter of seconds, Justice ran his tongue up the side of Believa's neck. Salt trailed from her tear ducts irritating her eyes, leaving no tears. Lacking energy from her draining earlier that morning, left her dehydrated and too weak to fight back, as Justice sank his fangs into her once more.

Instead of feeling the pull of her blood break through the surface of her skin, she felt Justice let go of her as she fell to his feet. He looked baffled as she scurried away from him as far as the doorjamb would allow.

"I don't want to kill you, Believa, but you cannot leave. Do you understand? You cannot leave me," he said.

Believa nodded her head and sat with knees pulled to her chest. Dusk had just fallen which made her fear factor run wild. Staring at her with a mesmerizing glare, Justice warned her once more.

"I need you. Do not make me hunt you down."

Discovering that night held the magic to make him stronger, Justice stretched his arms and legs.

"I'm going downtown for awhile," he called. "Have yourself ready for me when I get back. I want you ready all night long. Do you hear me, Cher?"

Again, Believa made the effort to nod her head, as pain gripped her from her sore neck. Satisfied, Justice turned and disappeared out the front door --- slamming it shut.

Finding her voice after she thought she was alone, Believa's scream nearly shattered her eardrums as she opened her mouth wide enough to pull a muscle in her jaw. It was a scream of captivity. A scream that lacked faith and hope, and one filled with sorrow and emotional torture.

Already having run a block away from the house, Justice smiled as Believa's scream filled his sensitive ears. Running with the night, Justice needed to feed and was soon on the prowl once more. "I am ready and feeling mighty fine tonight."

Heading west toward downtown, he allowed his legs to carry him faster than the human eye could see.

6

I Want To Know

Aches and pains that settled over me were the best I'd ever felt. Our binding ceremony was everything any bride could have dreamed of having in a storybook wedding. Tasting Nacio during our plasma exchange was a new experience. After going through the trauma of rape by Klein, I wondered whenever my wedding night came if my husband and I both would be robbed of matrimonial intimacy. The past is the past; therefore, I look only to my future with Nacio. He loved every inch of me, from head to toe. I love the fact that he provides me with a security I have never known.

One bite from Nacio caused unexpected physical changes. Sound, smell, taste, and touch had taken on new acuity. With the strong scent of passion lingering throughout our suite, our arms and legs are a tangled, woven mess as we lie in the middle of the bed. Taking notice of newly heightened awareness, I could hear the Frigidaire in the kitchen turn on its cooling cycle. A curious moth, had taken interest in a flickering porch light over the garage. Its fluttering wings had the clarity of soft helicopter propellers.

Touch is what I craved most. Nacio's caress brought

comfort --- best described as a strong sedative for an easy slumber. Nodding off is comparable to floating in a gentle stream. Once asleep, my name is whispered by a lovely familiar voice.

"Solis," my mother's voice called.

Feeling the corners of my lips pull upward in a smile, I continued to enjoy the peace I felt.

"Solis," another happy familiar voice called. "Wake up, child. Do you not hear us calling you?"

Yep, that was Grandma Olvignia's voice.

That command did it, bringing me forward in a trance-like state to realize I had nodded off to sleep on my wedding night to wake up on the other side, standing before my mother and no-nonsense grandma.

"Congratulations, Hammer!" my mother shrieked. "You have bonded with Nacio, and you are the new Mistress of our family. I am so very proud of you, honey. You don't know what this means yet, but you soon will."

Looking at her, I realized her beauty was even more breathtaking than when I last saw her in our last dreamscape visit.

"Did I die?"

"Naw, you are not dead, silly," Grandma Olvignia interjected. "If you were you'd look good like us!"

Still the firecracker even in the afterlife, Grandma Olvignia stood with her back straight as plywood and her knees locked back in the opposite direction, as a general readied for battle and on standby. This was and still is, even in the afterlife, her battle mode. Knowing from her previous life, this persona of Grandma Olvignia's was not a good one, I accepted the fact that this dreamscape visit was not a social call, but a warning.

"You need to clear your mind, child, and listen to what we say very closely," my mother proceeded. "It's time you knew of the truth of your heritage and all of the tragedies that comes with it."

Dreamily, I stood before my mother anxious to understand what lies ahead for me, "I'm ready to receive that knowledge, mama."

Grandma took her queue, raising her arm and touching my forehead as her voice carried me further away across time. She began to speak a chant that resonated in a low and steady hum, entrancing me further.

"Yeoway oma, Yeoway omu, Yeoway olo," Grandma Olvignia continued.

Grandma Olvignia's voice commanded full attention.

"You have the blood of the Ashanti people running through your veins. Your ancestors were strong, wise women blessed with supernatural gifts beyond reasoning or explanation. Our ancestors were beautiful women that were sought after and betrothed to marry the eligible warriors in the community."

Amazed at grandma's words, my mind captured her words as events of the past played out right before my eyes.

"Oded was one of our forefathers --- a young warrior in our village. He was strong, extremely handsome and sought after by many young women amongst the community. He only had eyes for his bride, Olinka, and loved her even though Priestess Auldicia had her raped."

My mother's face took on a troubled look at this point

as she moved in closer and took my hand in hers. Fixing her eyes on me, she took caution as she gathered her words.

"Hammer, you must understand when I tell you what is to come. Amongst our people there was one known as the Obayifo, a witch that roamed the village at night. We knew who this woman was, and knew that she would do unspeakable things with her body as she took young warriors as her lovers."

Although in a dreamscape, fear somehow worked its way down my spine as my mother continued.

"You see, the Obayifo, also had a cursed taste for blood and lust as well. She overtook our village slowly at first. Until another of our ancestors learned of her existence and set out to stop the evil which had befallen our community."

"Auldicia was the Obayifo was she not, mom?"

"Yes, baby, she was," my mother confirmed.

"The entire village was seized with fear and anguish. Our crops became diseased; our men fell ill with a sickness that left their reproductive organs impotent and diseased as well. We noticed that many of them lacked strength or the desire to be with their brides when night came, no explanation. Animals were slaughtered and drained of blood. Many young brides thought that Satan made his way into their huts and robbed their marriage of desire. In truth, it was Auldicia.

Continuing the history, an awful realization settled in about the Treemounts and Auldicia.

"Auldicia was a high priestess --- given her power after her pact with Vulkus. A demon that is lowest and least respected in murky depths of hell. Her pact with this demon was to wield extraordinary power on earth, in exchange for damning souls through lust and blood exchange with living humans. Vulkus would someday claim her body and soul for eternity. Only he knew the day and hour to collect the debt from the pact Auldicia had made. Only a woman as vain as Auldicia would use her body in such vulgar ways, that no man would want her. Lying in lust with men in the fields amongst the pestilence and animal waste was how she preferred to have her trysts."

My mother never stammered one word as she journeyed on.

"Oded discovered Auldicia was the Obayifo that had cursed our ancestor's village. Punishment for his revelation was severe, and she made certain to do it in the cruelest of ways. Testicles are a sacred part of a warrior's anatomy, in implementing his punishment, Auldicia tied Oded's testicles with soaked bamboo --- pooling the blood to make the sacs dangle heavy. A flat stone press heated on an open fire, then greased with animal fat to cause the wounds to sizzle. Oded's weighted testicles were pressed and smoked repeatedly as torture.

As these events unfolded as mama's words continued, fear retreated as anger filtered in and the need for battle took its place --- that's when grandma spoke once more.

"Auldicia created the World of free Hoedom as you know it today," she hummed. Grandma had such a way with vocabulary and splicing words together, as serious as this conversation is I couldn't help but giggle and try to correct her---a mistake on my part causing a sharp admonishment.

"Do you mean whoredom, Grandma Olvignia?"

"I said Hoedom and that's what I meant. Don't sass me, girl!"

Trying to keep it together, I kept my quirky giggles to myself as my mother chimed in once more.

"You see child, legend has it that Auldicia is a distant cousin of the mythical goddess Medusa. Vanity and seduction were a curse for her. Weakening the males in the village was her punishment to the females out of jealousy. Warriors continued with the sickness yet, there were no babies being born to those couples that had mated. Instead, a number of unexplained motherless children appeared along the edge of the shoreline. Some of the women questioned the spirits of these children --- naming them evil bastards of Auldicia. Many of the children smelled like animal waste and lie covered in filth. This sickness has perpetuated itself in many generations of our men. It manifests itself today in our men as slothfulness, cowardice, and laziness --- causing them to conceive children and not take brides at all, or worse they become rapists, as in Klein's case.

In disbelief, I found myself unable to speak. Hearing those words from mama, confirmed she knew of my stolen innocence. I feared the possible whereabouts of those children and what transgression they committed in the world today.

"Auldicia has power over certain elements and weather occurrences, Solis. You must prepare for any of these happenings, and you must discover them in order to defeat Childress."

"But how can I, mama?" I asked. "Childress's whereabouts are unknown at the moment. Can't I just leave all of this and go on with my life? I'm finally happy now, and I don't feel that it should be all my responsibility."

I had not heard my mother shout my name in many

years, but hearing her shout now caused apprehension, giving her my full attention.

"IT IS YOUR RESPONSIBILITY!" She interjected. "You must take your warrior and end this curse, Solis. You are the new mistress and you must carry our family name. You are the strongest and the most worthy, no matter what you think you have been through, this is your destiny."

Grandma put a new spin on things that I questioned.

"Your ancestor Olinka, one of my many grandmothers, had the gift of sight, as I did, and as you have now. Her gifts blessed her as the mistress of our village. Keeping the peace amongst our people is what made the little community flourish. She too possessed a goddess like beauty that naturally made her an enemy in Auldicia's eyes. Reclaiming control of her village was her main mission. Olinka led a group of women who set out to identify the plague that ravaged their community, and knew they had to work fast after what was revealed to her."

"Was she able to stop Auldicia?" I asked.

"Olinka followed Auldicia one night, deep into the woods. The Ashanti women of the community had muscular frames with height considerable enough to carry their blessings of muscles and hips. The Ashanti women's attributes caught the eye of warriors and even slave traders. What Olinka witnessed next is what set her into action. When Auldicia first journeyed into the woods her body was that of a normal woman, but once she stopped walking and turned to the largest tree in the woods, Olinka saw her lie in lust with another village warrior that appeared paralyzed at the base of the tree. After taking the seed of the warrior in her body, her belly was full with that of a child. Once her desire was fulfilled, she revealed her fangs, and delivered a savage bite to the young warrior's neck."

Shock was stingy in giving me breath, and I could not gather words to respond to what my Grandma was saying.

"Auldicia murmured a chant, *Ignabo, Ignabo azi* --- causing the sky to rumble with thunder and lightning as the woes of labor twisted her womb in agony. Bearing down on the surfaced roots of the tree, Auldicia pushed her mud cloth to the side, as the head of a wailing child pushed through her womb --- magically inhaling its first breath of life. If the labor and delivery of the child stalled, Auldicia would impatiently reach in and yank the child free of her womb."

Grandma stood firm with hands postured on her hips.

"Once the placenta expelled itself from her body, rodents that lived in the tree ran to secure the waste, and carried it off in the direction of the shore. Cord blood flowed from the baby, causing Auldicia's unending appetite to intensify. With predatory instinct, she bit her newborn causing the child to wail for its life --- sending the shrill cry into the distance of the black night. It is assumed those children were vampires.

"How did Olinka stop her?" I stammered. It was clear to me that these things were disturbing for Grandma Olvignia to recall, but she continued.

"Olinka realized that each time a child was conceived by Auldicia, her bloodline would be perpetuated and the curse would lead to a generation of evil souls on earth, and this has come true. You must stop any Treemount blood from spilling on sacred ground during death, Solis. Each time a child is born the legend remains true, and evil continues to dwell on earth. Once a child is born to a Priestess during an induction ceremony, and the child is a girl, that child is a legacy. The blood and birth waste passed from the child's mother would be all powerful --- making the new Priestess and her child unstoppable."

"This includes any drop of blood from direct descendants from Auldicia ---meaning Childress, Klein, Justice, and Erland.

"What happened with Olinka?"

"Auldicia realized that her evil had been discovered, though it was too late for the young warrior. Blood rushed from his body, as death came on swift wings to claim him. Auldicia shouted a chant to the sky, and she transformed into her true form that only a Mistress can see. Auldicia stood before Olinka at 8 feet tall, with spindly arms attached to hands with talons --- covered in scaly skin. Fangs, the length of hypodermic needles, gleamed fiercely in the moonlight, as black patent wings stretched across her back. Pustules filled with disease and bacterium lined the surface of her legs, as hoofed feet stabbed the ground."

"Grandma Olvignia, please just tell me what happened to Olinka!" I pressed.

"Oh, now you realize what's at stake here, don't you?" she patronized. "I thought it wasn't your responsibility?"

"Okay, Grandma, enough arm-twisting. What happened?"

"Olinka raised her hands to Auldicia and threw a mixture of rare Colloidal Silver and protection powder in her direction. Smoke began to rise from Auldicia, as her limbs started to singe right before Olinka's eyes. Screams filled the night as Auldicia tried to find her bearing. Olinka chanted a binding spell to drive Auldicia from the village. Not far from where the two supernatural beings fought, stood a patch of *Mikania Micrantha*, known in your world as Mile a Minute Weed. Olinka summoned loose strands of the weed to a waiting stitch needle made from a rhinoceros tooth. As Auldicia stood paralyzed, Olinka utilized her strength to stitch her womb shut, magically sterilizing Auldicia. Legend has it that no more children were born from her barren womb. She was driven away from our village community. It is said, she was punished by Vulkus because Olinka won the battle --- washing her footsteps from the earth's surface. She would smother in Hell for all eternity."

Awestruck, Grandma Olvignia held my attention --- rendering me useless.

"Knowing that she could not fight the power of Olinka's blessed gifts," Grandma Olvignia lamented, she retreated, but not without placing hex on Olinka. Auldicia made it clear Olinka's bloodline would always be haunted by the generation of children conceived by Auldicia from that day on, and this is one reason why the Treemounts possess such strong hatred for our entire bloodline."

"You said that is one reason they hated us so much, but what is the other?"

"Nacio of course, child," Grandma squawked.

"Your warrior was the most sought after in his far away community of the Canary Islands. Blessed with strength and prestige, he had his entire life before him. Excelling at all endeavors and challenges, Nacio had the pick of any female he chose, but that was not to be his fate. Slavery soon swept the coast of the western tip of the continent, and he became a victim to its consequences. Auldicia tried to turn Nacio into a vampire, but was unsuccessful, but later sealed his fate once in the new world, where you now are his bride."

"Did Auldicia leave earth?"

"It has always been assumed that she has been damned to hell since she has no longer been seen or heard from. The question is what happened to all her ill-conceived children? Olinka, although thorough in her conquests to end the life of the motherless children, there were still many that escaped into this world furthering the Treemount bloodline. This is your fate as the new Mistress, Solis. You must put an end to this evil or none of our family members will be safe. Do you understand now, child?"

Once Grandma Olvignia and mama explained things more clearly, I could not help but feel an invisible constricting weight placed on my shoulders. Doubt still racked the corners of my mind about my abilities and my strength. I prayed that someday I could move past this doubt. Knowing what lies ahead of me makes me wonder if my newfound happiness is in jeopardy.

"Is Nacio safe or is he still coveted by Auldicia?"

"Stop doubting who you are, Solis," my mother hissed. "You are the chosen one and you will succeed, my dear."

Grandma, as usual was brutally honest about everything.

"What you should be questioning is whether Childress wants him. Her motives are to change into a vampire. She wants him for this sole purpose and, of course, to punish you for whom you are."

"What!" I exclaimed. "I will slit her damn throat if she tries to touch him in anyway."

"Oh, I see that nearly woke you up, didn't it?" she truthfully jested.

As Grandma Olvignia found humor in watching me squirm like she always did to get me to focus and believe in my abilities, my mother's expression gleamed with what she told me next.

"Sweetheart, you will always have a connection to me and your grandma and you will never be alone. You have been blessed with the strongest of telekinetic abilities as well as telepathic abilities giving you control over animals."

Dumbfounded, I gazed at my mother with an imaginary thought cloud above my head filled with questions.

"Animals? Mama you of all individuals know that I am so not animal person. When did you ever see me petting a cat, dog or any animal for that matter?" My mother was so tickled by my response; she made sure to drag her humor out a little more.

"You have the gift of the alliance many do not share with animals. They will offer you protection in your time of need, and that is something that you should be proud of, Solis. Whenever you find yourself in a dangerous situation, you will find your new telepathic ability with animals useful."

Mama and Grandma both smiled as they each gave me a hug and kiss, as they began to fade way. They responded in unison, bidding me farewell.

"Sleep now, Solis. Never doubt yourself and always remember we love you dearly."

I enjoyed seeing the two most important women in my

life, but my heart yearned for them to physically remain with me. With questions still swirling in my head, one more inquiry slipped from my mouth. Curiosity had a continuous grip on my heart about her death.

"Mama, was your death accidental?"

Answering and sending reassurance with it, my mother put my fears surrounding her death to rest once and for all --- yet it was bitter sweet.

"Yes, my death was an accident. Your stepfather was not involved. However, the woman he is married to has Treemount blood coursing through her veins."

***

Awakening peacefully in the middle of our bed, vivid thoughts of my wedding night stirred my desire --- which made me smile from ear to ear. Rolling over, I found Nacio taking in an eyeful of my silhouette, conveying we shared the same sentiments. Our bed was a sexy mess, as we lie entangled in a ruffled heap of satin sheets. The area on my neck where I received my first passion mark was a little tender, but nothing to fret over. Nacio brought my hand to his mouth, gently kissing my fingers.

"Good morning, Mistress Puente."

"Good morning to you too, Hefe Puente," I said lovingly as we shared a kiss.

"How are my mothers doing?"

A fluttering feeling of butterflies twirled in my stomach as I blushed from the realization that I had become a bride, and had a new family member, whom I knew I would do anything for. Nacio's happiness is all that matters. Nothing is too great for him.

"Those two are quite well and are very proud of you… of us. They both told me of my ancestral history…and of yours. Auldicia's bloodline has wreaked havoc on several generations. Should she rise, there is no telling what the world's fate would be. What are we going to do, Nacio?"

"Nothing other than your happiness matters to me as well, Solis…nothing. Nothing will harm you. I promise. Our task is not an easy one, but a necessary one. We will be together as it is fulfilled, so enough for now. Let's take a moment to be a couple in love before going off to fight the world and all the Treemounts in it. So your mother said you could commune with animals. That is funny."

My sweetie's dry humor tickled my funny bone and made me smile. Rubbing my shoulders with the Jasmine scented sheets Bose made just for us as an aphrodisiac, my fears were put to rest…for a while."

"What would you like to do today, Mistress, besides lie here and allow desire to run free between us?"

"With an offer like that up for negotiation I could just take you up on that," I said knowing that desire would soon turn our smoldering embers of passion to a full flame with one more kiss. His lips met mine, and the flames raged.

***

My second awakening was that afternoon. Nacio held a hand full of my hair, running his fingers through my curly mane. In need of a bath; he was all too obliged to draw the bath water---filling it with Gardenias and Jasmine.

"Come, Mistress," Nacio commanded. "Let me wash your soft skin."

Giving him a "Yeah, right look", he reassured me he was strictly going to bathe me.

"I promise no tricks, okay?"

"Ummm, are you sure?" I teased.

"Promise," he said as he planting a wet kiss on me as I submerged into the hot bathtub.

With his huge frame, Nacio looked as if he were a giant sinking into the water as our bodies joined each other as one. His firm chest acted as a recliner for me as he poured a carafe of warm water over my head to lather and wash my hair.

It is true what they say about the sense of touch, we all need it. Although it had not been 24 hours, I knew that I could not live without his touch. Each caress of his fingers as they stimulated my scalp nearly drove me into an endless slumber. Massaging the temples of my head, brought a sense of peace ---something I had longed for over quite some time as well.

Eager to find out what was in store for us before it got too late in the day, I summoned courage to ask Nacio about my new acuities. Receiving one bite from a vampire can indulge your senses, receiving two bites seals your fate to transform into one.

"Sweetheart," I started. "What made you decide to take a chance and bite me? I'm not complaining about it. I am just curious."

A long silence filled the air as I turned to him and we looked deep into each other's eye. Smiling with his eyes, he cupped my chin with his hand.

"I could not wait any longer, my dear. I have literally waited a lifetime for you. Everything is so perfect. Some men might not have cared about a matrimonial ceremony, but I did, and I wanted to fulfill the dream with you. I do worry about you going through the change. Leaving the human world is a difficult choice to make, Solis. Please take care in making your decision."

"The choice was not a difficult one," I said. "I am here with you now. I made the choice. Eternity could not separate us, because I will follow you to the end of the earth."

"Alright, then we will turn in the direction of the endless horizon and live out our time together."

A sneaky little tear slipped from my eye down my cheek. As soon as it did, Nacio wiped it clear before it dropped into our bathwater. Many sleepless nights were now in the past. I knew I would never feel the loneliness I felt in the past. Trusting someone is not easy for me, but I trusted him with my life.

Trusting him is easy, but I know I want children and that is something that has circled my mind. Children are a blessing, and leaving the possibility of children behind when I leave this life is one I will mourn. It is a sacrifice that I will take into consideration, but for now I want to enjoy my groom.

Becoming an eager beaver to show him and my beautiful ceremony diamond ring off to the world, I decided where I wanted to go for the day.

"Baby, let's go to the northern part of the River walk. It's just been completed and I want to see."

His lips turned up in a greedy smile --- fangs gleaming in the sunrays spilling in from the custom blinds.

"Well then, we are off to see the river as you wish."

"I want to see the bats that live underneath the overpass by the river."

"Sure. As long as you don't expect me to turn into a bat," he grinned.

7
Cher Childress

"With child?" Childress blurted, "I'm not carrying a damn child. Surely you have been smoking this tree moss out here with your Slims, Aunt Bureau, because you have got me messed up."

"Who's the daddy, heifer? Do you even know? Seems like to me you would at least have sense of enough to know where you last laid your behind down at to know you are pregnant!"

Tension filled the muscles that covered her spine, as she took a defensive stance with her aunt. Erland's foolery saved their aunt from a possible strike to the face and an all out brawl there on the porch.

"Oooohhhhwwwhhooo," the oversexed eldest brother Klein cooed. "Childress, you are pregnant! Guess 'ole Bouvier was handling his business the right way before you hexed him and he shot his head off, huh?"

Flashing jade eyes fell on him, as he stood laughing at her in her moment of embarrassment. Balling up her fist, a right hook split the wind in his direction, only to have it caught mid air by Bureau with her cigarette dangling securely in the right corner of her mouth. Childress stumbled backward tumbling right into her aunt's arms.

"I will not have that shit out here! Look at you, heifer. You probably haven't eaten in days," an irritated Bureau accused. "You look like you haven't slept in six months. In fact, I know you have not slept with the law after you."

Childress pinned Klein with her eyes, hoping to put a hex on him that would give him a palsy that would paralyze one side of his face to slow his speech to a slur, but Bureau jumped in the middle of the two before it went any further.

"Man, forget you, Childress," He squawked. "I'm going inside and get cleaned up. You got an extra toothbrush and tooth paste, Aunt Bureau, because my mouth is funky?"

"Go look in the bathroom cabinet, Klein and leave us women be before you get hurt out here, fool," Bureau responded. "There's a red and white one in there."

Little did she know, Bureau had actually known the truth about her niece's loose wayward behavior with different men for years. Whenever Childress's mother Frances came to visit, Childress would go through local men like athletic socks. Even with that in mind, she wasn't about to let her nephew hit his sister in her condition and she needed to intervene before there was an all out brawl at the swamps edge.

"Urgata!" Bureau yelled, "Come on out here and say 'hey' to your cousins! Don't look like the law caught them yet, since they out here on my doorstep!"

Beautiful physical features are a trademark in the Treemount bloodline --- it has been for centuries. Urgata was one of Bureau's daughters with the very same seductive allure of her cousin Childress.

An inch smaller in height, Urgata's frame was leaner than that of her cousin's, but she could still pass for a sister to Childress. Flawless skin covered a fresh young face comparable to famous supermodels. Her hair was the same color, like her cousin's, only bone straight and shoulder length. Childress instantly resented her cousin's perfect looks. Bureau beckoned for Urgata's assistance.

"Hey, Childress, how are you?" Urgata asked sincerely.

Childress stood with the right corner of her mouth, turned up in an irritated scowl.

"Don't worry 'bout me, just you mind your business."

"Whatcha standing there looking at, girl?" Bureau squealed. "Fix this girl a plate of food to eat." As Bureau reached for Childress's arm, she noticed her clutching an old book with a worn spine. Bureau knew instantly what Childress held in her possession. This book held all of the history of the Treemounts and their skills and talents in the practice of Voodoo. This book gives its owner access to the skills and unyielding power into world of the underground.

"Where'd you get that book from, girl?" Bureau questioned.

"My mama gave it to me. Why?"

"I believe that book should be here with me. I'm the mambo in these parts is why and your mama stole it from me."

"I'm not giving you a damn thing."

"Watch how you talk to me in my house, tramp."

Looking in Klein and Erland's direction, one quick growl of a command and the two buffoons snapped to attention.

"Ya'll help me get this heifer inside, she hasn't eaten

but she is still heavy as hell."

Erland, halfway lucid, responded to his Aunt's plead "Yes, ma'am."

"Take my arm, Childress," Urgata urged. "I'll help take you upstairs so you can rest."

"I don't need any damn help from you so back off and give me 50 feet!" Childress warned as she made her way past Urgata.

Setting foot in Bureau's home quickly sent the visiting relatives on a trip down memory lane.

Crab parboil gently wafted through the air to the living room in the front. The smell originated from the kitchen located in the rear of the home. Childress quickly adjusted her eyes to the dimness of the room. Thick, bruise colored velvet curtains hung loosely all along the walls. The generations of Treemounts were many and Childress was quickly reminded of that fact, as she noticed all of her second cousins scattered throughout her aunt's living room.

Urgata had four boys, as well as her sister Tahiti making the living area look like a daycare without a staff to childcare ratio policy. Bureau's other two daughters, Tahiti and Menlo, were not at home when Childress and her brothers arrived.

Childress's mother Frances and her older sister Bureau had been close when they were growing up. When Frances hit puberty and started having children, her escapades with men drove a wedge between the two sisters, therefore Childress did not grow up around her cousins --- widening the gap the initial wedge had caused between their mothers.

Attempting to take a few step towards the stairs, Childress had her path blocked by a toddler who had found naptime comfort by crawling inside a lampshade for an afternoon snooze.

"Slide out of my way, damn it!"

Little Oakley was soon rolled out of the way by his brother Fleming who had found joy from eating a hot biscuit. The older of the two, he enjoyed the biscuit with some maple syrup by making a bowl out of cheap sunglasses. The child dipped his biscuit inside the lens of the cracked sunshades, trailing syrup from his mouth to his scalp.

Oh yeah, Childress was quickly reminded of what her childhood was made of and what the next few weeks of hiding out in Dogwater Swamp would be like.

"Can't you control your hellions?" Childress sniped, as she turned towards Urgata.

"Come on, boys, let's go out back."

"Yeah, take their little asses out back with the moccasins or something."

Making her way to the sofa, she sat down on the shiny, sunken grime-slicked furniture. She was about to close her eyes when she noticed a child with a head the size of a bowling ball hoist his head out of a cardboard box. The scowl drawn across his face clearly indicated his awakening from his nap occurred due to the hubbub from their arrival. Yes, little Moffit literally came into the world with a man's head on his shoulders.

"What the hell you looking at, Moffit?" Childress hissed. "Take your heavy headed ass back to sleep."

Moffit continued to stare at his squatting second cousin who had obviously invaded his space. The toddler stuck his tongue out at Childress and slowly lowered his head back to the depths of his pretend fortress.

Before she could respond to her little cousin's insolence, a wave of nausea hit Childress with the force of a gavel on a judge's bench.

"Ooohh, I am going to be sick."

If she had any doubt about being pregnant, the nausea confirmed what her aunt already knew.

"They said the entire tri-state region is on the lookout for ya'll," Bureau confirmed. "What were you thinking?

"Childress got us on the run from this chick she can't stand, named Solis Burkes," Erland said, teeth chattering from withdrawals. "You got some nerve pills, Aunt Bureau."

"Boy, tell me what the hell I look like feeding you some of my nerve pills?" Bureau interjected. "You'd better find your own damn pharmacy."

Bureau sat irritated as Erland went into one of his catatonic stupors. Losing patience by the second, she refocused on Childress as she jumped up and got in Erland's personal space.

"You are going to need a hospital bed if ya'll keep telling my business," Childress snapped.

"Tell me, child, what's the story with you and this girl?"

"I hate her and I always have. There is several dead relative's back home, auntie. I know they are dead because they first came up missing. Solis Burkes has something to do with it, I know. She's hooked up with a vampire named Nacio; I knew once we heard Dukane, Montclair, Judd, Hastings, and Duboc came up missing they were dead.

Bureau continued to stare at Childress, but was flabbergasted at what her niece was explaining to her about the believed to be dead Treemounts. She contemplated what to do next, and chose her words very carefully. Knowing that what she was about to say would surely send her power-hungry niece into a rage.

"The family mambo has to put a stop to this foolishness," Bureau stated. "We are Treemount women and have always dealt with our enemies accordingly. Since your mother Frances has past, I will step in and rid us of this girl and the police that hunt you for the things that happened.

Childress spun her head around and locked onto Bureau with a warning that made shivers run down the short woman's back.

"I know where the hell I come from and who I am," Childress sneered. "You are not taking over a damn thing as mambo for me and my enemies. That is *my* right --- it says so right here in this here book, Cher. Don't twist the truth."

Bureau only sat still for a few moments before she rebutted her earlier statement, in hopes of calming her riled up niece.

"I only meant that since I have been a mambo longer than you it would best if…" clipped by an outburst from Childress that rattled the windows behind the velveteen curtains, Bureau shuddered.

"Here me good, Bureau…just because you are older than me, that don't mean you are better than me," Childress blasted, crawling within an inch of Bureau's personal breathing space. "Do you understand me?"

Nodding her head was the only thing Bureau could do without setting off fireworks from hell in the living room. Proceeding once again, she threw in some ancestral trivia that was sure to make her niece take her words to heart.

"You now carry a child within your womb, Childress. I believe the child you carry is a female. If this is true, this female will be a legacy to our bloodline. In order to fulfill your destiny, you must take your rightful place as the new mambo for your part of the Treemount clan in your mother's honor."

"Don't lie to me, old woman," Childress barked, still within breathing distance from Bureau. "If I fulfill my destiny as mambo, I take over the entire Treemount clan. In doing so, I will crush Solis Burkes and the rest of her rats in her clan. With her out of the way, I will be sure to take Nacio from her… and you will step aside as mambo and bow down to me…you got that?"

"You need to be careful with the book you have in your possession, Childress," Bureau warned. "It is a powerful document and you need to treat it as such."

"Don't tell me what the hell to do! I know what I'm doing. Do you know what it is that *you* are doing?"

Without any hesitation, Bureau took heed to the warning Childress had bid her. Bureau was a rather clever woman. Bowing down to her deceased sister Frances' criminal children might well be the only way to save her own children from the clutches of evil that made its way to Dogwater Swamp.

"If you are willing to take the responsibility for the new mambo of the family, you will need to have your Ason ceremony soon. It will need to take place to fulfill your destiny, child, but first you will need to make certain you will survive the pregnancy, Childress. You haven't eaten in days, child. Eat the food that Urgata brought here for you."

Childress looked at the bowl of gumbo, as her nausea continued. Reaching forward she picked up the bowl and held it under her nose, paranoia set in and she followed her instincts.

"I'm not eating this damn stuff she brought in here. You think I'm crazy?" Childress sniped. "I know what kind of power it would mean to take over the family as the mambo priestess. You think I'm crazy? I'll fix my own damn food."

Once again, nausea caught Childress in a chokehold and sent her jetting to the bathroom. The downstairs bathroom in Bureau's home is just underneath the staircase. Running inside and slamming the door shut, Childress held her head over the huge commode that sat like a throne on a pedestal in the middle of the small space, as dry heaves refluxed up and down her esophagus.

After taking a few breaths for some relief, Childress leaned back against the peeling gold paisley wallpaper that had lost its adhesion many years ago. Looking at her reflection, she began asking herself some pretty life altering questions.

"What the hell am I going to do with a baby… dammit?" She wondered.

"I can barely look after these three damn fools. I know Justice has gone off and done something stupid, I can feel it, and now this? I cannot take care of a baby. If the child is anything like her dumbass, weak assed daddy then I am surely in trouble. That damn fool shot himself in the head at point blank range, surely any child of his is going to be an emotional failure to thrive child…a dumbass too."

Moments passed as Childress continued her confinement in the bathroom. A hot flash caught her next, and she turned on the faucet and splashed some cold water on her face. Klein had been in the bathroom brushing his teeth just moments before she had gone in.

Still pissed off from telling all her personal business about Detective Bouvier's death to Bureau, Childress grabbed the red and white striped toothbrush that sat in a little green cup on the vanity. Looking at the ring of lime that colored the rim underneath the commode, Childress made certain to take the toothbrush and thoroughly scrub the black ring from the commode. Feeling quite proud of herself, she then worked a spell to fix his wagging tongue and loose runaway lips.

"Telling stories is a big mistake, brother dear. May these sores that appear, make it clear when you talk my business it is me you will fear."

Quickly she returned the red striped toothbrush to its place. A maniacal smile stitched across her beautiful face, Childress rejoined her pirate relatives in the living room --- smiling, and keeping her secret to herself.

***

"Childress please eat," Bureau pleaded. "You said you were going to fix your plate, so go and fix your plate."

"I cannot eat that mess you got in there with that parboil."

"Well, I guess you having cravings is to be expected. What do you want to eat?"

Stomach pangs erupted deep in her gut the moment Bureau mentioned eating. After contemplating having a bowl of gumbo, a craving finally hit her just as she responded to her aunt.

"I want a steak…and I want it rare."

"What? A rare steak?" Bureau balked. "What are you going to do with a rare steak?"

"I am going to eat the damn thing."

"Well, the only reason I could think that you might want a rare steak is if you---," Bureau didn't finish her sentence before she switched her train of thought.

"The book you have Childress, there were some blood flakes from Auldicia in it. A puzzled look fell across Bureau's face. You didn't ingest them, did you? Did you ingest that blood? Please tell me you didn't?"

Childress studied her aunt's expression very carefully for signs of some kind of betrayal before she responded to her.

"Why?" she paused. "Look, that's my damn book. My mama gave it to me, and whatever was in it belongs to me to, you got that?"

"Child, no wonder you looked like a damn fool when you got here," Bureau explained, lighting a brown cancer stick. "You have started a chain of events that might have cursed us all. By taking Auldicia's blood into your body, you will become as she was, a vampire. You, too, will have the traits of Porphyria, light sensitive skin and craving blood for your own satisfaction."

"What the hell are you whining about now, Bureau?"

"You will need to provide the Loas a sacrifice in order to complete your transition as the new Priestess, if not you will not completely fulfill your destiny and you will always be weak and vulnerable to your enemies. You will be nothing more than a back wood trickster, instead of a powerful mambo."

Having heard that from her aunt, Childress knew this to

be true and considered what her options would be.

"Well, alright," she responded. "I will sacrifice this baby."

Bureau's raspy voice cracked with irritation, "I won't let you, Childress," Bureau shouted. "She is too precious to our bloodline. You cannot do this, I won't let you."

In the blink of an eye, Childress crossed the room in an instant, sneering with her arm stretched out grabbing Bureau by her chubby face and threatening her."

"Just what do you plan to do about it, Bureau? Huh? You cannot stop me on anything I plan to do. You think you are better than me, huh? Smarter than me? Well, I have news for you, do what you will, but if you interfere, I'll put you in the ground out back with the rest of your clan --- cross me if you dare, Cher!"

Frightened, Bureau became short winded. As tremors seized her, she quickly banked the burning embers at the tip of her cigarette. Childress held on to her face the way an umpire holds a ball in a baseball glove. If Bureau had ever known trouble in her lifetime, she knew without a doubt that her niece being in town had brought trouble with the law and the voodoo gods to her doorstep.

Knowing she would not win the argument with Childress, since she had made up her mind, Bureau explained the sleeping arrangements for her extended family's stay.

"Childress, you need to sleep downstairs with Urgata and Tahiti across the way from you in case you need anything at night. Oh yeah, and you need to figure out a way to get some food in this house for ya'll. I know those two fools will eat the shingles off this roof if we run out of food, so make some kind of plans for a disguise to go to the food stamp office here tomorrow."

"Yeah whatever, I don't care about that, just as long as---," Childress had her thought interrupted as a knock on the screen door caught her attention.

"I'll get it," Urgata called out.

Urgata opened the door, and a gorgeous latte colored man with a shoulder length curly black ponytail waltzed through the threshold---Nayphous Aljeaneux. Strong, with broad shoulders housed a muscular 6'3 frame. Nayphous had been a childhood playmate to Childress and her cousins back in the day, and here he was, all grown up. Known for his fierce skills on the saxophone, he had become a renowned jazz artist in the south. Shifting her weight from hip to hip, Childress was mesmerized.

"Hey, baby," Nayphous said, smacking Urgata on her lips. "You ready to go? The show starts in 30 minutes."

"Yeah, just let me grab my purse."

Just then, Klein and Erland came in from the backyard and greeted Nayphous. They all passed a smooth fist bump around and gave a manly hug to each other.

"What's been up, man?" Klein squawked. "Long time my brother."

"It's you man, it's you," Nayphous responded. "Erland is that you brother?"

"Hey man, what's happening?" Erland squealed. "You looking like money, man."

"Naw, man, just taking it slow and I've been---," Nayphous froze as he looked past his lovely belle Urgata and followed his eyes to Childress, who was now fluttering her eyelashes, as she played with a long strand of hair.

"Hey Cher," she greeted. "It has been too long since I last saw you."

Licking his lips in response to the tender figure that stood before him, Nayphous had to catch himself, before his lust gave him away.

"Hey, yourself."

The crackle of sexual electricity filled the air, as Urgata stood helpless as her man's eyes lingered over Childress. Acting quickly, she spoke up before anyone said anything more.

"Well, we had better get going if you are going to make your gig tonight, baby."

Erland and his slow-to-respond self chimed in, "What gig, man? You playing somewhere?"

"Yeah man, I'm taking my baby here to The Suga Shack. You want to tag along?"

"Heck yeah, man, let's roll," Klein said. "Just let me run and brush this catfish out of my teeth."

"I'm coming too," Childress said inviting herself along.

Urgata looked up after her cousin willfully became a fifth wheel, and that is when Bureau stepped in to run interference for her daughter and her beau.

"Uh, Childress you still haven't eaten, and I just thawed out this steak. Come on and eat, girl, because you surely are going to make it to the hospital from dehydration before you make it to the Suga Shack. In fact, the food stamp office is still open. It shouldn't be many people there, why don't you go ahead on and fix your disguise and you can take my car to go get some help?"

Seething and pissed off that she was not invited, Childress had no choice in the matter. She went upstairs and reapplied her deep brown foundation, and glasses. Again, the authorities were looking for someone who looked the total opposite of the way she looked now.

***

Bureau had been right, there were only two other females ahead of Childress in line with an appointment at the food stamp office. The Department of Health and Human Services had never had so few folks waiting for assistance. She felt her disguise just might work out after all.

A tall, heavy girthed in-the-middle man draped with soft love handles that hung over his belt called for Childress to come into his office for her interview.

"Number three."

Childress started down the hall with her ridiculously over exaggerated walk. The name on the door of the caseworker stated, Mason Merionette.

"Please have a seat," Mr. Merionette said. "State your name."

"My name is Bureau LaDeaux," Childress said, sticking firm to her alias.

"Identification, please"

"Well, Cher," Childress started. "My identification burned up in a fire after Katrina hit, and I haven't had a chance to replace it.

Mr. Merionette, let out a long hot breath, and then rolled his eyes to the back of his head as Childress sat and stalled with excuses.

"Ma'am, no identification, no services, plain and simple."

"I told you I don't have I.D."

"No food stamps."

Before another word passed between the two of them, Childress grabbed the man's stapler off his desk. Holding it in hand, she lunged for Mr. Merionette and stapled his testicles together --- then stapled them to his inner thigh, leaving him wailing in pain as a pool of blood seeped through the surface of his Pier slacks.

"You are going to fix me a food stamp card for a thousand dollars; you got that, damn fool? If you don't, I'm going to make Testicle Etoufee out of your jewels. You understand me? Now start typing and activate it."

Holding the heavy-duty stapler in her grip, Childress stood firm, as the automatic card reader sputtered and spit out a card with the name of Bureau steno-graphed across the bottom.

Yanking the warm plastic card from the machine, Childress turned and looked directly at the bleeding state worker as he sat arched in pain. Mr. Merionette cried as a child would during punishment. Grabbing a hand full of the hollering man's hair, she commandeered his thoughts.

"Forget you saw me…you will never remember me ever again."

Happy with her accomplishments, Childress blew a kiss to Mr. Merionette over her shoulder and switched her hips down the hall and out the door. As usual, she was happy with her trickery to get her way.

Once inside her aunt's car, she cranked the volume up

on the stereo and let Boney James's "The Total Experience" serenade her, as she gunned the Cadillac back to Dog water Swamp.

8
Blissful Best

After rolling around in bed all as long as possible, we finished our bath and got dressed. With his back to me, I caught my breath as I watched him cloth himself in a sexy loose fitting brown silk short set. His muscles rippled over his back, while his buns flexed when he put each leg in his shorts.

"Do you like what you see?" he asked. Embarrassed at getting caught drooling, he encouraged me by giving me his approval.

"No need to be shy, my love. Whether you accept it or not, my body is your claim and yours alone."

"So are you saying I have papers on you, sir?"

"Papers and a receipt too," he said, caressing me once more. "If you keep up this enticement, we will never get out of this suite."

"I am sure the rest of our extended house family won't mind our absence. After all, we are newlyweds."

"So you don't think they will wonder where we vanished?" he said, between wet kisses.

"Trust me, they won't care, and speaking of vanished, during our binding ceremony, I saw you materialize right before my eyes. I'd like to know all that you are capable of, Mr. Puente."

Breaking our embrace, Nacio stepped back from me and flashed a smug grin. Amusingly, he laughed at the request as he threw his shoulders back and brought his chest forward like a five star general.

"My dear bride, nothing would pleasure me more than to show you just what you are dealing with. Brace yourself…I don't want to frighten you. It's been awhile since I've done… tricks."

I ran and jumped on the bed and readied myself for the unexpected. Sure enough, I was not disappointed. Slowly, wind began to ruffle the palm trees in the four corners of the suite. Taking my eyes off Nacio for only a second proved far too long. He had turned into a mere cloud of dense mist, transparent against a dark background.

"Oh my, honey you are truly amazing. Everything on you from your clothing to your hair is invisible."

Stunned, but only because it had happened while I sat nearby, I walked over to where Nacio's voice was the strongest. This same ability is the one that I am most familiar with.

"Show me something else, anything, I don't care."

The vacuum sound of wind rushing in filled the room as he reappeared, as handsome as a statuesque work of art. Raising his arm to touch the wall behind him, the room around me turned into the library down the hall. We had moved from our room to the chaise that sat in front of Nacio's executive desk in the library.

"Wow, I can't believe it!" I said. "Did we travel to the library?"

"No, my love, we did not. Glamour, as it is called, has allowed me to remain in this city for decades without revealing my identity to the world. It has provided a great convenience to Bose and me."

"Is it ever physically painful to transform to mist or to transform a room or anything like that?"

"Not at all," he said, holding me in his gaze. "The only painful things for me are the different forms of silver…and not being near you."

Now I was the one with a smug smile plastered across my face, as the vacuum sound of wind filled the air, and our suite returned to its original décor. Questions still crowded the corners of my mind of what was to come.

"I feel stronger, Nacio, far stronger than ever before. Will this continue to happen to me, or will I go back to the way I was?"

"You now have a drop of my blood running parallel with yours. New abilities and strengths with continue to increase within you."

"Will I need to feed?"

"As long as the process is not complete, you will not need to feed. But I must be honest with you, Solis the physical turning process of vampirism is extremely taxing on your body. Your organs shut down, one by one --- bringing excruciating pain. Oxygen deprivation of your organs makes the process unbearable. Any unfiltered toxins saturate your organs bringing a slow and painful rebirth."

Although I was a bit shaken at what he told me, I was able to accept it as the truth --- I still wanted to be with him. Struggling through my doubts and thoughts about what was to come for me, again, I thought of not being able to conceive children. I also would miss eating. Those things seem shallow, but they are part of being human --- which I still am human.

"I can live and be reborn with knowing the consequences of my choices."

"Are you sure, Mistress? You'd be stuck with me forever," he teased.

"I'd better be."

A knock at the door slowed our love games to a grinding halt. Bose had prepared our first meal as newlyweds.

"Pardon my interruption, Hefe, but your meal is ready."

Nacio was fully dressed, but my ensemble was not quite complete. Heading in the direction of the closet, Nacio stopped me.

"I have a surprise for you," he whispered. "Look over your shoulder."

A beautiful bone colored maxi sundress lay across our bed. Sleeveless and sleek, I wasted no time dropping the bath sheet that covered my undergarments. Made of Egyptian cotton, the sundress fell softly over my shoulders.

"It's beautiful honey, thank you." He pulled me close for a sizzling kiss.

"We had better get downstairs before we begin where we left off, and if that's the case, you won't be in that dress for very long."

***

As we arrived downstairs with our fingers intertwined, Nacio sat me next to him in the dining room. Bose had the usual meal set up for Nacio --- a crystal clear goblet with warm blood plasma sat in the middle of a gorgeous Noritake plate. For me, Bose has a wide variety of entrees to choose from, French toast, waffles, scrambled eggs, sausage, and a fresh batch of oatmeal and raisin cookies. Yes, indeed, I would definitely miss these things once I become a vampire. The Caraways continued to have their meals in solitude.

"Everything smells delicious, Bose, thank you," I smiled.

"I made certain to add extra vanilla to your treats, Mistress."

"She is beautiful, is she not, Bose?" Nacio inquired. "My destiny is fulfilled and I will never know happier days for the rest of my existence."

"Agreed, Hefe," Bose said, winking at us both.

As we both finished our meal, Bose let us in on a little surprise he had for us as well.

"I, too, have a gift for the two of you and everything is set to go," Bose said. "Please follow me this way."

Nacio and I looked at each other with anticipation as we left the dining room.

Bose led us out back to the gorgeous west garden of the estate. With two sitting stools positioned for a portrait stood an easel and canvas, in the middle of the garden. Bose joined us with his painter's cloak on, and his sleeves rolled up ready to begin another masterpiece.

"My gift to the two most important people in my life is a portrait to last through the ages."

Overwhelmed with emotion, I gave Bose a hug and light kiss on his cheek. The talent he possessed was undeniably extraordinary. His work greets me each time we set foot in the foyer of the mansion. Remembering the day Nacio first brought me to the mansion, the first thing I saw entering the foyer was the portrait of Jesus with little children around him. At that moment, I became a loyal follower of Bose and his talents.

Our sitting took a little under 45 minutes. Extraordinary, indeed---vampire talent most definitely, no human could paint with such precision and exquisite detail. The result of the 72 x 84 portrait brought more tears to my eyes. Bose had captured Nacio and me facing east and embracing each other, with the sun going down over our shoulders. The desire captured in Nacio's eyes is conveyed the vivid colors that burst from the canvas, as he held handfuls of my hair, and as I held his face in mine.

"My friend, I cannot thank you enough," Nacio said to Bose, embracing his arm. "You never cease to amaze me, my brother."

Gathering my wits, Nacio took me took me in his arms and dried the rest of my tears.

"Bose will be back after a while. I'm presenting my mate to world," he said. "Actually, we're headed to the River walk for the evening.

"Yes, Hefe, I will continue to finish mixing the formula needed for the *hunting expedition."* Bose air quoted, indicating the chemical weapon he had engineered to use against the female Treemounts.

***

We arrived at the corner of Travis and East Houston at the Allright Parking Garage. Nacio parked the Lexus on the top floor of the building.

"I love parking up here. It gives us privacy and no car dings," he said throwing a sexy wink my way. I had never seen my mate as happy as he appeared. Grinning non-stop since I had awakened, Nacio's spirits were on a cloud nine high.

"You know, Solis, you've made my existence meaningful once more. I have never had this kind of joy before in my life, not before I was turned into a vampire nor after. When I look at you, it reminds me of how good the sun feels in the morning…what rain tastes like on my tongue...what your soft hot lips feel like against mine…," he whispered as we kissed.

"If you keep this up, it will make me want to cut our visit to the River walk short, and I will want to go back home and get tangled in our sheets --- just keep it up I warn you," I smiled.

Watching him bask in victory over my response to his physical gestures, Nacio ran over and opened my car door. Seductively, he extended his arm and I obliged, sliding my arm under his as I was led down to the elevator to begin our honeymoon stroll down the River walk north.

"You look enticing my, love," Nacio said admiringly, licking his lips as thirst settled over him. "I will have to pace myself with you. I can't let my thirst run away with me."

We walked arm in arm out of the parking garage headed to the river below us. Dusk had fallen over the horizon as we entered the River walk north at the corner of Lexington and McCullough. Tropical plants lined the path of the River walk as busy tourists stopped to stare at the architecture of the tiled cobblestones in the sidewalks. Although beautiful and clear, the daytime temperature was a searing 105 degrees --- the evening temperature 103 degrees and cooking.

An all-too-happy tourist found a pillar to photograph. The pillar held a beam to an overpass which had the rivers architectural history inscribed on it. A short blonde curly headed man, with ten extra teeth in his mouth, stood with his tongue hanging out as he aimed his digital camera at the pillar for the perfect shot of the structure.

Casually dressed in a blue short-sleeved Polo, khaki shorts, and clear Crocs on his feet, the eager vacationer continued with his photography as sweat slid down his temples. The sweltering heat in the atmosphere caused steam to rise from the sidewalks in slow billowing puffs. Unaware of the severity of the climate, the man stood in his shoes as they melted right underneath his feet. Capturing his photo, the man took a step forward causing the sole of his disintegrated shoe to smear into wax on the concrete.

Passers-by sniggled at the befuddled vacationer, teasing him about his naked foot as his jellied shoe dangled from his toes. Others pointed to the puddle the melted Croc made in the middle of the river's walking path.

"Hey, man, that's you back there in that puddle!" the heckler shouted. "That's you! You are in San Antonio, Texas. Don't you know you can't wear jellies on your feet? The sun will get you every time!"

Embarrassed into retreat, the vacationer quickly gathered his remaining dignity and sought comfort underneath an oak tree. Some of the river's landscaping is quite exotic. A rich anonymous oil developer had sponsored a section of the river that had a patch of Birds of Paradise near a cascading waterfall, near the old Pearl Brewery. Any visitor coming to this part of the River walk felt the tropics from the humidity and the water.

A dark patch of brush distorted the beautiful scenery. Covered with piney needles and horrible smelling leaves, the brush seemed sinister in nature. I couldn't take my eyes off the patch of brush as the shamed vacationer wandered closer to it, limping after putting his foot on the hot concrete. Nacio stopped in his tracks, sensing the danger I had as well.

"Sweetheart, I don't like what I'm feeling here," he cautioned.

"I feel it too. In fact, I feel awful. Nacio, something is moving in that bush."

An arm reached beyond the foliage of the brush, snatching the vacationer by his neck, stifling any scream for help --- or a warning to anyone else that happened to be near.

"It's another vampire, Solis, get back!" Nacio yelled with his fangs in full view.

With unprecedented agility, he stalked the menace inhabiting the bush. Pulsing forward, without making a sound detectable by the human ear, Nacio stood at the foot of the bush and pushed the leaves back.

Hard headed and not listening to what I was told, I glimpsed at what stared back at us. In full view stood the new youngling vampire Justice Treemount, as he greedily fed in public, only yards away from other humans. Interrupting his feeding, pissed him off, as he looked at Nacio and me with green eyes the color of neon lights. His fangs were comparable to sharks teeth, sitting like crooked wind chimes in his mouth.

"Justice, stop what you are doing now!" Nacio called.

Caught in a feeding frenzy, Justice unclamped his jaws from the gaping hole in the vacationer's neck as blood showered the bush roots below his feet. With a rattlesnake's hiss, blood dripped and sprayed from his lips. Justice looked past Nacio and laid eyes on me.

"Hey there, Solis, baby. It's good to see you again. Look what I can do. You like it? I sure hope so, because you're next."

Before 'go to hell bastard' slipped my lips, a female bystander screamed at the blood that ran across the River walk path. Others joined in, causing police officers that stood above on the street level to point their flashlights in our direction and blow their whistles. Nacio zipped by me, plowing into Justice --- both vampires shattering their shoulder blades as an undead death match began.

Nacio cut through the wind, striking Justice in the face, sending more blood through the air, painting the stone structure next to a waterfall blood red. Uncontrollable and uninhibited with arms, fists and feet moving in a blur, Nacio was a destructive fighting machine. Justice flew back from the impact --- crashing into the concrete.

"Is that all you got, punk?" Justice taunted with a bloody smile. "You hit like a girl!"

Now I was pissed off and wanted to get a blow in of my own. Looking around for anything to pick up and lay into this bastard, I soon found a suitable weapon. A wrought iron barstool from a nearby vendor was enough to fulfill my purpose.

"You mean he hits like this?" I said, letting go of my own fear and allowing anger to control my emotions.

Adrenaline fueled my reserves of strength as I reared back and swung the barstool at Justice, striking him between his shoulder blades --- swinging him around like a tethered ball.

Just then, an opportunity presented itself for Nacio to kick Justice in the middle of his back shattering his spine on impact, but it didn't even slow him down. Nacio reached out to catch Justice by his arm, only to be blocked and instead Justice caught hold of Nacio's forearm --- twisting and fracturing it instantly.

"Nacio!" I screamed, before going into hysterics, and realizing now I had to do something as the two fanged menaces continued their battle and humans were getting closer.

Needing a quick solution without drawing more attention to myself with my telekinetic ability, I decided to trust my instincts. Underneath the overpass, evening had just fallen and it was time for the nesting bats to come out. Remembering what my mother and grandmother said about my connection to animals, I looked in the distance towards the overpass and summoned the awakening bats to assist me.

"Please help us! Please!"

Not knowing what to expect, the bats took flight from their nest swarming the River walk path. Several picked up silver forks and knives from the fine dining areas of restaurants that lined the river's path. The bats honed in on Justice, firing the loose silverware like spears and arrows. The cutlery must have been real silver because it worked.

"Aaagggh!" Justice screamed, as the silver delivered

acid like burns to his flesh, causing him to release Nacio from his deadly grip.

Turning in my direction, Justice staggered and attempted to lunge at me, but was thrown backward as gunshots rang out through the night. Bullets scuttled in from the Southside of the river's path and nicked him with three rounds one after the other.

I looked up to see a stealthy Detective Menlo Kildare running with open fire blasting from her weapon, holding Justice as the target bulls eye.

"Dammit, that hurts!" he winced in pain, as his back bubbled and sizzled. "I'm going to get you next, bitch," he cried as he turned and ran north passed the brewery and vanished into the night. Detective Kildare continued in pursuit, as the rest of the San Antonio Police Department blocked off the area to maintain civilian safety.

"Sweetheart, are you alright?" I asked, looking at the damage Justice inflicted on Nacio's arm. It wasn't long before his arm began to heal.

"I'm fine. Dammit, he's gone!" Nacio shouted. "One good thing about his dumbass, he's clueless and we'll catch up to him soon."

"So Justice is definitely responsible for the rash of serial murders in town," I said. "Did you see his eyes? I guess Basira did turn him before he poisoned her."

"This appears to be the case," Nacio said. "One thing he didn't count on is the fact that he killed her and she was the one to turn him into a vampire. He will forever mourn her death, especially since it was by his own hand. Justice will be in an eternal state of insanity, making him a ruthless killer."

A vaguely familiar voice joined our conversation. "He was ruthless to begin with, now this makes it worse." Nacio and I both looked up to see Detective Menlo Kildare standing a few feet from where we were, slowly holstering her recently fired weapon.

"Detective Kildare," I said, stunned. "What are you doing here?"

"We need to talk."

"Uh, yeah," Nacio said. "But not out here in the open. Plus we don't know if we can trust you."

"I know I just saw Battle of the Fangs out here, I think you really have no choice at this point."

"Babe, I'm willing to go on a little faith," I stressed. "But we need to get you out of the open so that your wounds ---," I stopped speaking immediately, noticing the wounds Nacio sustained were gone --- as if they were never there.

Detective Kildare glanced at him, shaking her head in disbelief yet not running for cover or alerting her police squad for backup.

"Oh yeah, we need to connect," she said. Nacio decided to reveal his location. I had to trust his instincts about Detective Kildare, although he sensed my apprehension.

"Be at the corner of Cedar and Pereida at midnight," he told her. "Someone will come and pick you up where we can talk."

With little hesitation, she accepted the rendezvous and was ready to join her fellow law enforcement agents. Checking her perimeter before she dashed off to assist her squad with the now mounting crowd, she left us with a warning that I took to heart.

"Good, that will give me the time I need to answer questions about firing my gun, and it will be perfect for me to develop a cover that will stick for my reports before leaving duty. We are all facing hellatious danger, I hope you are ready to do what you need to do, Solis," she warned.

Feeling as if she had spoken directly to my deceased relatives, the weight on my shoulders just tripled, burdening me with more to carry than Atlas himself.

9
Pretty Poison

Detective Kildare quickly vacated the area, as Nacio grabbed me teleporting us back to the parking garage. Before I could ask any questions, he had placed me in the car, started the engine, and peeled out leaving tire marks on the asphalt. The ride home was tense, leaving him hyped up for more battle and on edge.

"We are out of time, Solis. We have to hit the Treemounts now with all speed. Justice is loose and menacing anyone in his path. He has no clue what to do as youngling vampire, which means he kills for no reason at all. If we don't stop them, there could be several other vampires running around before the end of the week."

"I know, but what are we going to do? Bose hasn't perfected the formula with the Dieth yet, has he?"

"I'll find out soon," he said, bringing the sedan to a stop at a red light. Nacio closed his eyes for a brief moment --- looking as if he were meditating.

"I've just finished sending a message to Bose. I told him to round up the Caraways and get them ready to meet as well. We have to do this tonight, Solis."

"I'm with you just tell me what to do. Justice was awfully bold to threaten me that way," I said, stunned. "What do you think Detective Kildare knows?"

"A whole lot more than what she pretends to know, and it will definitely change our plans."

"You must trust her somewhat, am I right?"

"She is trustable to a degree, but there is something that still does not sit well with me, but we are going to find out just what it is real soon. The last statement she made about Justice was a little too close for comfort, such as the fact she said 'he was ruthless to begin with, now this makes it worse'. Detective Kildare definitely knows more than she pretends to, and soon we will know what she knows," he reassured.

"It's as if she has a hidden agenda that is all about her," I explained. "Well, one thing is for sure, she seems to want to get to the bottom of this as much as we do."

***

When we arrived back at the Puente Mansion, Bose, Armando, Patience and Basrick took up various places in the library. Each household member, anxious to get the attack against the Treemounts underway, waited for directions.

Patience looking ever so chic in a long forest green tie-dye blouse and skinny jeans, finished with black Stilettos. Heavy long brown ringlets of curls shimmed with every tilt of her head. The grief in her face was partially replaced with relief, once she was summoned to the study at Nacio's request to strategize against the Treemounts this evening.

Armando paced wildly like a lion ready to spring free

against his captors, yet still in mourning himself. Blonde tresses fell over his shoulders each time he swung a turn in the other direction, as his footsteps put wear on the carpet. Decked in a blue designer pullover t-shirt and creased designer jeans, he looked like a male model waiting for his cue to hit the catwalk. Although there could not have been an easier solution for what happened to his daughter Basira, Armando carried the burden of guilt that comes with grief.

Wearing traditional mourning black seemed to be the only clothing Basrick appeared in lately. A simple designer button down, boot-cut black designer jeans and black elf loafers that turned up at the toes were the only efforts he could make to cloth himself and join the rest of his family in the library.

Basrick wore his grief across his chest without any apologies. Death of a sibling, and a twin sibling at that, tends to hollow the survivors, but in Basrick's case, he considered his twin his better half. Basrick's soul had been hollowed out after her death --- shelled for the rest of his life without his twin's connection. Like his father, he too carried the burden of guilt and grief.

The night she was poisoned, Basrick pleaded with Basira not to see Justice once he knew that is what she was doing. When Nacio and the Caraways first started exterminating the Treemounts, Basira would always be the last to return to the mansion. She had been killing the Treemount men, and afterwards she would go and spend time with Justice. Basira traveled to see him in the form of a condor sized bat to fly home quickly after her visit.

On her way to the mansion from visiting Justice,

Basira fell from the sky---turning into silt soil. Basrick and his parents watched as their beloved Basira disintegrated. In the manner which the decomposition of her body took place, Armando knew immediately it was poison from Colloidal Silver. It brought his daughter to her death.

Silt covered the Caraways as their beloved fell, her final remains landed in Armando's arms. Armando's screams of sorrow seemed to fill every corner of the globe on that painful night. Yes, indeed, the Caraways were ready to strike back full force at the Treemounts.

Last but certainly not least, Bose stood fixated at the television as news anchor Vanaya Austin delivered the coverage of the shooting blood bath that occurred this evening on the new portion of the Riverwalk North:

"*...this was the scene earlier tonight that brought a tragic end to vacationers and other bystanders this evening. SAPD discovered the remains of a young woman and young male believed to be in their early twenties.*

Both victims had been mauled by what authorities are calling a wild animal attack. The young woman was identified as Elbithea Diseno, a resident of the 500 block of East Nolan Street. The identity of the young male is pending until next of kin can be notified.

Police officers were in pursuit of an unidentified suspect that bystanders explained fled the scene, gun shots rang out after the suspect threw a sharp weapon at one of the officers in pursuit.

Parts of the newly opened River walk North have now been closed indefinitely until authorities can fully investigate the origin of the attack, and to clean up the horrific crime scene left behind…In other news…"

When I heard Elbithea's name, I grabbed Nacio's arm for support as my legs turned to cement, paralyzing me. A Treemount has murdered another friend of mine and it must stop. I prayed, hoping for mercy.

"Oh father, help us," was all I could say without having a meltdown, but it did not stop the tears.

My own gut was twisted with grief from the homicidal tendencies of the hellish family. It appeared every other week the bloodshed was becoming more random and more precise with each day that passed. I have to put an end to the madness before anyone else dies.

Having felt the same sentiments, Nacio spoke to break the tension in the air. "Bose, we are expecting the arrival of a Detective Menlo Kildare --- it appears she has information that will be helpful in our quest. She has just arrived and is stepping out of her vehicle now, so please pick her up at the end of the driveway. We don't want to keep her waiting too long and frighten her."

"Yes, Hefe," Bose replied. "I'll only be a moment." Bose left everyone standing and waiting impatiently for relief as anxiety continued to weigh heavily on the shoulders of those in the room.

***

Detective Kildare waited at the parking lot across Cedar Street waiting for her transportation to take her to meet with Nacio and me. Going to the Police substation allowed her a chance to change into a different set of navy blue slacks, with a white blouse and navy blazer. Mid-heal navy blue pumps clicked and clacked as she paced steadily until she saw the headlights of the Lexus flash across the parking lot at her.

Instinctively, she grabbed her service revolver as a means of security and warning in case the headlights turned out to belong to someone else, instead of the transportation she was awaiting. She did not know who or what to expect, especially after what she had saw tonight.

Bose slowly turned the big sedan into the parking lot and glided to a smooth stop. The driver's door opened; and what Detective Kildare saw was enough to make even a tough-as-nails woman like herself gasp for breath, as every towering inch of Bose stepped out of the car. His stride was confident and alluring as he made his way over to where she stood.

"Detective Kildare?" Bose inquired.

"Yes, that's me," she said, as familiarity settled deep within her.

"I'm Bose Puente, caretaker of the Puente Estate. I'm here to transport you to where you and Mistress Solis can speak in private."

"I'm ready," she said, not taking her sparkly aqua eyes off Bose, as she licked her dry lips as though a desert drought caused instant dehydration.

Attraction had her in its grip and Detective Kildare could not understand her own emotions. Never had she laid her eyes on such a dashing creature as Bose. Safety was something she had always provided for herself. However, in his presence she found it to be an overwhelming pleasure.

"Come with me, Detective," he said, low and seductive. "There is no need to fear me. You can let your hand relax off your revolver, trust me, you won't need it."

Hypnotically, Detective Kildare slipped into the back seat of the sedan and slipped into serious infatuation with Bose. This made things easier for Bose as he positioned the car to the entrance of Puente Lane driveway. He would not have to worry about putting a spell on her, nor worry about her asking questions about the mysterious lane as they drove the two-mile distance to the mansion sitting at the end of the road.

Breathing rapidly, but not loudly, the detective sat and stared at Bose from the back seat, catching glimpses of his green eyes as he glanced back at her intermittently. Losing herself, she stared at his build, the strength noted in his chest muscles and enormous thighs; Detective Kildare wondered if Bose found her attractive.

Questioning his attraction to her, they rode to the mansion in silence. Bose looked up at her in the rearview mirror and smiled with delight, causing her to blush and turn away from his gaze. This feeling did not seem to diminish in anyway, even after the soft tap of the vehicle's brakes brought the car to a stop.

Bose got out of the car and chivalrously held open the door, as she tried to contain her emotions. Extending her gracious long legs, she found her hand settling in the middle of his huge palm guiding her out of the vehicle. Looking into his eyes, made shivers vibrate slowly up and down her spine. Smiling, he had extended his other arm beckoning her to follow him.

"Right this way," he said, leading her to the entrance of the mansion. Detective Kildare was lost in thought as she continued to stare at Bose.

"Who are you?" she asked, perplexed and dazed.

"The answer to your question is 'yes'," he said.

"What question?"

"If my attraction to you is mutual," he reiterated. "My answer is 'hell, yes'."

Again, her response to him was dry lips, gasping breath, a fluttering heart and a tingling spine. Scientifically, she figured it was total arousal. Bose continued smiling as her responses increased.

Taking her by the arm, Bose led Detective Kildare through the house quickly, as he felt the tension coming from inside the mansion. Calming her, but not dousing the flames, he stroked her cheek as they arrived just outside the library door.

"Hold that thought as we take care of some business first, okay?" He asked.

She could only nod in response, as he pushed the door handle and the door flew open to all that were still standing where he had left them. Bose spoke as everyone moved forward to greet the detective.

"Detective Menlo Kildare is here to speak to you, Mistress."

"Thank you, Bose," I said, as I motioned for Detective Kildare to come in and sit down.

"Welcome to our home, Detective Kildare. I didn't have a true home the last time you and I spoke, but now I do. It seems that each time you and I see each other it is always in the midst of some tragedy," I said.

"Yes, it appears that way," the Detective said, now with a little more liberty from her arousal, yet her attraction to Bose remained obvious. Clearing her throat, she was able to reclaim composure.

"Wow, now I see why you couldn't be contacted unless you called us."

"Well, now you understand my need for discretion," I said.

"I do, get a much clearer picture of your situation now, especially after tonight."

"I wanted to know what it is you know about Justice Treemount."

"Yes, we'd all like to know," Nacio spoke, stepping from the shadows by the fireplace. Dark, murky and black, the life sized fireplace seemed as though it led to a different dimension in the mansion --- it screamed haunted mansion.

"Well, I would like for you to hear me out before you judge me," Detective Kildare said. "Do I have your word?"

I looked at Nacio and then at the grief in the faces of the Caraways, and knew somehow solemnly vowing to keep my word might cause conflict within our home, but it was a chance I was willing to take.

"I promise, Detective."

Silence fell over all present in the room as my own rapid breathing filled the air, for what was said next.

"My name is Menlo Kildare Treemount La Deaux."

Nacio and all the Caraways growled deadly and low when Detective Kildare revealed her true-identity to us. I even caught a sound of resonance in my own throat, after the shock of this explosive detail. I held up my hand to silence my mate and the Caraways, whom I considered extended family.

"I can certainly understand why you would not reveal

your true identity, but surely you must have realized that it would be discovered and your own safety would be at risk?" I said.

"Keeping my identity hidden was my own doing since I hate my mother's side of the family," she said. "I am the daughter of Bureau Treemount La Deaux. I dropped Treemount and La Deaux use only my middle name as my last name. My mother and my aunt Frances were sisters. Childress, her brothers and I are first cousins. I have more of my father's features. Brown hair and aqua eyes marked my father's side of the family, which makes me look different from my cousins who are marked with green eyes and blondish hair."

With my mouth, hanging nearly to the floor from all the disclosure, I pulled myself together to ask a question.

"Aside from the fact that you have homicidal criminals in your family, what is your relationship with them like today?"

"My aunt Frances was a whore and a thief," Detective Kildare interjected. "She often stole many things from my mother and would never admit to doing it. Our family has a history that is as damned as it is sacred."

"Then you know that you come from a long line of demons then, correct?" Armando spoke up, grief and anger selecting his words for him.

"Yes, and you are?"

"Forgive me, Detective Kildare," I said. "This is Armando Caraway, his wife Patience, and their son Basrick." The Caraways stood panther-like and ready to pounce on the detective for her disclosure.

"Justice killed our daughter Basira," Armando hissed.

"I would be lying to you if I did not admit that I have sworn to avenge her death --- your cousin Justice is on borrowed time."

Aimed in the direction of Armando, Detective Kildare continued her storyline.

"I do know that I come from an accursed family, but I have fought all my life to distance myself from them and make amends as a peace abiding citizen and law enforcement agent. I have never condoned what Childress, Klein, Justice, and Erland do in their spare time when they are not stealing or terrorizing people. Theft is in their blood."

"Don't forget murder," I spoke up.

There was a pitiful softness in the Detective's face, and it was obvious what she explained was true about not wanting to be affiliated with her awful family.

"Yes, including murder," she said. "I have to apologize for all of my cousins mishaps. It is the main reason I went into law enforcement to begin with. It is the main reason I will stop at nothing to bring all of them down. The last time I saw my mother Bureau was nearly 20 years ago. I never forgave her for all the things she did to my father; I believe in my heart she sacrificed him to the Loas for her reign as the mambo of Dog water Swamp."

Captivated by what the detective said, we all listened in silence.

"I was raised by my father's sister Vidalia, and she was the one to tell me about my wicked mother and her sister Frances. Our family kept two books of the family tree and the generational curse that has plagued our bloodline for centuries. One of my ancestors, Priestess Auldicia, has been my family's curse for all the future generations of her bloodline. The

Treemount name has a long branching history. A large, dead tree near a village is where Priestess Auldicia lived. The tree is the origin of where she gave birth to a generation of bastard children that were damned as vampires on earth. Diseases of slothfulness and crime festered in their blood. My Aunt Vidalia said the rest of the Treemount family history is in multiple volumes of leather case bound notebooks. The books were lost over the years. One of the books had been in my mother's possession but was stolen by my Aunt Frances. I heard of her death not long ago and fear that the book now belongs to Childress."

"How did you know about Justice?" I asked.

"I hadn't seen my cousins in many years and have only recently come to Texas myself. I knew there might be a connection with the recent deaths at the Texas Taste Tease and the recent crime victims had been found with bite marks and blood, after some deductive reasoning I figured sure enough, the Treemounts are linked to the late Detective Bouvier's death. Finding out that Justice is a vampire was not something I could believe at first, but then I saw you and Nacio at the scene tonight, and everything else fell into place."

"Well, I can see how you uphold the name of San Antonio's Finest," Bose said, with a look that I had just come to learn in his eyes. Bose had a thing for Detective Kildare.

"I want to help put an end to this terror from my cousins, especially Justice. I know that he has been responsible for the rash of fires we have had in the older eastside neighborhoods as well. More John and Jane Does have also turned up. I believe he's feeding on the victims and then leaving them to be found. He never was too bright."

"Can we trust you?" Patience spoke up.

"You have my word."

"Good, we need to get to work tonight before anymore damage can be done," Nacio cut in. "Bose, what's the status on the formula?"

"It's ready for disbursement Hefe," Bose confirmed as he handed Nacio folders of the information on the locations of the female Treemounts. The goal is to stop as many of the Treemount women as possible since their voodoo power was the strongest with the women in the family.

"Armando, Patience, and Basrick," Nacio called, "we need you to set up to strike tonight."

Nacio divvyed up the assignments of the various city locations of the Treemount clan, and Bose continued to pull information on the generation's family tree and unfurl the biological weapon he had created.

"Friends, I present to you Formula Diethmifex," he said. "This weapon will be dispensed in the form of tranquilizing darts. Just three milliliters of this chemical mix will not kill the female Treemounts, but it will make certain to render any future reproduction of those females impossible. Should any of the females currently be in the midst of gestation, the child they carry be it male or female would be born with the inability to reproduce children.

Everyone in the room stood mesmerized as Bose continued.

"Congenital birth defects would ravage future generations --- carrying breast cancer in both female and male children born," Bose stated. "Other reproductive congenital birth defects, such as transsexual characteristics along with diseases would put an end to the family reproduction."

Nacio spoke with a triumphant glint in his eyes, "Yes, this would be our goal to end the reign of terror --- nixing future generations."

"How soon would the mix take effect?" Armando asked.

"Yes," Patience inquired. "How would we measure the results of the Formula Diethmifex?"

Patience had a point. There would be no way of knowing if the inoculation took effect. Bose reassured everyone in the room and he provided the mourning Caraways a sign to watch for during our expedition.

"The formula is fired from a tranquilizer pen with the projection range of 100 feet from the target. Once the formula is dispersed at an intramuscular injection site and infiltrates the blood stream of our targets, the pregnancy maintaining hormone is suppressed and the male hormone testosterone rapidly fills the blood stream, causing the abdominal cavity of the females to distend and hang---rendering them unconscious," Bose explained. "The females faced would round out, and the jaw line would fatten on contact. Estrogen instantly evaporates, as the vial and the casing it is in disintegrates---leaving no evidence behind."

There were no more questions asked. Everyone understood the severity of the situation at hand --- embracing the mission. Nacio made his sentiments clear.

"Each of you is responsible for delivering the poison package to the females in the home to stop the reproduction of anymore of the accursed children, understand?"

Just then, Detective Kildare spoke up in question.

"So let me get this straight," she said, "the plan is to find and kill all of these females?"

I stepped in to give clarity, "No, the goal is to use a chemical weapon that has been enhanced to kill off or greatly alter the reproductive systems of the females so that no more children are to be born, thus ending the curse on earth."

"Well, sounds like a plan to me," she said. "I can help by giving you the address to the location of these females and," she paused by throwing a sexy look over her shoulder at Bose before she continued, "I can help do research with Bose."

Bose had a luminous smile to match his eyes that locked onto Detective Kildare's like high beams. Of course, Nacio kept focus, cutting through the lust quick and dirty.

"Yep, good, let's all go over to Puente Masonry to lock and load," he said, reaching for my hand and kissing it once he held it.

Before I could look back at everyone, they had all cleared out. Patience and Armando slipped out of the study and headed downstairs. Basrick simply opened the study balcony and shifted into a Condor sized bat. Bose stood looking at Detective Kildare. Holding the door open as she slid her body past his, Bose shuddered as the scent of her perfume lingered past him.

Our mission is set to begin tonight, but Bose had other physical needs that needed tending. Watching the sparks fly in the room, I knew they had an agenda that only included the two of them. Nacio and I went to the car and headed a little further south to Puente Masonry.

***

Strolling slowly down the hall past the Egyptian Suite in the Puente Mansion, Bose walked ahead of Detective Kildare with her right on his heels. Suddenly, he stopped in front of the Old English Suite, the room with the life sized wall to wall portrait of Buckingham Palace --- he stepped in and she followed.

Magnificent walls towered over the furniture, confirming the suite was definitely fit for royals. Bose turned and looked at Detective Kildare, licking his lips as his fangs descended to fill his mouth.

"Allow me to demonstrate the answer to your question," he said. "My attraction to you is more than I've known in two centuries and several decades," he said, telekinetically shutting the door as she turned to look over her shoulder as the sound ricocheted off the walls.

Rather than being afraid, Detective Kildare found herself loosening her belt and casually dropping articles of clothing on the floor. Bose heard every beat of her heart, as he hardened in response.

"I feel as if we've known each other for some time," she said. "I've never responded to anyone this way in my life. Are you influencing my thoughts in anyway, perhaps?"

Another smile rippled across his face as he shed the last of his own clothing. "All that you feel, is real because you wish it to be real. Allow me to deepen your emotions," he said, taking her in his arms --- kissing her fiercely.

Detective Kildare's yearning for Bose was undeniable, and yet frightening. She jumped, straddling her legs around his waist as they barely made it to the California king standing in the middle of the room. She adored his body, down to the exquisite vine shaped birthmark that encircled his belly button.

Without control or warning, Bose pierced the surface of her neck, sending showers of ecstasy over her as she lay beneath him. Shuddering with a low incessant moan, Bose's satisfaction hit him the same time blood plasma sweetly washed down his throat.

"You taste so good to me."

"More," she said. "Please take more, don't stop."

"I won't turn you into a vampire, Detective. That's not something I'm willing to do."

"Menlo, call me Menlo."

"Alright then, Menlo," he said. "I won't hurt you and I won't take your life from you. Do you understand?"

With great hesitation, Detective Kildare agreed, but she still had no control over her desire.

"Okay, it's fair, but I want to be with you. Together we can stop Childress and her brothers. I want to be part of that. I can help you with your research. Will you let me help you?"

"It seems reasonable," he said, reaching for her once more.

They continued to make love as time slowly crept away, bringing dawn closer to the horizon.

***

Puente Masonry stood red-bricked and four stories high with blacked out windows that spelled the initials PM on the face. Behind the building, Lake Mitchell sat serenely as coastal birds made stops there along their journey back to the Gulf of

Mexico.

Humongous mixers and vats stood alone in a field behind the building connected by a piping system that flowed in and out from another set of huge vats just inside the building. Nacio smiled proudly at his life's accomplishment as I stood by him arm in arm. Amazed, I allowed my eyes to take in the entire structure.

"Mistress, behold our wealth," he said. "Every freeway, arch way, and multi-story building and hotel in San Antonio was birthed from Puente Masonry, as I've explained before. It also houses the chemicals to the formula Bose put together. It is impossible to keep a biochemical weapon that potent at the mansion."

"Did Bose create it in the vats out back?" I asked. "What's going to happen if we no longer need what he has made?"

"Don't worry, Solis. We will utilize all we have made. I will not stop until our quest is complete and all the Treemounts are no longer a threat to us. Allowing them to exist the way they are now is too great a price to pay. All of us will be doomed if they are not stopped. Bose's ingenuity has allowed us a way to compromise. We won't kill them all, unless it's necessary, but they mustn't be allowed to reproduce. I feel that's fair enough."

I had never seen Nacio in such an uproar. I knew that he meant every word, and it wouldn't be long before Childress and her clan were be wiped out.

Just then, a hard thump hit the automatic door and in flew Basrick. Scary up close was an understatement. Levitating low in mid air and lurking as sinister as a black shadow, Basrick's red eyes found us, as he morphed back into his former handsome persona, turning his eyes blue once more. Nacio greeted him, as Armando and Patience misted in and morphed back to their human forms as well.

Bose and Detective Kildare arrived late. Jokingly, everyone knew why and continued with business as usual. Nacio laughed as he led us down to the basement where the laboratory was located. He held up his hand to the seven-inch thick steel door, pressing an entry code to gain access. We all followed him in, gasping at the hundreds of loaded holsters of Formula Diethmifex darts that laid across the several lab countertops. Nacio began to dispense holsters and cartridges to everyone, just as Bose and Detective Kildare decided to join us.

Admittedly, Bose looked all too pleased as he walked in hand in hand with Detective Kildare. They must have truly enjoyed each other, because he walked in with a lean, and she came in with fresh curls in her hair. Their time alone with each other must have been good.

"Uh, thank you two for joining us," Nacio smirked. "We wouldn't have dared to interrupt your, uh, 'research'. Hello, Detective Kildare."

Armando and Patience giggled with their fangs showing as Nacio jested with his brother and his new friend.

"Oh, excuse our tardiness," Bose gushed and smiled, as he looked at Detective Kildare whose responsive blush looked like circus clown rouge.

"Oh, please call me Menlo," Detective Kildare requested. Insisting on a first name basis confirmed her alone time with Bose was more than good.

"Alright, Menlo, welcome," Nacio greeted. "Let's roll out, folks. We need to move while we still have the element of surprise on our side."

Anxious and ready to move out, I reached for a vial-filled holster and Nacio stopped me the moment my hand landed on the holster.

"And what do you think you are doing?" he asked.

"Oh, come on, Nacio, this is my fight," I said. "You and I have already had this discussion and it's closed for anymore feedback on the topic." He looked me up and down, and cracked a smile that made me make plans for our next love making session.

"You think you're tough now, don't you?" he smiled. "You stick close to me, you understand?"

"Yeah, blah, blah, blah, I love you too," I laughed.

The Caraways took the north and northeastern corners of the city. Basrick chose to work alone and took the southeast and southern tip of the city. Bose and Menlo took the southwest and west, and Nacio and I headed through the downtown and northwestern areas to pay visits to the Treemount females, and deliver the inoculation to them. We were also hoping to run into Justice if possible. Somehow, I didn't believe we would run into him though, Nacio was dead set on taking him down.

***

Driving up to the first subdivision in the middle of downtown shocked me. A little red and white house at the corner of Frio and Guadalupe streets had the address 1411 Guadalupe etched on the curb.

"Castiana Treemount Vargas, her husband and two children live here," Nacio explained. "Bose left notice that this woman is the sister to the late Monteclair Treemount, who died as a result of Nacio's strike against our enemies. He described her as a miserable, controlling, abusive spouse who claims to be a local curandera, or folk healer or Hispanic shaman, according to Hispanic folklore. Voodoo from New Orleans was passed down through the Treemount generations, now she wants to expand her practice here, meaning there will be trouble should Childress find out she has competition."

"So what is the action to this plan, Nacio," I said. "Do we just ring the doorbell and shoot her with the Formula Diethmifex?"

"Actually, that was the plan, yes."

Looking doubtful and hesitant, he read my thought cloud and reassured me there was little to fret about.

"Mistress, do not worry," he said. "We'll get them and this will all be a bad dream, and we will live out our lives together," he said lightly stroking my cheek, and quelling my doubts.

"Let's go do this, baby."

"I'm with you," he said.

Nacio and I got out of the car, moving rapidly towards the gated front door of the little bright red and white house, which was reminiscent of the one in the fairy tale Hansel and Gretel. In spite of its appearance, there were no gingerbread windows to entice visitors. Instead, grime and vines decorated the home's facing; while one window hide covered in black tarp with a pair of chicken feet dangling above from bamboo strips.

In haste to get to the front door, I narrowly missed the corner of a cracked commode that had seen its last days, as the seat lay askew atop the porcelain opening. Flies claimed home to the inside of the vestibule, forming a fierce swarm that hummed like jet fighters in pursuit.

Nacio turned into a heavy blanket of mist, as I approached the door. Nervously, I rang the doorbell as the sound of shuffling feet approached. The skipped cadence of the footsteps that ended at the door were dull and heavy, possibly that of an obese individual. The door handle rattled just before a hateful warning stopped the person from opening the door.

"Paul," the hateful woman's voice bellowed. "If you touch that door, I will make the right side of your ass hurt for the next three months. Move away from the damn door."

Adrenaline kicked in, as I reached for the loaded tranquilizer pen. Nacio lingered through the air on standby in case something went awry. The door flew open and there stood Castiana with a wrinkle creased down the middle of her forehead in aggravation. Patches of hair were missing on either side of her head as she wore a poorly tended auburn wig that clashed with her green eyes and fair skin. Waif thin, short and gangly, Castiana was nowhere near the category of attractive.

"Who the hell are you and what the hell do you want?" the bizarre woman barked as she stepped out onto the small porch.

Moving without hesitation, I held up the pen and aimed for the woman's unguarded right shoulder giving her a departing message.

"I want you and your family to go straight to hell," I said firing the loaded dart and watching it make contact in the woman's right bicep.

Castiana made a small yelp as she slowly sank to

the grimy cement porch. As promised, the effects of the Diethmifex were undeniably amazing as it went to work on ravaging the women's reproductive organs, evaporating her estrogen, and leaving her virile with a manly appearance.

The potency of the chemical mix in the Diethmifex was swift. Castiana's midriff began to expand, while the small hips she already possessed seemed to disappear completely. Her sharp, gaunt facial features thickened with rubbery fat that gave her a round frying pan face. Castiana's eyes bulged from her head as her lips turned up in a fierce grimace. While the physical changes took place and tremors ravaged her body, she lay paralyzed on the cement --- wailing in protest. Her once high-pitched hateful voice filled with bass comparable to that of a man --- startling her.

"What have you done to me, dammit?"

"Oh you'll figure it out real soon," I said, as Nacio touched her forehead, putting her in a light trance as we made our escape.

Watching the Diethmifex take effect gave much needed reassurance that we would be able to complete our mission.

"Did you see that? I asked Nacio. "It worked."

"I told you it would. I have total faith in Bose. I have trusted him with my life, and I always will."

I hated causing harm to anyone, even the hateful Treemounts, but I knew this was the only way to flush Childress and her brothers out for the big battle. Once she is aware that the rest of her family is marked for extermination, she will have no choice but to come forward and stop hiding behind cowardice. Hyped up and ready, my trigger finger itched to fire the next dart, as I glanced at Nacio.

"Well, baby, we are on to the next one," I said, as he pulled away from the curb ---burning rubber down the street.

***

Northwestern San Antonio had lots of city nightlife, as every nightclub was jumping with throbbing bass. Many of the Treemount females thrived on conceit, believing every man in town wanted to lie in lust with them --- truly the twisted thoughts of sick whores. It was only natural the next victim would be found in one of the swankiest adult entertainment clubs in town --- Club Stunner.

We didn't look out of place at all as we drove past the valet attendants and parked the car ourselves. Nacio knew we needed to keep our keys for the quick escape we planned after we delivered the Dieth.

Club Stunner owner, Living Treemount, known as the head whore and main entertainment attraction at the club, never let her patrons down when she did her dance routine --- packing the house every night. She is the sister of the late Dukane Treemount; another of Nacio's victims. Standing unusually tall at 6'1 with beautiful figure eight curves accented by a small waist and thick hips, Living's waist-length red wavy hair swung around her shoulders, as she snaked down the chrome dance pole that stood in the center of the huge stage, wearing only a tiny g-string.

Rather than landing on her feet, Living allowed her agility and flexibility to take her down to the stage surface in a perfect horizontal split. Executing her seductive signature move caused a shower of money to rain through the air from the eager male patrons, as they released a ripple of coyote howls through the audience.

"Ya'll like that, huh?" Living inquired, as she recovered from her painful looking unladylike split. "Then ya'll are going to love this."

Nacio and I stood looking as Living turned her back to the crowd and bent over, sticking her head between her legs, mooning the audience. Disgusted and eager to kick her butt myself, I took the opportunity to do the next best thing. The pen I held was loaded with a dart and the aim was perfect. Nacio looked at me and nodded in approval.

As the many patrons continued to holler and howl, I discreetly held up the pen and fired. The dart made contact with Living's bare butt, striking her left cheek and exploding the Diethmifex into her gluteus muscle. Living fell to her knees with her head still between her legs and her butt up mid air. Her left butt cheek started to swell as inflammation quickly set in. Tremors rocked her body as her other cheek and hips started to shrink.

Living fell over, as her abdomen began to swell expanding her waist --- ripping the tiny g-string that looked more like a shoestring as it dangled from her body. Her breasts began to flatten as her face rounded out, extending her jaw line. With the changes occurring as rapidly as they did, the howling ceased instantly as the patrons watched in astonishment. No one made a move to attempt to help Living. Soon, the silence was broken by sneers, as the patrons soon looked at the drinks in their hands and threw out the alcohol on the stage.

"Damn, she's looks like one of us now," one confused clubgoer said. "I want my money back." Soon other men joined in and dived for the money thrown all over the stage, starting a fight and making our exit easy as Nacio and I left the club unnoticed.

Once back in the car, we looked at each other and confirmed that what we were doing was easy…or so we thought.

***

We were the first to return home. Things were quiet, as Nacio went to the kitchen to feed. I took some time to reflect on my newly deceased friend Elbithea Diseno. Attending San Antonio College was a lot easier with her around. Now, she was gone. Just like everyone else that had been dear to me. I wanted to call her family, but new it was too early in the morning to have such an intense conversation with her parents.

I needed to talk to someone who would give me some answers to questions that seemed to keep ping ponging in my head. My uncle Nuke Henderson would surely give me those answers and he would surely forgive the wee hour in which I am calling.

Nuke Henderson is my mother's youngest brother, who had recently implemented a hostile takeover acquiring all of the funeral homes in the San Antonio area, making him the wealthiest conglomerate funeral home owner in the southwest. I called my uncle knowing he would have all the information about the funeral arrangements of yet another of my friends. I knew I could not stomach another funeral in such a short time.

"Here, who is this calling this time of morning?"

"Hey, Nuke," I said. "I hate to call you so early, but you

got the body of one my friend, Elbithea Diseno."

"Solis, is that you?"

"Yeah, Nuke, it's me."

"Said Elbithea Diseno, huh?" He asked. "Yeah, they brought her in last night. Man, she was messed up pretty bad. They said a tiger escaped from the zoo and attacked her and that tourist. The only thing about this is that all the tigers are caged, and were never out. Blood remains stained on the pillars of the overpasses down the on the river. There's no telling when they'll get that cleaned up."

I hated to ask him, but I needed some reassurance that all of Elbithea's funeral arrangements would be paid in full.

"Nuke, I will be paying for the services, please make certain her family has whatever they need. Can you do that?"

"No problem, I'll let you know when the services are," he said. "Have you talked to Chase?"

"Yeah, I've talked to him recently. He is still recovering. How are you?"

"Well, it's slow boogie, but it's going?"

"Alright, Nuke, thanks for everything, love you."

"Love you too."

Just as I ended my call with Nuke, the Caraways made their way into living room. Their mood seemed to have lifted some. The strike against the Treemounts seemed to give them some empowerment to manage their grief.

Nacio joined us in the living room with a tray of warm blood and plasma in fluted goblets, with one holding blackberry wine in it for me. Would I ever get used to the sight of others enjoying goblets of blood. I still had trouble picturing myself doing this for the rest of eternity. Bose and Menlo came in last, wielding the same look of triumph on their faces. Nacio set the tray down on the table, as he proposed a toast.

"To our success at our first night of extermination and to our forged new family," he said. "Cheers."

"Cheers."

We all drank our libations as Armando gave his debriefing to us on the accomplishments he and Patience had achieved.

"We hit everyone that was on our list for tonight, Nacio. Soon the city will be free of any newborn Treemounts. We need to lure Justice out as soon as possible."

"I agree," I said.

"We'll get the chance to hit Justice," Nacio said. "He's not very bright, and because he does not know what it is he has done, he will make a move that will cost him dearly. Let us celebrate our victories as they come. We can't afford any mistakes."

"Well done," Bose said. "Menlo and I will continue our efforts to find the family's history."

The Caraways glanced at Nacio and I with a little smirk, indicating Bose would find much pleasure in having Menlo assist in finding genealogical information on the Treemount family tree.

"Let's retire for the evening and set out again tomorrow."

We all headed upstairs to our suites, with our mates in tow. Basrick continued to sit by the fireplace, keeping watch over the mansion.

***

Delivering the Formula Diethmifex over the next few

months continued without any problems. Eventually, our hunt went to the outlying counties and on to other cities throughout the state and country. No evidence left at the scene of the crime, leaving authorities baffled and making statements from those bold enough to be witnesses difficult to piece together.

Justice kept a low profile, yet there were unidentified bodies that continued to turn up intermittently. There had been no contact or information on the whereabouts of Childress and the rest of her brothers. Nacio insisted on continuing with our plans to take small steps, with a huge reward in the end.

10
The Enlightening

"Help me, please somebody help me!" Klein shouted, rattling the floorboards in the old swamp house as the rest of the family slept. He emerged from the bathroom with the worst case of mouth pox ever seen.

"What the hell you hollering for, fool?" Erland said, rubbing his eyes only to buck them at what he saw as he looked at his brother's face. "Damn man, what happened to you? I thought you said you only had a toothache."

"My mouth has been hurting for a few months, but this morning I woke up like this."

Erland moved within two feet from Klein with his eyes squinted looking at the sweltering pus-filled blisters that lined the inside and outside of his brother's mouth. Inflamed and rupturing, the pustules began to ooze and run down his face. While Erland continued to gawk at his brother's face, Bureau made her way out into the hallway to gander at Klein. Immediately, she knew a spell had caused the outbreak on her nephew's face and in his mouth.

"Looks to me like you were cursed into silence, Klein," she said. "Guess you better keep a muzzle on that mouth of yours, or else you are going to have more than pox to worry about."

"A curse?" Klein asked. "Who the hell is bold enough to put a curse on me? I got something for whoever it is."

Just then, Childress sashayed in with her huge baby bump, nearly flattening Erland as she rounded the corner.

"Ooohh lookie there, Cher," she howled. "Looks like you got a little fire going there in your mouth, boy. You want some hot sauce to bust them pustules?"

In pain and seething with resentment, Klein reached for the toilet plunger and started down the hall after Childress.

"Witch, I'm going to whoop your ass for putting this mess on me," Klein shouted. "Take it off me now."

Childress stood against the wall and smiled as Klein tried to rush towards her with the plunger.

"Oh, so what do you plan to do with that wood in your hand, Klein?" Childress asked.

Klein always seems to forget his sister can outwit him at anytime, and this situation was no different from others. Childress was still highly aggravated with her brother's loose lips and she punished him for it. Now, things have worsened for her eldest brother, and it appears he still has not accepted that she will always be a step ahead of him.

Childress braced herself, as she whispered more black magic that brought more pain on her brother. "Beat some sense into him to let him know, I'm ahead of him, always."

The wooden toilet plunger Klein held in his hand quivered as his grip tightened on it. Before he could comprehend what was happening, Klein's right hand slammed down on the right side of his face, bursting three pustules and leaving the residue on the handle.

Each knock on the head from the wood in Klein's hand sounded comparable to stones hitting a roof --- making him holler with pain, as a string of expletives left his swollen lips.

"Aunt Bureau, get this girl out of here before I hurt her," Klein pleaded with his aunt, as the blows to his head intensified. Seeking shelter from his possessed hand, he staggered down the hall and out into the backyard hoping the elements would help him.

Bureau stood dismayed at the strength of her niece's power. Knowing what it would mean to her own safety, she knew it would not be long before the time would come in which she would possibly have to destroy Childress.

"Childress, that's your brother don't hurt him."

"I don't give a damn he's my brother. He needs to keep his mouth shut, or else that toilet plunger is going to turn into a mallet hammer."

"I told you before," Bureau interjected. "I'm not going to have this hell in my house."

"And like I told you, Bureau, I don't give a damn."

Not liking the idea of admonishment in her home, Bureau spoke a Cease Spell, to undo what Childress had put in motion.

"Be still and move no more."

Luckily, for Klein, Bureau heard the last knock to the head as he simmered down in the backyard.

"Erland, take this peroxide out there to your brother and help him with that damn pus, and wipe the pus off my walls when you finish, you hear?"

"Yes, ma'am," Erland conveyed, now having a break

from the withdrawal symptoms he had experienced.

Elation from having regained control of her home environment did not last long, as she turned and nearly walked right into Childress --- standing right in front of her protruding stomach.

"Who the hell told you to undo my curse? Huh? You had better watch yourself old woman. I do not have time to keep pretending to play nice with you, Cher. You got that?

Bureau, gasped as she quickly sidestepped her niece running towards the kitchen. She heard hateful words come from Childress as she fled.

"And bring me a steak and make it rare. I'm hungry, dammit."

It had been years since Childress last visited the home. During her absence, Bureau had a small pantry built within the kitchen wall. Kept in secret from her children, Bureau used the small pantry for praying and working spells that needed supreme power behind them. She took the opportunity to work one now as she whispered in solitude.

"I need to find out what happened to Justice. I know he would tell me more than what this heifer told me. I cannot let her continue to cause trouble and destroy my family, or take my reigning power. I have to summon Justice."

On bended knees, the small round woman lit a candle at an altar that was against the wall. She poured some protection powder out on the center of the altar, and spelled Justice with her finger in the powder, chanting his name --- summoning him.

"Justice, hear me," she said. "Hear me, and come to me. I need you to come to me. Contact me; I need to hear from you now."

Bureau continued her chant, blowing more protection powder over his written name on the altar, closing her summons. Quickly, she grabbed a handful of the protection powder and stuffed it in her cigarette pouch. As she finished up, she heard Childress make another request for some food.

"I said I'm hungry, dammit."

Confident her spell would work in due time, Bureau continued with business as usual in the home playing Hostess to her fugitive niece and nephews.

***

Childress watched as Bureau came in with a huge Porterhouse steak freshly thawed and swimming in blood, garnished with parsley on the side. Pregnancy increased her appetite two fold, and anything she could get down her throat she did --- as long as it came with a side of fresh beef.

"'Bout damn time you brought my meat, Childress barked. "I told you I am hungry as hell."

Bureau slowly put the tray with the steak down on the nightstand where Childress was reclined in bed with her swollen elephant ankles.

"Stop fussing child I said I was coming," Bureau replied, just as her cigarette pouch slid off the tray and fell to the floor, as Childress immediately planted her eyes on the hefty pouch.

"Sounds to me like you have a little more than cigarettes in that there case."

"My cigarettes and a little sage is all," Bureau quickly

lied, turning her reaction away from her inquiring niece's eyes.

"You need anything else?"

"Naw, but I'll let you know if I do."

"Alright, well, I'm headed over to Istimia's to play bingo," Bureau lied again. She needed a quick cover to make certain she had time away from the house to invoke her summons to get in touch with Justice.

Bureau hurriedly, grabbed the pouch, lit a cigarette as she did her usual stroll out of the room and down the stairs, careful not to give any indication of her betrayal towards her niece.

Once out of earshot, Bureau ran as quickly as her small legs would allow her to. Spotting her keys on the kitchen counter, she snatched her purse and headed out the door. She jumped into her car and gunned it down the dirt road, away from Dog water Swamp.

Three miles down the road, Bureau turned down Grosse State Trench Road. A clearing in a field that stretched off the road caught her eye. Once she reached the clearing, she sat her purse and keys down, and reached for her cigarette pouch. Taking a handful of the hexed protection powder, Bureau chanted a call to Justice in hopes he would respond to her summons.

"Racooroo, Madaoo. Justice, hear me, hear my call to you. What say you when I call your name? Come forth, come forth, come forth."

The short woman opened her hands allowing a breeze on swift wings to carry the protection powder in the western wind. Circulating with the velocity of a cyclone, the protection powder ascended into the sky and vanished. Now all she had to do was wait for him to respond --- knowing Justice would not be able to resist the summons with his name in it.

Night would be falling soon and she knew Justice is the only one that could help end the misery that was squatting in her home.

***

Several months had passed since the night Justice had run into Nacio and Solis down on the river. Still confused and dazed from the silver that had been plunged into his back from the swarm of bats that attacked him, he had been hiding out at Believa's trying to recuperate. Silver remained lodged between his shoulder blades, rotting his flesh--- preventing the wounds he sustained to heal. Weak as a human, Believa could not retrieve the silver from its buried location in his back.

She had been by his side the entire time. Having sense enough to know that multiple vampire bites would turn her into a vampire, Justice decided to keep her human to lure other human victims for him to feed on. With an insatiable appetite, he kept Believa busy.

"Put on the red pants, dammit, and go out and get me some simple sucker to feed on, you hear?"

"But you ripped the crotch out of the red pants. I can't go out there like that," Believa squeaked.

"Either you put them on like I said, or I'll sew the crotch shut with you in them. You got that?"

Without any further hesitation, Believa listened to her fanged pimped out lover as he planned to put her on the stroll amongst prostitutes and drug addicts for the evening. Terrified of the consequences, Believa put on her bait and made herself up with heavy make up to entice would-be Johns as they approached her. Although weak, she knew Justice could still muster enough strength to snap her neck. She left him on her couch as she went out to find sustenance for him to continue his painful existence.

Working the corner of Third and Broadway downtown, Believa wore the gapped pants praying that she would not run into anyone she knew. That was wishful thinking for her, because who else would come strolling down Third Avenue none other than her old Sunday school teacher, Deacon Mac Moan. Considering he was a lecherous pervert, things just got much easier for Believa, reeling him in would be quick and dirty.

"Hey, Deacon Moan," she greeted, presenting her D cups under the street lamp. "How you doing, sugar?"

Looking as though he had one too many from the club around the corner, Deacon Moan pulled his britches up high as he could without bringing them under his arm pits as he approached Believa.

"Well, hey yourself, sugar," the lit up man said. "And please, call me Mac."

"Alright, Mac, you looking for some fun tonight, baby? I sure could use a good time," she said, playing with her heavy hair as she tossed it over her shoulders. "Why don't you come and party with me," she said, turning around and bending over to touch her ankle strap on her right shoe, exposing the missing seat of her pants.

Believa knew it would be easy to lure Deacon Mac Moan to Justice. He once fondled her under the small desk when she was eight and knew nothing had changed with him. He took the bait.

"Come on, sugar. Let's go to my place. I don't live too far from here."

"Yes ma'am, I'm with you."

"You can drive, baby, because my hands will be busy getting to know you."

The intense petting session continued for the entire drive, as Deacon Moan's lead foot slammed down on the accelerator, cutting the ride to Believa's house to mere seconds.

Justice could smell the lust rolling off Deacon Moan as he and Believa made their way inside the house. Attempting to get off the couch proved to be a task for him, as he staggered to hide himself in the shadowy corners of the living room, Justice could barely manage to walk. He slumped into a corner just as the mismatched couple made their way inside.

Deacon Moan's hands were exploring Believa's folds in the crotch less pants, as she put her purse on the couch. Predatorily, Justice positioned himself to feed while his fangs cut through his gums --- thirst burning his throat.

"Sit here, sugar, while I go and finish removing the rest of these clothes."

"Yeah, you do that, baby, but don't leave," the in-heat man said, seating himself on the couch. "Stay here and peel those clothes off."

Knowing Justice was somewhere in the shadows, Believa took care not to make any sudden moves. Removing herself from what happened next, she encouraged a little role-play with the hot man.

"Let's play a little game, honey. Close your eyes and

imagine what I look like, and open them when I countdown."

"Alright, I can do that."

She slowly started counting backward from five, rubbing Deacon Moan's chest. Justice appeared behind her, waving her out of the way while he continued to unbutton the man's shirt.

"Four, three, two, one; open your eyes," Believa's voice quivered.

A smug smile stretched across Deacon Moan's face as his eyes slowly opened --replacing arousal with a scream of horror. Before he could attempt to escape, Justice flashed his fangs and took a bite out of Deacon Moan's right shoulder, severing his subclavian artery --- spewing blood from ceiling to floor surface.

Justice bit into the man so hard, torn blood vessels trailed down the man's back, sending Believa into retreat, as she tried not to scream --- fearing the same fate. Drinking non-stop, Justice made sure to pulverize the man's body, leaving little fluid inside him.

Believa sat slumped on the floor in a fetal position and near shock. She usually dealt with what she saw pretty well, but tonight was different. She hadn't expected to see Deacon Moan, and thought she would enjoy punishing him, but it actually had the opposite effect. She sat on the floor slowly, giving regret enough time to settle in, followed by guilt.

"Damn, that was good," Justice growled, as he picked the man's flesh from between his fangs. Believa sat looking at the mess all over the living room, as her stomach churned.

"More," he said, sliding his tongue across his fangs, and then licking his lips.

"I want more."

As long as the silver remained buried deep in his flesh, he remained a slave to gluttony. His perforated wounds oozed fluid, as he dropped onto the couch from weakness.

"Open the window and let some fresh air in here, Believa," he said. Believa's delayed response time from her catatonic state earned her a snarl from Justice.

"Now, dammit."

"Uh, yeah," she said. "Okay, I'll get the window."

Believa scurried over to the tiny window in the living room to release the security latch, letting in the stale and humid night air.

Justice listened as a gentle breeze whistled in through the screen. Even after his feeding, his wounds were slow to heal --- prolonging his convalescence. Needing comfort and finding none from her captor, Believa left the bloody living room to curl up in her bed.

A sudden gust of wind blew through the screen, tearing the mesh from the seam and scattering books and newspaper on the bloody floor. On high alert and ready to strike, Justice heard his name from a whisper in the wind.

"Justice, I need you to hear me," the voice said. "I need you to answer me. I need to hear you."

After listening to the message in the wind, Justice suddenly had a bad case of longing for his deceased mother. Rather than taking another destructive trip down memory lane with agonizing memories, he decided to do the next best think---call his Aunt Bureau.

"Hey, Believa, where's your phone? I have business to

take care of."

***

Although her belly hung swollen and the size of a pumpkin, Childress kept her figure --- and a glance from behind would not indicate she was carrying a child. The longer the days were in Dog water Swamp, the more anxious she became.

"I'm bored as hell in this sewage dump," she mumbled to herself. "Guess we gave the Feds the slip. I know none of them are stupid enough to come down to this mud hole…I need to find something for me to do, dammit. I'm getting tired of sitting here day in and day out."

Devilment was something she thrived on, and her intentions were always self-centered and the same.

"Nayphous looked good enough to eat the other day. He has no business with Urgata --- with her simple basic ass. She still sucks her thumb at night and wears stockings with her dresses. He needs a real woman, someone who will serve him just right. I know just who that person is. Suddenly, I have an urge to go hear some jazz tonight."

Childress needed physical attention and Nayphous was her next target, but not before her stomach growled once again, indicating the baby had wiped her out and she needed to refuel once more.

"Bureau, bring me some more meat," she called. When there was no answer, Childress began cussing loud enough to send the mosquitoes to the other side of the swamp.

"Dammit, do have to do every damn thing around her?" she said as she and her belly made way to the kitchen.

***

After a few rounds of Bingo with her friend Istimia, Bureau headed to The Suga Shack to hear Nayphous as the opening act for the evening. Time seemed to pass so slowly while she waited for Justice to contact her. She knew he would be able to give her a better understanding of what was happening back in Texas.

"I sure hope that boy hasn't gotten himself into any more trouble than these fools already have," she murmured. "I have got to find a way to get them away from here. The Loas are going to punish us all for the foolishness they have caused, I just know it."

Bureau was confident her summons to Justice would work. She was The Mambo in these parts. People from far and wide would come to get her wisdom. Her abilities with spells were strong and she normally would not doubt her ability, but deep in her soul, she knew trouble was coming hard and fast to her doorstep.

"I pray Justice hears me. I pray he hears me. I pray

he---," her phone rang, interrupting her chant. Without hesitation, she pulled off the road and took the call. She cautiously, reached for her phone as her hand trembled, feeling the unspeakable evil on the other end. She flipped the device open.

"Hello."

"Hey, Aunt Bureau, it's Justice. Something told me to call you. What's going on?"

Bureau had to take a moment to gasp for breath, which reminded her to breathe. She knew her nephew's voice, but knew his soul had long left his body.

"Justice, what have you done to yourself? You've sold your soul."

"Auntie, I haven't done anything I---," she cut him off with two words.

"Don't lie," she said. "Don't dare lie to me, damn fool. What's happened back there?"

"I'm different, Aunt Bureau. I'm different. I don't want you to see me like this. Several of our family members are dead here. Childress believes one of her enemies is killing us off one by one. Her name is Solis Burkes. She's with a vampire and I'm scared, Aunt Bureau."

"Childress is pregnant Justice," Bureau explained. "All she eats is bloody steak. She swallowed your mother's blood and the blood of our Ancestor Priestess Auldicia, and now she is developing the signs of Porphyria, blood cravings and peeling skin. Klein said she is pregnant by some detective, but he said that the man shot and killed himself. Childress hexed him."

"What? Aw, man this is bad, Auntie," he said. "What is she doing now?"

"She is trying to run me out of Dog water Swamp as The Mambo. She plans to sacrifice the baby to the Loas as soon as she's born. By the child being a female, it makes her a legacy, and her birth will make Childress invincible. You've got to stop her, Justice, only you can help with that."

"What is it you want me to do, Aunt Bureau? I'm scared myself."

"I will summon you again when the baby girl is born. This child is a legacy in our family. The birth makes us strong against our enemies. Now get off the phone before they find you."

The phone went dead. He stood there perplexed, but with a new agenda.

"Oh yes, payback is very sweet sister dear, very sweet indeed," he said to himself.

"You've gone and gotten yourself pregnant, how about that? A tramp like you as a mother --- what is the world coming to? Oh boy, this has just raised the stakes for me. Yes, sir."

Bureau abruptly ended the call. She hated to hang up, but could not take the chance of having the call traced. Speaking to Justice put her at ease. Knowing that Justice would be the strongest of her nephews to challenge Childress gave her hope that her sister's troublesome children would soon move on.

"I can relax a little bit now," Bureau reassured her conscience. "Justice will be the one to whoop Childress's pregnant ass if push comes to shove. My children will be safe from her, and we can get our lives back."

Her fears subsided in one aspect, but raced uncontrollably in another. Unspeakable evil had fallen on Justice. Bureau knew her nephew's soul was no more. He had become a child of the night.

"That damn boy has gone and unleashed part of Priestess Auldicia's curse upon himself and he will be doomed to hell for it. As long as he rids us of Childress, he will have to deal with the curse on his own. I will not risk my family's safety."

Bureau decided to leave the fate of Justice up to the Loas, and she continued on her way to The Suga Shack to hear Nayphous play his saxophone. Playing the venue at The Suga Shack had sky rocketed his career and he had a loyal following from the locals. She and the rest of her children are looking forward to a fall binding ceremony with Nayphous and Urgata. The question is how long would it take before Childress started her tramping and mess things up between the couple.

Not wanting to ruin the evening, Bureau put the thought of Childress out her mind as she went to listen to her future son in-law blow his horn. She arrived at the club and went inside to her usual spot. Urgata arrived earlier, taking a seat at the table near the stage and flagged her down when she saw her walk in.

"Hey, mama," she greeted with a kiss. "Nayphous is getting ready to take the stage.

"Get me a drink would you, baby?" Bureau asked her child, ready to relax.

Across the club, she saw Klein and Erland wearing extremely loud print clothing that made them look like lost members of the Earth, Wind, and Fire Band. Erland stood next to a young woman who was as catatonic as he was. Neither of them said anything to each other, and stood still as mannequins.

Klein sat at the bar trying his best to get a date to party with after the club closed, but could not get any interest from any female in the place. His mouth pox from the hex Childress put in place made all the females avoid him like the Swine Flu. He sat frustrated, lashing out at every woman that turned him down.

"Aw, screw you then, tramp," Klein barked. "I can get any female I want." His attempts and insults only made him the most avoided man in the club. He finished his drink just as the MC took the stage.

"Ladies and gentlemen, I'd like to welcome you to The Suga Shack tonight. Please put your hands together for our very own headliner tonight, Nayphous Aljeneaux. Go ahead and blow, Mr. Aljeneaux, blow."

Nayphous didn't waste any time commanding the stage. He counted off, and belted a sexy note from jazz artist Euge

Groove's song Chillaxin', as the crowd roared with applause ---herding them to the dance floor. Hoisting her short and near-to-the floor legs up, Bureau swung her hair over her right shoulder as she flagged her usual partner to escort her to the dance floor.

All was well for the evening, until a sense of dread crept up her spine. Nayphous had just made the bridge of the song when the crowd parted and the spotlight swung in the direction of the club entrance. There stood Childress in one of Urgata's dresses that cocooned her body leaving little to the imagination.

Wearing the dress was one thing, but Childress had taken it and completely tricked it out. Flesh seeped out of shreds that she cut into the cotton material, giving on lookers a peek-a-boo sideshow. The plunging neckline of the dress past beyond the collarbone, show casing her breasts that oozed over the top --- spilling over the edge.

Bureau stood seething as her niece walked in rocking her hips as she swayed towards the stage. Nothing interrupted the band as Nayphous continued his solo. Childress moved her lips slowly --- mouthing words that Bureau only figured was a hex that she was conjuring. Not wanting to alarm the bystanders, Bureau tried to run interference, but was unsuccessful. Childress dropped some protection powder around her, blocking any attempts from Bureau to stop her.

Childress reached the stage and stood there as Nayphous continued. He walked to the edge, and blew his horn in her direction as the crowd roared.

"Blow, baby, blow!" she hollered, as she walked up on to the stage. Taking her usual tramp dance routine to the next level, she turned her back to the crowd, and bent over --- shaking her hips one way, as her swollen belly went another. The lecherous men that were on the prowl for the night squealed with delight, as Childress shimmed on stage.

Bureau nearly burst from anger, as her niece let her true colors show. Urgata made her way to the table and set her drink down as tears began to form in her eyes. Childress did not let this stop her. Once she saw that her cousin had made her way back to the table, she slowly turned and walked off the stage, but not before looking over her shoulder and waving her finger at Nayphous to follow her backstage. Unable to resist, Nayphous surrendered to the lust cast upon him by the seductress. He left the stage as the band played on. The MC immediately stepped in to clean up the mess that could have ended his career.

"Oooh, folks, looks like this is a hot one tonight," the man crooned. "Go 'head, Mike, take us out of here." The bass player took over as maestro, as Nayphous slipped back stage.

Childress slipped out the back exit and waited for Nayphous to follow. He did not disappoint her, as the door swung open and the look in his eye cued her to wave him over to her once more. As she walked over to his car and got in, he followed, cranked up, and left the club in the moon light. Childress was satisfied her spell worked, and she was ready to intimately bring the night to a close.

Back at the club, Urgata wiped her face as the hot tears

fell into the drinks she had just brought to the table for her and her mother. Bureau was pissed, as her heart broke for her child as she cried.

"Mama, that bitch has not changed one bit," she cried. "Now she's ruined things with Nayphous. I am going to put a spell on her to maim her ass."

"No child, you cannot do that, because you will bring destruction down on us all. Be patient, child. I might have a solution to all our problems soon. I hate you have to suffer, but trust me, it might be our only hope of surviving."

Not knowing what else to do, Bureau and Urgata left the club riding in silence all the way home --- dreading to return to Dog water Swamp.

***

"Take me to your place, sugar," Childress crooned, as Nayphous punched the accelerator, arriving at his place rock hard with plans to have a long and hot night with Childress.

"I see you are ready for me. It's about time you woke up and let that weak mouse of a cousin of mine go. You need a real woman. Now that you got me, what are you going to do with me?"

Unable to make it out of the car, Nayphous grabbed Childress and kissed her exposed breasts. Anxious and hating the interference from the steering wheel, he jumped out the car and ran to the other side, yanking open the passenger side door and carrying her into the house.

He kicked the door shut with his feet, still entranced and not having spoken a word all night, since before she walked in the club. As he turned to face her, all that remained of her was the dress she wore that was now in a pile on the floor. Childress had made her way to the nearest bedroom.

Nayphous ripped his shirt from his chest, and dropped other remnants of his clothing while accepting her invitation into his bed.

***

Dawn was turning over the horizon just as Childress walked in the house at Dogwater Swamp. Bureau sat in the recliner under a cloud of smoke, flicking the dangling ash from her cigarette. A crumpled pack lay at her feet, while she rocked slowly in the recliner.

Childress trudged into the living room, caught off guard by Bureau reclining next to a black partition. Her twisted dress could not hide the fact she had spent a lustful night with her cousin's fiancé.

"Well, well," Bureau hummed. "Look what crawled out of a hole and waltzed in here."

"Leave me alone, old woman, before you find yourself crawling out from somewhere nasty."

"Why would you hurt Urgata like that, Childress? You knew they were getting married in the fall. Things were fine, and then along you come tramping and being a hoe all over again."

Childress snapped and made her way across the room, now standing two inches from Bureau's nose, hissing fierce morning breath.

"Have you lost your mind, Bureau?" she asked. "Don't let this pregnancy fool you. I dare you to say one more thing to me, and I promise you I will take the skin off your ass and make a soup with it, you understand me?"

"You are going to destroy us all. Why is it that you cannot see what you are doing?"

"I told you, Bureau, I know what I'm doing. Do you know what you are doing? Before you answer that, I'm hungry. Get me a steak and do not let poisoning me cross your mind. If it does, I'll know, and then that is when I'm going to put a cross bone on you --- marking you for death. Got it?"

Bureau sat unable to breathe well, nearly choking on the smoke she ingested. Things were going downhill for the family and nothing could stop it.

11
Who?

Locating Treemount families in Texas was nearly complete. Our next stop was to head to Louisiana to deliver the Formula Diethmifex to the rest of the females in the family. Those that received the inoculation had visible physical results that were astonishing.

Bose kept follow up research on those that had received the formula. Extreme weight gain, acne, deepening of the voice, and hair loss were just a few of the noted side effects of dangerously high levels of testosterone in each female --- leaving them unable to reproduce. Several Treemount females suffered an increase in aggression from the testosterone excess leading to increased crime, which in turn led to an increase in arrests. Nacio was pleased at how smoothly our plans were moving along.

"We are making excellent progress, Mistress. Soon we will have wiped out all except Childress, Klein, and Erland. Justice will have his eradication as soon as we identify his whereabouts."

"I agree, sweetheart," I said, enjoying the fact that I looked forward to happiness with my mate, and knowing that I would no longer be plagued by the Treemounts.

Our lives were coming together wonderfully. It seemed Bose had finally found a mate of his own. Nacio only wanted the best for his kindred brother, and Detective Menlo, although a Treemount female, she appeared to be a suitable match for him.

"I have never seen my brother more happy and content in all of our decades together. Menlo seems to be very fond of him. She's strong, independent, and a cognitive match for his scholarly abilities. They will be very happy together."

"He appears to have come alive in a way I never imagined," I agreed. "Our home is alive with love within these walls; despite the fact danger lurks outside of our protective fortress."

"It wouldn't matter what I had to face," Nacio said. "As long as you are with me, the world could stop turning."

We embraced, sharing a tender kiss that seemed to last forever until Bose knocked on the door.

"Hefe, breakfast is served."

"We'll be right down," Nacio responded.

"I guess we'd better go and join the rest of our family."

"I guess we should," I said.

We both left the suite and started down the hall, when we ran into Basrick. Nacio and I both greeted him and surprisingly he returned the salutation.

"Good morning to you both," he said. "If it's possible, sire, I'd like to have a word with Mistress Solis?"

"Certainly, my friend," Nacio responded, kissing me as he stepped between us. "Please excuse me."

This was truly a bright good morning. Basrick had

spoken few words over the past several months and now he is requesting to speak with me.

"Mistress Solis, please forgive me for my grief and behavior over the last several months. Losing my twin has made me ache for a vengeance that is beyond reproach. I have never meant any disrespect towards you or the sire. I am asking for your leniency and mercy," he said as he knelt on one knee and kissed my hand.

"Please rise, Basrick, there is nothing to forgive," I said. "We love you no less than before. Your loyalty is appreciated."

He rose, and then bowed once more. "I will continue to assist in finding the Treemounts and execute the plans."

He disappeared down the hall, heading in the direction of the library. I felt things were turning around for us all. Basrick is kind and wise. It pains me to see him in such agony over the death of Basira. I truly believed him when he said he would seek vengeance against Justice.

***

Downstairs in the dining room, everyone had their usually sustenance. Bose had prepared French toast for Menlo and I, and a fresh batch of oatmeal and raisin cookies for me to nibble on for the day, and of course blood for the vampires. Nacio was anxious to continue our quest.

"Bose, what have you got for us today?"

Briefly taking his eyes off Detective Kildare, Bose explained the results of his recent find.

"There should be approximately two hundred Treemount family members left," this includes the children

Klein has not claimed. We must come to a decision determine what to do with those children as our quest comes to a close."

Nacio looked at the Caraways seated across from us and then at Menlo. It seemed he struggled a bit with the idea and decided to put the decision on hold.

"I see. Well, let us get closer to that point and by then we should have some clarity, and some deductive reasoning that will support our decision."

One thing held true, Nacio had a way with words that seemed to blanket and comfort everyone, even though it is a situation in need of a resolution. Menlo cleared her throat and looked over at Bose, breaking the small amount of tension that hung in the air.

"Whoa, look at the time. I have to get to the substation before my phone starts blowing up," she explained.

"In such a hurry, my sweet," Bose said, already lonely for her and she hadn't even left yet. "When will you return?"

"Don't worry, honey. I'll be back at the end of shift. You know I cannot stay away too long," she said, smiling slyly.

"Well, I have enough to do today, so I will be quite occupied in your absence," Bose said. "It will help me during my longing for you."

"Hey, save some of the work for me to do," she said, reaching to kiss him goodbye. "I'll be on my way. I want to follow up on a few John Does that have turned up once again. I'm certain Justice is responsible, but I don't think he's working alone. He's been underground too long, but we still can't find where he's hiding out at."

"Anything you can do is appreciated, Menlo," Nacio said. "But don't worry, we will get him soon enough."

"Alright, I guess I will see you all a little later," Menlo said, waving goodbye and taking Bose's hand.

"Come on, honey," Bose gestured. "I'll drive you back to the entrance."

Although Menlo had decided to assist us with ridding us all of her family, she still carried with her the burden of guilt for her family's transgressions. It is obvious, whenever decisions have to be made in our action plans against the Treemounts. For Menlo, being a member of the Treemounts is sort like living on the same block with people your siblings stole money from --- but like the saying goes, "blood is thicker than water."

Even though your siblings don't live on the block anymore, but you still do. This means everyone drives slowly past your house pointing, or staring at you while you are out on your front porch, or egging your house while you sleep at night. She would always carry the curse of the name Treemount.

Bose led Menlo towards the front door, where he had parked the car out front. He had sworn himself to a whole days worth of work to look up and locate the last 200 Treemounts. If this took Bose a whole day to complete, it would probably take near two weeks for the average human to complete this task.

"When I return, I'll retire to the libraries for the rest of the day," he said.

"No problem, Bose," Nacio said, waving the two off.

***

Bose made it to the driveway entrance that led to Cedar and Perieda streets. He hated leaving Menlo.

"I know you have to work, but I sure wish you'd stay a little longer."

"I will not be gone too long my dear," she said. "I just want to check out some leads, that is all."

"Well, you call me when you are back here tonight, understand?" Bose asked. "I have programmed my phone in your phone, so you can get in touch with me; and I know what you taste like, so I'll know exactly where you are always."

"You are making me weak," she said. "And I have to go to work."

They shared a long, steamy hot kiss before she broke away to drive off. Things were heating up between the two of them; Menlo had not known a greater satisfaction before she met Bose.

Bose stood at the end of the entrance, licking his tongue across his fangs, reminiscing about the love they had made. He anxiously awaited her return for more.

***

Daylight crept by, as everyone eagerly awaited the return of nightfall. Bose spent the majority of the day in the downstairs library. His neatly arranged stacks and files are as he had left them, allowing him to pick up right where he had left off. The last volume of information he perused was of a slave ship's manifest. It contained information about the cargo on-board. The spine of the book appeared genuine and authentic, possibly several hundred years old.

The last entry Bose looked at described the traveling conditions of the slave galley below:

"...disgusting, filthy conditions has brought disease upon the crew, many will not survive to dock. Something has befallen a few of the bodies on-board. The doctor discovered the bodies had no blood remaining as they decayed. It is feared that Satan has stowed away on the ship and will soon take us all to hell. There are several abandoned children on board with no mother to claim them. Many captives wandered loose on the Northwestern coast near the Canary Islands and Morocco. The bastards will sell to the highest bidder as a slave that will tend the land. One child in particular, with eyes green as jade and skin fair as snow will fetch a wonderful price for the voyage. This bastard makes the smell of shit and vomit more bearable.

The entry about the young green-eyed child along the Canary Islands and Moroccan coasts piqued an interest with Bose. It led him to believe the source of a very important part of the Treemount family history connects to this one child slave. The description of the child's eyes and skin color indicated there is a definite link between the child and the Treemounts.

Bose continued to read the entry about the auction of the slaves once the ship docked:

"...finally arriving in Louisiana from the Mexican Gulf. Metal clanked and rattled as the slaves unloaded the remaining dead and dumped them in the ocean, making way for the others to line up on the auction block. One wealthy French landowner stood beside his wife on the pier and watched as the slaves stood shackled and whipped. As the auctioneer began

his count, the landowner's wife took note of the baby that clutched the bosom of one naked female slave.

The child's Lilly white skin, stood out in shocking contrast to the rich brown skin of the slave's. The landowner's wife whispered to him to purchase the child and the slave the child clutched so tightly. Each landowner brought their own branding iron and had it heated with fire from a pier side Blacksmith. Once the sale was final, the child and the slave received a brand on the belly button marking them as property of the slave owner. The child wore a brand made with a ring the landowner wore on his pinkie finger. Both were loaded into an open wagon, as both wailed from sizzling skin. Doing this kept the slaves from escape attempts. This particular landowner's symbol came with notoriety throughout Louisiana. Name and symbol was..."

Pages were missing from the manifest, interrupting the information Bose read. His mind began to race, needing to find the rest of the pages to the manifest. This particular volume came wrapped in a golden cloth tie. With its particular length stretched to its current size, indicated to Bose there were more volumes.

Bose began cycling through the information knocking over stacks and skimming through the books, and then tossing them to the side. The racket the books made from toppling over, alerted Basrick to possible trouble in the library. He stormed in to find that Bose was in the midst of disarray, which was so unlike him. Basrick stood in the sea of books and mayhem looking perplexed.

"Is there trouble, Bose?"

Bose allowed his obsessive-compulsive disorder to

kick into overdrive as he sifted through the scattered volumes of books and periodicals strewn about --- searching for the missing parchment from the slave ship's manifest. Bose hardly noticed Basrick standing in the middle of the library.

"Uh, naw, man everything is fine. I just seemed to have lost an integral piece of archival evidence."

Basrick made an effort to reach out to the rest of the household members, and this effort to assist Bose appeared to be a social gesture.

"You mind if I take a look at what you found so far?"

"No not at all, here you go," Bose said, handing him the ship's manifest. "It appears we had this particular ships manifest in our library archives. This is the first I have read of its contents. It explains during a slave auction, a child was nursing from one of the captives, but it was uncertain if the child was hers or not. The description of the child fits that of the Treemounts. I have read the entire volume except for the last few pages and now I cannot find them, and it is driving me crazy."

"Maybe I can help," Basrick said taking the manifest from Bose and looking through it.

"Yes, skim through it and see if perhaps we can piece together some other missing links. A few years back, I cleaned out the shelves here and donated a few of the books to the Central Library, and to the Witte Museum, perhaps those missing pages were stored in those boxes."

"It's certainly worth a shot to check it out," Basrick added.

"Yeah, well I'm on my way. Let Nacio and Solis know I won't be long will you?"

"Alright man, that's cool, see you later."

Instead of teleporting away, Bose went down stairs and headed out the front to take the car where he had left it. Basrick began his own investigation, reading the ship's manifest in detail. Many of the entries were astonishing, especially the description of the child.

"These entries never mention whether the child is male or female," he spoke to himself. "This finding needs to be discussed with Nacio and Solis."

Basrick quickly finished reading the manifest and drew his own conclusion. The sex of the child will need to be determined. He knew this would take their hunt in a new and perilous direction and put them closer to annihilating the Treemounts for good. With a few of his own obsessive-compulsive tendencies, Basrick set out to determine the sex of the child that survived the ships voyage. The child's resistant strength to all the disease and pestilence on the ship left a remarkable impression on Basrick, and raised more questions.

"How is it this child survived the mysterious plague that had stowed away on board the ship?" He asked himself. "The blood drained bodies might have been caused by a vampire."

Anxious and with more questions, Basrick quickly decided to assist Bose by checking out the history of the slave owner, and what link he and his family played in the Treemount family tree.

"I'll search for information on the web while Bose is downtown at the Central Library. This ought to make gathering information faster. It certainly will help bring some peace to our family. We can all rest once we put the Treemount bastards in the ground where they all belong."

***

Bose arrived at the Central Library and went straight upstairs to the Genealogy section of the library. He quickly scanned the library stacks for the set of books that he graciously donated to the library with Nacio's permission. It was not long before he zeroed in on the properly catalogued treasures that were once property of the Puente Estate.

"Ah, here it is," Bose mumbled. "*Manifesto de Marina* surely this has the remaining few pages of the ship's manifest."

Gambling on the fact that those few pages could open his eyes to new understanding proved to be true. He found a table and continued his investigative probe. The torn fringes of the page were from the other volume that remained at the mansion. He knew they matched, due to the scrawled quill ink and calligraphy that allowed him to continue reading right where he left off. He recalled the last words from the previous volume were *Name and symbol:*

"*...were the choices of the owner.*"

"Dammit," Bose murmured, careful not to startle any of the patrons within close proximity to his workstation. Anger crept over him, as the statement seemed to be a dead end. No matter for him, Bose understood how this type of investigative work gives promising leads that can lead nowhere.

"I must get a grip on my impatience. I wish nothing but happiness for Nacio and Solis. I wish this to be over. I am going to find the root of this evil and put a stop to it myself. I have to complete this task for my brother and for his new bride. They and the Caraways are my only family, and I wish them no harm."

Bose continued to peruse the stacks next to the ship's manifest. Running his hand over several volumes of information, he found his hand stopped at the moth-eaten volume of a slave narrative thick with faded quill text. He stood mesmerized at the clarity of the text he read. Slaves reading and writing was treasonous and against the law, however, the particular owner of this slave took good care to make certain this slave could survive. Bose allowed his eyes to follow along the calligraphy entries of text, as his mind seemed to go down memory lane:

"...I am no longer called Adesewa Ojonto. My name is now Manette Treemount. I do not know how old I am, but I look young and my skin is brown and not folded. Ma'am Vivienne liked the name Manette, said it was her mammie's name. Master Estes said it was good to have his land name to identify us if we ever tried to run. Since the day we came off the ship, I was glad not to be beaten anymore. Ma'am is good to us slaves. She does not let Master hit us, and we get the left over pieces of pork, that is not burned bad, and she made us read and write our name. I miss my old name. I will always be Adesewa Ojonto. Ma'am Vivienne and Master Estes are called Creole, said it is called mulatto. They have African, French, and White blood in them, but they look all white. No color in their skin allows them to fool white folks into thinking they are white too. They are rich and have many slaves like me."

Bose sat still as a cobblestone as his eyes tracked the text back and forth, left to right taking in what lie before him. A sense of peace blanketed him as he continued his journey through the young woman's words:

"...I miss my home, with all my brothers and sisters. I miss home, but I am glad to be away from the motherland. Obayifo had come and taken her share of the men in the land. She drained the blood of many of them and made many children with them as well. Many brides were unable to conceive children with their grooms due to the Obayifo's ways. She was a witch and a drinker of blood, sent from hell below. Her name was Priestess Auldicia. Many of us lived in fear of her and became captives by the slave traders fleeing her vengeance. The children she had from lust came aboard the ship. The villagers were afraid of the children. Many Voodoo priests and priestesses sought to kill the children that wandered the coastline. Villagers feared that because of the evil that gave birth to the children, letting them live would bring more vengeance upon the village. Many villagers killed the motherless children on sight."

Bose continued his journey, as he silently wept for the souls of those children that paid a high price for Priestess Auldicia's evil. Maddening as it was to continue to read, he did so vowing to curse the family himself.

"...On the night of my capture, we saw the great battle with Mistress Olinka and Priestess Auldicia. It was an awful sight. Mistress Olinka was powerful and defeated Priestess Auldicia who had just given birth to a beautiful, but cursed child. The child received a bite from its Hell-sent mother as she drew blood from the baby several times, cursing the child as she carried the curse for blood lust. As the battle between good and evil raged on, a storm brewed in the night sky, sending the hidden on-lookers further toward the coastline into their capture.

Herded like goats and thrown below into the ship, some slaves were unaware of the battle that had just taken place. On the ship, I noticed the small child that the Obayifo, Priestess Auldicia, had just given birth found its way on the ship below. I knew the child was Satan's spawn, and that black magic ran through the child's veins. Only a few hours after giving birth, the child was the size of toddler and growing. Born with the most beautiful green eyes and hair like golden corn flour, I knew the child should not be allowed to live. As my voyage continued in the bowels of the ship, a strange plague ravaged the captain's men and the slave cargo. The dead began to fill the air with stench as the seawater carried us to the new land.

No one could figure out what was killing the slaves. The ship's captain was angered and beat many of us, because he said we caused the death and disease. In my soul, I not only knew what caused the disease aboard, I saw it when it happened. Death came for those poor souls at the hands of the baby that had boarded the ship. I will continue on the next morning. Ma'am Vivienne calls for her tea."

Bose closed the back cover on the last sentence of Adesewa Manette's narrative. Amazed at the courage of this young woman, he felt a sense of pride after reading the words from the text. For him, her words had opened a floodgate of emotions that only made him long to know more about her life and what answers she could provide to he and his family.

In need of more to add to his investigation, Bose checked the rest of the stacks on the shelf only to find they them missing. Irritated, he made his way to the front desk to inquire about the whereabouts of the next volume of Adesewa Manette's narratives. The librarian stood behind the desk, staunch as a statue as she looked over her glasses at Bose.

"Might I help you?"

"Yes, my dear. I need to know the location of the next volume of this book."

"Well, it says here, it is checked out and on display at the Witte Museum."

"Thank you. I will be taking these with me as well."

"I could put an in-transit request on it to have it returned here for you." the librarian, smiled and flitted her eye lashes that rimmed blue eyes, as her own blond locks fell to one side of her bobbed styled hair.

Bose's charisma had obviously caught the angelic face woman's eye, but his heart clearly belonged to Menlo and he quickly finished his business in the library and headed to the Witte Museum.

"Uh, no, thanks, I'll drive there and finish my research."

Leaving in a hurry, he left the wooing infatuated librarian behind the desk as her eyes followed him down the stairs.

***

Exhaust from school buses lingered above the trees in the parking lot at the Witte Museum. Hordes of unruly elementary school children kicked and prodded each other while waiting in line to gain entry into the museum lobby. St. Bernard's School Parrish chose to spend the day at the museum, and from the looks of the faces on the nuns the end of the day could not come soon enough.

A stick-thin boy with big brown eyes and teeth that

resembled a bottle opener, winced in pain while a wrinkled, gaunt faced nun griped his left ear; pulling him to the end of the line for yanking one of his female classmate's pigtails.

Bose quickly passed the agitated crowd of little ones, but not before catching the all-knowing eye of a nun elder. Both he and she stood eye to eye. Fear filled her eyes as she spoke to him in Spanish, gripping her rosary.

"Un Vampiro," the nun said. "Un Vampiro en la ciudad." The nun had called Bose a vampire and mumbled that he was a vampire in the city.

Not allowing her to alarm the children or the rest of her order, he warned this woman to shut her mouth, as he waved his hand in front her to wipe her memory clean of seeing him at all.

"Callate la boca, mujer."

Hastily stepping past she and the children, Bose made it inside the museum lobby and up to the front where the curator stood ushering in the day's patrons.

"Sir, what floor can the exhibit of the African American History Slave Narratives be found on?" Although Bose could have just probed the man's thoughts, he chose to conduct himself as civil and human like. Others of his kind would have probably done the opposite of his approach.

"Third floor, second exhibit hall on your left."

"Thank you, sir."

Bose headed off and found exactly what he had been searching to find. Adesewa Manette's narrative stood in the center of a large roped off pedestal. A camera overlooked the narrative volume, controlled by a remote sensor that projected the text of the narrative on a screen for human eyes to read, but not for human hands to touch. The delicate nature of the narrative binder called for the museum to provide extra measures of preservation. Acids and oils from human sweat glands would further degrade the priceless document if it were touched.

His quest for knowledge grew, and he did not have time to spare by flicking the remote sensor to turn the page of the video reading device. He telepathically disabled the equipment. Flashing behind the barrier, Bose read the narrative, and found he was only more agitated and anxious after his discovery Adesewa Manette's entry continued the next day recalling the events of her life in the new world:

"...my body lay next to another female who also had her body joined together with several husbands. The ship captain was her husband for most of the voyage, but some of the other tribes men were her husband, as they were mine at other times during the voyage. When we made land, our bellies started to fill with a child. I often wonder which of our husbands fathered our children. It did not come to be that I would bear a child, as the savage beatings caused me to bleed my seed out.

While we lay amongst the filth and disease, the child born from Priestess Auldicia made its way into my arms one night to feed. I lay in fear I would have my fluids drained and would rot once death claimed my soul. That was not to be my fate. Instead, the child's hand found my bosom and began to suckle milk. Although the child continued to drain blood and fluid from the slaves as we lay in the midst of squalor, this child also needed milk.

Death should claim the child of Priestess Auldicia, but bleeding my own seed out would not allow me to bring harm to the little one. Instead of harm, I chanted the words of protection and peace to guide and watch over the little one. My milk had not gone sour from losing my own seed, and it provided sustenance to this little one. In the motherland, we practiced Voodoo religion for protection and prosperity, never for evil. This child might take my life someday and I needed to raise the little one to turn from evil. I asked the gods to be merciful and protect the little one as I sacrifice my life. My prayers fell on open ears that night. The child would never know from whom it was born, nor ever do evil again. I knew a price would have to be paid for my prayer, and the hour payment is to be rendered would be unknown to me. We made it safely to shore, yet still in bondage."

Adesewa Manette's narrative ran to the very corner edge of the final page of the volume. He quickly grabbed the narrative and tucked it under his arm. Still not satisfied, Bose quickly maneuvered down stairs to find the curator once more.

"Excuse me sir, where are the remaining volumes of the slave narratives?" he said careful not to leave the narrative in plain view.

The curator looked miffed as Bose appeared in front of him without warning, causing the frail man to gasp for breath.

"Gracious, you scared me, or rather; I wasn't expecting you to be standing here."

"Where are they? Where are they?" Bose demanded, stepping into the curator's personal space while his eyes pierced and probed his mind for any indication of lie.

Barely able to respond and with eyes the size of golf balls, the curator managed to whisper the answer to the question posed to him as Bose floated past him.

"The rest are on display at The Institute of Texan Cultures."

Although frustrated and anxious to see Menlo, Bose continued his quest fueled by his yearning to protect his family. This was the only excuse he could come up with for his course behavior with the curator --- that and the fact he had not fed yet. As he drove back towards downtown, he reflected on all the text he had reviewed for the day.

"I hope this is the last stop for the day. I miss Menlo and can't wait to wrap myself around her once more. It will be time for her to end her shift soon, and tonight I think I will let her play nurse and I will be the on-call doctor for her needs."

Entertaining the playful thoughts of he and Menlo caused him to harden in response. The last few months have been the happiest in his existence, and he enjoyed every moment with her.

Bose parked the car in a VIP Parking space near the International Flag display out in front of the Institute of Texan Cultures. The Puente Estate had donated to the University of Texas for many years, often funding many of the exhibits that came to the city, so parking the car as close to the front door without driving it into the museum itself was a doable thing.

Giving a nod to Linda, the gum-popping cashier was his usual entrance routine when visiting. Matrix Security Company had Robert guarding the door as usual while patrons padded across the carpet, admiring the exhibits. Bose threw his hand up greeting Robert, as the security guard waved him by.

Bose went to the downstairs level, where new exhibit assessments and cataloguing takes place before going on display. It was not long before he identified what he needed. Surely, this was Adesewa Manette's final narrative. Satisfied that he had accomplished his goal, Bose settled in and quickly read the young woman's text from the volume:

"... Upon arriving to the shallow shores of port Louisiana, I noticed my irons had caused disease to settle in my wounds where I had taken the whip. My little one would not let me go. The child's nails sunk deep into my shoulder flesh, frightening me but I knew that one of my prayers had been answered. My other prayer was that the child and I both would find peace with a merciful master. When my turn came to stand on the auction block and we were purchased, I saw Ma'am Vivienne's face and new there would be some peace, until her husband came at me with the slave owner's brand. The brand still had the burned flesh from another slave cooking on its tip end, yet mine was to be next. The brand was in the shape of a tree with many branches, Master Estes seared the brand on to my belly button leaving a scar for life.

Master Estes had some heart and thought twice before he branded my little one. Ma'am Vivienne begged him not to do it at all, but told her it was best to get it over with now, because it would be worse and might cause the child to try to run once it grew. Master Estes had no heart, as he heard other slave masters tell him what to do as they hatefully called us names. Master Estes took off his pinky ring and had it heated over at the pier side blacksmith's shop. He told me to hold the baby as I stood in pain, and begged him in my old language not to do this, only to be slapped making my wound bleed.

Master Estes took the heated ring, now a fire hot brand, and branded the child's belly button. The men stood and laughed as the baby screamed in agony, no mother felt more pain than me, as the little one shook with misery. Just then, I felt the child being pulled from my arms as Ma'am Vivienne grabbed the little one and walked away as the screams continued. Through my own tears, I watched as Ma'am Vivienne asked me what the child's name was. I could not speak the language as I do now, but somehow I knew she was asking about the child's name. I had not thought about it, but I called out to her "Bosewana". She seemed to understand, but felt "Bose" would do just fine for the beautiful baby boy.

Bose shuddered at the words that flashed in his mind, yet the text clearly stated the knowledge he had sought for so long. Denial set in quickly, as resentment washed over him.

"This is an error only a slave could make. Surely, she did not spell the words correctly in the entry."

"*It cannot be true*", is the hook to the song he sang over and over in his mind, while Bose fought hand to hand combat with his conscience as the swarm of truth stung like angry hornets. He lifted his shirt and looked at the peculiar marking over his belly button. For years he thought it to be a birthmark or skin imperfection.

"Dammit, this cannot be true. There is no way I am the son of Priestess Auldicia," Bose stammered to himself. "This is an error, it has to be."

After losing the emotional combat with his conscience, his inner core began to twist from the truth and the uncontrollable bloodlust that seemed to worsen matters. Nonetheless, he continued reading. Adesewa Manette's narrative acknowledged what Bose was, yet she kept his secret:

"...I know that my child is a blood drinker, yet I have asked the gods to keep him safe. He has grown so quickly that I hardly recall him as a baby. He is a man now, and I fear for the worst. I have seen blood lust rise in him, and yet the invisible

bind remains in place to keep him from killing. He is very handsome and many of the other slave girls make eyes at him, showing subtle affection. Although he cannot speak with them face to face, he steals glances at them. He works in the house most times, but also works outside in the wheat and cotton field. I have seen him feed on other humans as a baby, and I am afraid once he kills someone as a man, the protection prayer will be broken, and he will become a full blood drinker like his mother, Priestess Auldicia."

The entry ended as Bose wept silently now. He had done rather well keeping it together this entire day and sought to read the last entry. Adesewa Manette's writing scrawls in jagged lines that web across the page from corner to corner, indicating distress:

"...My fear has come true. Today, payment is due for my protection prayer. Bose has reached manhood and has taken the life of Master Estes. Master tried to force me to take him as my husband. Bose saw what Master did, and before I could stop him, tiger sharp fangs punched through his mouth and he bit Master in the throat. Ma'am Vivienne tried to shoot Master, but Master pushed me in front of him, making me take the wound for him. Bose turned on Ma'am Vivienne, and took Master's new hand sickle and split Ma'am Vivienne in two.

The gate-keeping god Guede appeared before me in his ethereal form, claiming the lives of my slave owners. I paid my gratitude, but feared for my son's life. Once Guede rendered the fallen lives a payment in full, I know it would not be long before my own life is joined with those of my fallen masters. Bose has been caring for me over the last day or so. I know that I must..."

The writing trailed off once more. Bose had held it

together, but he began to unravel; pacing slowly at first then, the click clack of his footsteps sounded more like machine gun rounds. He traveled in a circle until smoke came from his feet wearing the floorboards down. Finally, the emotional pain and hunger ripped through him at such a velocity his scream echoed throughout the museum, shattering the glass windows on the two upper levels.

It would not be long before the Robert, the security guard, would have the place on lockdown. Bose knew he would have to make a move quickly. He found the exhibit assessment log to find out where the last of Adesewa Manette's narrative could be located. The catalogue indicated the last narrative is on loan to St. Bernard Fernando Cathedral.

The beautiful jade green hue that normally colored his eyes was no longer present. A soulless, blood red covered his entire eye socket, making him look possessed by a demon sent straight from hell.

Driving was too slow a mode of transportation for Bose to reach his final destination. Teleportation won out over the choice to make his short drive to St. Bernard Fernando Cathedral. Again, he carefully carried the slave narrative under his arm.

The Cathedral doors remained open during the day to all who needed confession, and others that needed prayer. Bose stood in the foyer of the cathedral as he continued to weep. Passing through the threshold of the beautiful structure, memories flooded his mind of when he painted Jesus and the children on the ceiling of the Puente Mansion.

Several empty pews lined the cathedral, as he made his way down to the basement that housed historical archives. Upon first entering the basement, he immediately spotted the volume that he was certain held Adesewa Manette's dying words. The narrative bind was similar to the others Bose had retrieved information from earlier in the day. He carefully placed all of the narratives side by side, while reaching for the last text. Bose realized his hand shook just before touching it:

"...make certain that Priestess Auldicia never rises from her grave. Bose is the direct descendant of the Obayifo Priestess Auldicia, should any blood be spilled from a direct descendant on hallowed ground, legend has it Priestess Auldicia will rise from hell. The world as it is now will end and hell will be unleashed on earth. Lust and the disease it generates will ravage the world over.

The legend of Priestess Auldicia says that her body resides in a watery grave, but the location is not certain. She must not rise from her grave and no spilled blood over hallowed ground. No blood, no blood, no blood."

Bose realized this was the end of his life as Bose Puente. Bits and pieces of memories from the day he took the lives of his caregiver's slave masters filtered in, but an interruption from his thoughts caused him to snap back to reality. The nun he saw earlier at the Witte Museum stood before him, still fearful.

"Vampiro."

Before she could scream, he hissed and his fangs peeled from beneath his gums as he sank them in the side of her neck. Bloodlust had finally won over the protection prayer Adesewa Manette had prayed for him centuries ago. The nun's blood flow crashed into parched areas of his throat reviving him --- easing the emotional blow of his discovery. The num lay at his feet drained of all blood and plasma, as death settled in making its claim.

The power of killing gave him such a rush that his eye rolled wildly in his head as light flashed through the basement. He lifted his shirt and found the scar of the slave owner's brand over his belly button --- a faded mark of an Oak Tree symbolizing his heritage. All he days of his life he only thought of the mark as a birthmark. Discovering all the identifying information had filled in missing pieces of his identity.

"The protection prayer Adesewa Manette prayed must have blocked memories only this discovery could recover, and now I know who I truly am," he said.

Black and gray mist floated in the air above, forming phantom white eyes that stared at him. The shapeless mist spoke aloud, bidding freedom.

"A sacrifice has been made and all debts are clear --- live freely as you are, Vampiro."

No longer weeping, he stood tall as the sinister black mist slowly settled and soaked into his skin. His laughter filled the air as he stepped over the murdered nun, smearing some of her blood on the bottom of his shoe as it trailed across the stone floor.

"Now that I know my identity, I now know my true mission. I will raise my mother. My true mother, the almighty Priestess Auldicia and there will be true power on earth. No one can stop me or the rise of my family. As we take full reign over this world, all of my enemies will be crushed. The Treemounts shall live on, as all those in the Puente Mansion shall die --- starting with Solis Burkes."

Bose realized in order for him to gain power to raise his mother, he must save all of her children.

"I must find Justice and make certain he remains alive.

He and his siblings have the strongest Treemount blood flowing within them, second to my own. I can protect them, and I will teach Justice the ways of our existence and our family history. Being a new vampire is not easy and he does not know how to exist without drawing attention."

Confusion clouded his mind while he destroyed all of the archival evidence that revealed his heritage. Sharing what seemed a lifetime with Nacio changed to falsehood and resentment now he knew the truth. Bringing Priestess Auldicia back to the world she once reigned in fed his appetite for power in ways unmeasured. Bose laughed again ---tickled at the idea of his new beginning.

***

"Bose found a ship's manifest in the library?" Nacio asked. "That is amazing, but not too surprising. As a scholar, he cataloged books and periodicals for years. It's a wonder we never discovered this sooner."

"Who would have thought this information was catalogued here for this long, and it took something as tragic as this to find it." Basrick explained. "I took this as a lead to find out more about the slave owner that purchased some of the slaves from that ship ---his name was Estes Treemount. He was a wealthy landowner living in Louisiana, near the marsh and wetlands. He bought and purchased slaves and kept them on his land, breeding others as well."

"Excellent work, Basrick," Nacio praised. "We will continue our hunt tonight. Bose should be back soon, and Menlo will join us as well."

"I will continue to find missing information on this Estes Treemount until it's time for us to roll out for the night," Basrick continued.

Dusk began to settle in over the horizon, as we all prepared for the nights hunt. Nacio began to wonder what was causing Bose's delay. It wasn't like him to be late.

"I wonder what Bose is into?" Nacio inquired. "I bet he and Menlo have made plans and might be a little late getting started tonight."

"Well, if they are half as happy as we are then we have to give them their space. After all, I know I can't get enough of you, my dear."

"There you go again. You are going to get yourself caught up in a very compromising position that involves a back bend and toe touch."

"Oooh, you promise?" I teased, grabbing and holding him in an embrace as we kissed. "I believe it's time for more honeymoon activity."

Before he responded, Nacio teleported me to our suite. Below his waist, his hardened response to our kiss let me know he meant what he said about me being in a back bend as we made love.

"Yes, it is time for an extended honeymoon." He quickly removed his clothing, dropping them to the floor.

His rippling six-pack core muscles contracted while he carried me to our bed.

He commanded me to stand in the middle of the bed.

"Stand up and slowly remove all your of clothing." Waving his hand to power the surround sound as Gerald

Albright's *Bermuda Nights* filled the room I slowly peeled layers of clothing off, dropping them to the floor.

Once the last shred of clothing hit the carpet, he commanded me to finish my performance.

"Now, show me how flexible you really are. Turn towards me and bend over backwards."

A sly smile inched across my face while I stood with my feet apart and bent over backwards, exposing my naked body. Sweet moans of pleasure escaped his lips, letting me know he appreciated the view. Lovingly, he returned the pleasure as his soft lips found a warm spot to settle into, sending shudders over my legs making it difficult to hold the statuesque pose. We made good use of our time while we patiently waited for Bose to return.

***

"What the hell's been up with you over the past few months, Kildare?" Detective Prestwick Tausch hollered. "You going soft on me or what?"

"Soft? Who the hell are you calling soft?" Menlo sheepishly grinned at her partner of 10 years. "Can't a girl have a little fun? Or are men the only one's allowed to have needs?"

"Oh, I'm not saying that. I'm just saying you look happy for a change, you know, like you finally found what you been looking for. I'm happy for you, girl, just don't mess it up."

"I believe I have found the missing link in my life, oh and don't worry I won't mess it up."

Both detectives had a whole-hearted laugh about Menlo's new love life just before dispatch cut the conversation short.

"All units, all units," the dispatch operator called. "A citizen reported a John Doe at 1604 and Benz-Englemann. Please respond."

Detective Tausch responded to the call, making certain of the location.

"Detectives Tausch and Kildare, Homicide in route."

Menlo turned on the siren, and punched the accelerator as the Charger's hemi engine roared and the 400 horses got the two detectives to the scene in no time.

Arriving at the scene reminded Menlo of the night she witnessed Nacio and Justice slug it out on the Riverwalk. A dismembered male victim was scattered across a farm in far eastern Bexar County. Menlo knew her fanged cousin had been hard at work, feeding when he needed to on any innocent soul that happened to be at the wrong place at the wrong time.

Detective Tausch walked around as the Crime Scene Investigation team scoured the area, stringing crime scene tape from corner to corner across several acres of the abandoned farm. Pools of blood soaked dead weeds on the open acreage just a few yards from a house that sat off the road.

"I would say it was a grizzly bear but there are no bears around here. Plus, the pattern of bite marks looks too similar to the previous Does we've seen over the last several months," Detective Tausch said, looking at Menlo in the distance as she knelt over the victims head, as flies and gnats fought a turf war over the flesh.

"What have you got, Captain?" Detective Tausch asked the lead Crime Scene Investigator.

"Well, looks like an African American male, mid forties, 6'5 200 pounds, arterial spray 25 feet from the dismembered head, other limbs scattered over the acreage, and last but not least, intestinal tissue dragged another 25 feet south of the torso."

Cool and collected not to let on she knew the perpetrator and the source of the killing, Menlo remained silent as she tried to get a handle on where her cousin was hiding out, as she thought to herself.

"I know Justice is out here somewhere, I just wish I knew where," she whispered quietly. "He can't be that far away. This man was killed within the last few hours, and he could not have gotten far."

"Hey, let's let these guys finish up," Detective Tausch said, watching in the distance as Menlo rolled the victim's head over for the Crime Scene team to finish up. She acknowledged her partner's request.

"Yeah, alright let's wrap it up guys."

The CSI team finished up and left the scene, as Detective Tausch and Menlo remained behind to piece together the case.

"Let's go in and check out the house again," Detective Tausch said. "We might have missed something."

"Good deal, there might be more to it than what we have seen over the last few months."

Eager for answers, both detectives headed inside the dilapidated house in search of any evidence that might yield answers to what they were dealing with, although she had the answers.

A thick blanket of dust and cobwebs covered splintered remnants of wooden furniture, and shredded draperies that hung slanted in the windowsills. Covering her nose, Menlo held back a sneeze

"This place looks like a front for Doctor Frankenstein."

"No joke. I wouldn't want to get caught hanging out it this rat shack."

The wooden floors creaked as they cautiously shuffled through the house. Bending with each step taken, the wood underneath their feet indicated that the house might soon be in need of demolition.

"Careful Kildarc those floor boards are giving a little too---." Detective Tausch tried to finish, but fell through the floor as he tried to warn Menlo.

Detective Tausch, crashed through the floor with such force dust came from below in cloud of smoke. He had fallen into a basement in which the police department hadn't thoroughly checked out prior to leaving the scene.

"Tausch! Tausch are you alright?"

"Yeah, I'm good, but I think my leg is broken!"

"I'm coming down, hang on and try not to move."

The dirt floor of the basement had broken Detective Tausch's fall as much as possible, but not without injury. His fall caused him to land in stagnated sewage and mold from a broken pipe that had a steady leak coming from a cesspool. The owner's had not emptied the sewage for quite some time. Menlo knew she had to get her partner out of the situation quickly.

"Hang in there, Tausch; I'm going to get a flash light

from the car."

"Alright, hurry up, would ya?"

"Just hang on buddy."

Menlo dashed out the front door and back to the end of the driveway to her patrol car, popping the trunk for her toolbox. She found the flashlight and headed back towards the house. This was so not how she had hoped things would turn out for this investigation. Several months had gone by and she was no closer to finding Justice than she had been when she first started. Using her car radio, she called dispatch to send for an ambulance. Leaving the scene was not an option.

"Dispatch, this is Detective Kildare, Homicide. Officer down, I repeat officer down. Send an ambulance, stat."

Rushing back toward the house, she knew every second counted to get the help her partner needed. Finding Justice interrupted her concern for Detective Tausch.

"I wish there were some clues as to where he is," she mumbled. "Eventually, we will find him, and when we do---it's lights out for you Justice."

Detective Tausch winced as his open thighbone fracture protruded through the skin of his left inner thigh. It wouldn't be long before infection set in, putting him at risk for contracting deadly flesh-eating bacteria. Pain throbbed with each beat of his heart, as his skin began to wrinkle from sitting in the filthy water, waiting for his partner to begin her rescue efforts.

"Ow, damn it." Pain from the injury throbbed in sharp waves. "Hey, Menlo, hurry up."

Complete darkness made the basement more

uncomfortable. He could only wait for Menlo to return with help, and then he would concentrate on the unbearable pain in his leg. He continued to sit absolutely still, scanning the room in the dark as best he could. Detective Tausch sat motionless as dread settled in over him as he heard something splash in the sloppy sewage water. Realizing he was no longer alone, he desperately hoped it was Menlo coming to save him.

"Menlo, is that you?" There was no answer.

Reaching for his service weapon, Detective Tausch held the weapon with wobbly hands, wishing his eyes allowed him to identify what shared the darkness with him. Squinting across the dark room, he locked onto a pair of glaring red eyes as they seemed to float into focus, closer and closer until…

***

Menlo quickened her pace to reach her injured partner. She had just re-entered the house when she heard his gurgled scream shake the walls of the hollow structure. She knew from his pitch, his life was in danger. Justice had returned to the scene of the crime.

"Tausch, talk to me."

His scream choked off, as she found the door leading to the basement near the kitchen. Bracing herself for the worst, she took her other loaded pistol from behind her back. This pistol is loaded with silver bullets especially for Justice. Accepting this day would eventually come, she charged into the basement for her destiny.

At the bottom of the stairs, she stood in the dark

listening to the pitter-patter of the leaking pipe. Remembering the flashlight, she turned it on and aimed it to the center wall of the room. There in the middle of the room, Justice had Detective Tausch's neck hyper-extended, exposing a huge bite mark on the right side.

"Justice, don't do this."

Her cousin only looked at her with red eyes and smiled, as the last breath left her partner, leaving his eye fixed in fright as death came to claim him.

12

Make a move

Bose decided to move forward with his plans to reunite with his family. Finding Justice is his only priority --- the sooner the better.

"Where, oh where are you, Justice?" Bose asked himself. "I will find you soon enough."

Impatience had set in, and Bose began to conjure a spell to locate his distant relative. He shouted to the open sky.

"Macdoob, ohma. Blood of my blood, show Justice. Reveal him to me now."

A blast of wind blew through the air rattling trees. In the distance, approximately 30 miles away, a scream floated into Bose's auditory range, and he knew he had just located Justice, as the smell of death wafted through the air.

The spell indicated the place where Justice had recently instigated a savage attack and fed from a victim. This sent Bose into overdrive, causing him to follow the wind and teleport to the exact location. Deep in the woods on a rural property located out at 1604 and Binz-Englemann, Bose felt his own blood bubble the closer he came to him.

He also sensed another blood source nearby as well.

Menlo was in the same vicinity, and she was frightened. Bose stood outside the little farm house, ready to attack if it came down to that.

"What is Menlo doing here? I'm not ready to face her, but she will learn soon enough of her destiny as well. She will have a choice to make, and she had better choose correctly."

Another scent in the air that Bose did not recognize caused him to take on a predatory stance to feed as he entered the small wooden frame house. He slowly made his way through the house, taking caution against the huge hole in the middle of the living room floor. Following the sound of Menlo's voice, he knew she was arguing with Justice.

"I said, don't do this, Justice. You are going to regret this."

"Says who?" Justice lamented. "You are supposed to be my first cousin, and you would be the first one to turn me over and stab me in my back or worse shoot me."

"You have hurt too many people, Justice," she said aiming her gun right between his eyes. "This needs to end right now."

Justice found his cousins request to be a joke, and taunted her every word. "Hahahaheeheeheeehee," his laughter irritated her. "You don't know who the hell you are fooling with, girl. I can snap a man's neck like I snap my fingers. Just what the hell do you think you are going to do with that gun, Cher?"

Tension lingered between the two as the standoff seemed like an eternity. Unaware of the brainwashed accomplice that lurked in the dark, Justice acknowledged his consort.

"Believa, baby, come on out here and meet my sorry ass first cousin, Detective Menlo Kildare Treemount La Deaux."

Menlo turned her flashlight in the opposite corner to see a sickly brown-skinned woman slosh forward coming towards her. Two huge crusty scabs were visible on her neck as she continued in Menlo's direction.

Holding her pistol in place on Justice, Menlo was not afraid of Believa and bid her a warning before she took another step.

"Don't move, bitch. I said don't move, or I will drop you in this liquid shit. It's up to you, but I'm telling you. Don't move."

Believa only smiled as she lunged forward, as Menlo fired her pistol at Justice. She knew the silver bullet would cause a huge exit wound. To her dismay, instead of firing her weapon and hitting Justice, Bose teleported across the room and apprehended her weapon from her hand. He stood before her examining the firing chamber of the pistol, looking at the silver bullets meant for Justice. Smiling from ear to ear, he too taunted Menlo's attempt to kill him.

"What have we here? Solid silver hollow point bullets are not what San Antonio's finest is suppose to carry---shame, shame, shame on you, Detective Kildare."

"Bose, what are you doing? Why did you take my weapon? We are supposed to kill this bastard, not save him."

"Ah, but you are so wrong, my dear. We share the same blood."

"What are you talking about? You are not a Treemount, Bose. You must be mistaken."

Justice wiped blood from his chin, as he moved in

closer to Bose, shaken and still weak from the embedded silver festering in his wounds. He stood face to face with Bose looking eye to eye.

"Oh, so you two know each other? Who the hell are you, man? You are no kin of mine…are you?"

"I am Bose Treemount, born from the womb of the mighty Priestess Auldicia. We are from the same bloodline."

Confusion veiled his face, but Justice continued his inquiry. Soon he acknowledged the physical Creole traits of his heritage in Bose.

"Wait, wait, wait, a minute man," he smirked. "You mean to tell me, you are born straight from my ancestor, Priestess Auldicia? Man, this shit is crazy. Where have you been all these years? What happened to her, and how did you survive, and she didn't?"

Bose could only give Justice a small blanket answer considering the situation at hand.

"You will have your answers soon enough. Just know that we are her descendants, and our family shall rise again. What do you say, Menlo. Are you with us?"

Stunned as tears slid down her face, Menlo stood before her enemies wishing death upon them, and in disbelief at what Bose had just disclosed to her. Disgust swirled in her mind as the realization set in that she had consummated a relationship with a centuries old a maternal relative.

"Bose you can't mean what you are saying. What about Nacio? What about Solis? They are your family?"

"Solis Burkes?" Justice questioned. "This is about her ass again? She's the one that needs to be dropped. I'm sick of hearing about her ass."

Bose looked at Justice in agreement and offered an alliance to him.

"Our family shall rise again. You will need to learn how to survive as a youngling vampire. Soon we will reunite with the rest of the Treemount bloodline and take back what is rightfully ours. Menlo, are you with us?"

Choosing her words carefully, because she knew they might be her last, Menlo stood firm.

"Hell, no, I'm not with you. Both of you go to hell with your bitch dog mothers!"

Silence fell over everyone in the sewage-filled basement. Bose looked at Justice and nodded a command that set off a tragic chain of events. Justice acted immediately.

"Believa, honey go ahead and handle this hoe."

Taking orders from Justice made the zombie-like Believa light up with glee. She took her own .22 caliber pistol from her back jean pocket and fired three shots, striking Menlo in the front left temporal lobe of her skull, one in the upper left shoulder, and finally, the last bullet centered in her chest. Menlo went sailing backward as blood and plasma painted the mold covered brick wall.

Her wounded body slid down the stairs, plunging her feet into the murky ankle deep sludge that covered the pasty dirt floor. For a moment, Bose flinched as his beloved crumbled to her death, but sirens in the distance prompted him to clear out.

"Let's go. Menlo called for backup."

Justice didn't hesitate as he motioned for Believa to join them as they left.

"Priestess Auldicia, huh? I hope you can show me a

thing or two since I can't seem to get this damn silver out of my back."

"Yes, I see that," Bose acknowledged. "This must have been from some trouble you've had."

"Yeah, I can't get it out, and Believa is not strong enough to pull it out."

"Where have you been hiding out at all these months? We will need to go there now so that I can remove the silver."

"Well, we've been at Believa's house in the old neighborhood, it's pretty safe."

"Then we must go there now or you will eventually expire like Menlo here. Let's go. Grab hold of Believa and don't let her go."

Bose and Justice linked elbows as they teleported to the old neighborhood to Believa's residence.

***

Although Justice had just fed, he was weak once more. The silver had truly taken a toll on him, and his strength did not last long leaving him exhausted.

"Lie down here on the table," Bose told Justice. "Don't move."

Justice sprawled faced down on the dining room table as Bose held up his right hand, as his fingernails extended three inches from the nail bed. Justice looked on in amazement.

"Damn, I didn't know I could do that with my hands. It that something you can show me?"

"Be still, nephew," Bose demanded.

Justice lifted his t-shirt as Bose examined the bulges on

his back. The silver was beginning to liquefy into pus-filled poison. Bose took his fingernails and cut an incision in one of the three wounds. Using a hand held shovel, he scooped the silver poison out. Justice screamed in agony as Bose continued the same procedure for the other two wounds.

"Dammit, man, that hurts."

"I said, be still or else you will make the poison go deeper."

Believa stood looking at Justice as he had his unsanitary surgery performed right in the very spot she had her breakfast earlier that morning. Nauseated, she tried to excuse herself from the room.

"I think I'll be back a little later."

"Don't move, dammit. Stay exactly where you are," Justice barked.

Believa timidly sat down on the couch while the botched surgery continued. With the silver removed, the wounds Justice has sustained started healing right away. The results were amazing and the restored strength gave him an invincibility he had never known. He gave Bose a tooth fanged smile of gratitude.

"Hey, man, thanks. So let's see, you said you are a distant relative of mine, and you are the son of Priestess Auldicia?"

"That's correct. I am her son."

"Man, where the hell you been? My mother surely would have known who you are, yet this is the first we have heard of you."

"I was born a vampire. Priestess Auldicia gave me the gift of immortality. Soon all of the Treemounts will rise up and voodoo black magic will set our family apart from all the rest. We will be invincible --- crushing our enemies under our feet."

"Well, yeah, yeah, whatever man," Justice negotiated. "That's all fine and good and everything, but I need some money, you understand? My old lady here needs to get her neck and hair fixed. I went a little too deep on that last feed and nicked her too close to the bone. Now, she's not healing right. You understand, don't you?"

Bose's red tinged eyes looked at Justice, and his right hand reached for his wallet throwing a gold plated money clip filled with several hundred-dollar bills on the table next to him.

"Surely this will cover whatever petty expenses you seem to have incurred over the past few months. Use it wisely."

Greed put a smile on Justice as he picked up the money clip. Believa purred with delight, running her fingers over the shiny new clip.

"Does this mean, I can throw away the red pants and get some new ones?"

"Whatever you want, baby girl," Justice said. "Thanks, man. I guess you deserve a little respect. How 'bout I call you Uncle Bose? Yeah, that will do just fine."

Running his tongue over his teeth, Justice continued smiling as he pulled a ghoulish looking Believa close, kissing her wildly. Bose cleared his throat, interrupting the passion.

"Pardon me nephew, but we have an agenda to carry out. You understand, don't you?"

Pulling her face apart from his own, Justice released his consort and sent her on her way with a slap on her butt.

"Looks like you need to get you a woman Unc," Justice

teased. "You can't have mine."

"Shut your damn mouth," Bose roared. "You don't know what the hell you are talking about."

"Cool man, don't blow a fuse," Justice chirped, standing down in the middle of his uncle's outburst. "I just meant if we are going to roll together, you might want something that is soft and smells good next to you is all."

Bose caught himself, realizing his outburst stemmed from the last time he saw Menlo's beautiful face. Her eyes fixed in terror as bullets riddled her body, taking her life and sending her to the basement floor. They left the scene in haste, rather than disposing the bodies. Things had gotten out of hand, leaving Bose to panic. Menlo wasn't supposed to be there. Their love affair was one he treasured and held close to his heart, but she made the wrong choice. Nothing must stand in the way of resurrecting his mother. Dealing with Menlo and the fact that he had been intimately involved with a distant relative shouldn't have bothered him so much, but it did.

Overwhelmed by loss, Bose stood before Justice with pain shooting back and forth from his heart to the side of his head. Remembering the joy he shared with Menlo over the last several months made regret swim through his mind…but only briefly.

"I have greater things to think of now," Bose reminded him. "Beginning tonight, we will stop Nacio and put Solis out of her misery. No further harm will come to any more Treemounts. My mother shall live again. That is a promise."

"I can dig that," Justice agreed. "But what do you plan to do?"

Bose stood and glared at his nephew and then laughed

for his own amusement.

"I plan to kill Solis Burkes tonight. Her destruction will seal my fate. Nacio will join her in the afterlife as well. As for the Caraways, they too shall meet their end."

"The Caraways?" Justice asked. "Who the hell are they?"

"You killed Basira, Justice. You mean you don't remember that? If you loved her, you had a deadly way of showing her."

Justice turned and flashed his fangs at his uncle at the mention of Basira's name. It was his turn to be ultra sensitive, causing him to get in Bose's personal space.

"I do remember her. I loved her. Childress made me kill her, I loved her, do you hear me?"

Bose smirked at his nephew's advance toward him. He had to swallow the giggle that was now forming in his throat, as Justice flashed his fangs. Bose flashed his, making them draw down past his lip, warning Justice there were consequences for his insolence.

"Watch it, youngling. My fangs are longer and sharper than yours and you might get cut. You feel me?"

Justice considered the consequences and turned from Bose to sit on the couch, as misty tears came to his eyes.

"What the hell do you expect me to do, man? I loved her, and that bitch sister of mine made me take her out."

Now realizing he no longer cried tears Justice looked at Bose in astonishment.

"What's wrong with my eyes? I don't have tears anymore?" he asked his uncle.

"No, you don't, Mr. Idiot." Bose said. "You have a lot

to learn, so very much to learn."

"Well, learn me, I mean teach me then, instead of laughing at me."

"You need to learn not to draw unnecessary attention to yourself, Justice. One of the reasons we've existed as long as we have is because we know how to live in the shadows while walking side by side with humans. You do realize you are no longer human, do you not?"

"Yeah, gotcha," Justice replied. "I cannot stop drinking once I start feeding."

"Well, you stopped after biting Believa, didn't you?"

"Yeah, so?"

"Well, looks like you are learning something. Now it's time to see what else you are capable of. Follow me and do what I say do only when I say do it. You understand?"

"Alright, Unc, teach me."

Bose took Justice under his wing to show him how to exist quietly. Out in the front yard of Believa's small house, Bose took off running at a steady pace down the road. Justice struggled to keep up at first, but soon caught his uncle and met his pace with each step.

"Very good, Justice," Bose said, as they ran side by side. "I will teach you how to focus your thoughts to learn Teleportation."

"Telepo what?" Justice squeaked. "I can't think that far ahead, Unc. I smoked too much of that stuff growing up and my thoughts are shorter than other people's. So you see I can't do what you said."

"Alright, since you can't do it, meet me in Pletz Park in 15 minutes," Bose said. "I'll be waiting there. Teleportation cuts your travel time down, dummy. You shouldn't have been smoking that stuff."

Bose vanished in a flash of light, leaving sparks in his tracks. Justice continued to move at preternatural speed, but couldn't keep up with the spontaneity of teleportation. Staying high was one of several regrets Justice had to contend with as a mistake he made. He kept running to the southeast side of town to Pletz Park. The park was covered in blackness, with no street lamps lit.

"I wondered what kept you," Bose's voice spoke to Justice from a nearby Oak Tree. "What took you so long?"

"I took the scenic route."

Two men were sitting in a car in the park, smoking the very drug Justice had sworn off. Bose needed to feed and felt his fangs slide into place.

"You see those two jerks in that car?" Bose asked. "Let's get them. Follow my lead and watch me. You need to learn how to feed without killing. Let's go."

Bose teleported across the park to the driver side window of the 1987 Oldsmobile Cutlass Supreme, and reached in and snatched the joint out of the driver's hand. The startled man was so lit up from the joint he had no clue of the danger he was in and laughed. His blurred vision made Bose look as if there were two of him standing in front of him. Little did the man know each breath he took was closer to his last.

In training and learning to stalk like a true vampire, Justice arrived at the passenger side of the Cutlass a short time later; he reached in the car and yanked the younger of the two men through the passenger window, nearly snapping his neck.

"Careful, dammit," Bose said. "Make it a clean swift

motion, not so jerky. You'll kill him before you even feed. You must not be so messy with your business. Got it?"

"Yeah, I got it."

"Bite like this," Bose said, as he let his fangs sink in at an angle on the laughing man's neck. The man's giggles soon turned to sobs as he felt his life flow from him.

The fresh catch Justice had in his hands acted opposite his friend. He hollered, screamed, and flailed his arms and legs making it difficult not to attract attention.

Bose stepped in with important advice. "Hold your hand over his forehead to silence and entrance him. That will shut him up. Do it quickly so you can feed and move on."

Justice followed his given instructions perfectly. He held his hand over the man's head, putting him into a light sleep. Wasting no time, he pierced the surface of the younger man's neck without any more resistance.

Both vampires feasted until they had their fill. Bose pulled from his victim and dropped his limp body in the dirt.

"You see that?" Bose asked. "He still lives, because I did not take the last drop of blood from him. You will need to stop feeding now, so that he will live, understand?"

"Yeah, I got it," Justice confirmed, as she slowly released his victim. "So it has to be done like this every time?"

"Correct. Now, let's go. I want to show you where Puente Mansion is located. It holds all the wealth we'll need."

"Yeah?"

"We will have all the financial resources needed to bring our family together and celebrate my mother's return."

"Cool, let's head out."

Bose took Justice by his arm and teleported to the

corner of Pereida and Cedar. They stood at the end of the spell-hidden driveway leading to the Puente Mansion.

"The mansion is at the end of this driveway, but is hidden to the human eye. You are never to come here, unless I summon you, understood?"

"Alright man, but what if I need to get in touch with you? Or what if there is an emergency?"

"If there is trouble, I will know. Other than that, you will not come unless I summon you. Now head back to Believa's. When I call you, we will head to Louisiana to join the others, got it?"

"Yeah, man I got it."

"And meanwhile stay out of trouble, will you."

"Yeah, yeah, I heard you."

Bose started down the long driveway, working towards accomplishing his next agenda item --- terminating Solis Burkes.

"It won't be long now until my true mother is resurrected and she will reign once more. All of our enemies and Solis will bow to all the Treemounts. Her back will serve as our footstool. She cannot do anything to stop us, and Nacio will serve as my keeper and that of my mother," he thought to himself.

"Childress, Klein, Erland, and Justice will serve to protect Priestess Auldicia from harm. Getting rid of Solis will be as easy as baking a recipe --- her favorite recipe. I will make certain she has an extra batch of her favorite treats. That will surely knock her off," Bose thought as he continued to plot.

13
Demonic Justice

The wee hours of the morning looked the same to Bose. He went out back to the trash dumpster and found pieces of the dead chicken carcass that was used for the baked chicken dinner Solis and Menlo ate earlier in the week. Bose quickly found the remains and carried them in the house.

Taking precautions to be neat in his quest, he knew he could make oatmeal and raisin cookies for Solis while everyone was out delivering the Formula Diethmifex to the female Treemounts. Bose quickly found the Oyster industrial machine used to pulverize and puree meats and vegetables. Pulverizing the chicken carcass was easy, but covering the smell was another matter.

"I will need to put extra vanilla in the batch to mask the smell of the decaying poultry. The cinnamon and raisins should cover the smell well enough not to alert anyone of the strain of Type C Botulism. The symptoms will do well as a subtle illness at first, then Solis will get progressively worse, and then she will die," he mumbled. "Her stomach will wretch and heave, and paralysis will settle in --- immobilizing all of her muscles and her lungs. Her life force is over.

Bose continued creating his concoction. The house was quiet except for the soft wind that blew by him as Basrick entered the kitchen. He should have known everyone would be gone except for him. Now, he needed to remain calm and not do anything out of character.

"Hey Basrick, man. Everything cool?'

"Uh, yeah, man, we waited for you as long as we could, but we figured you and Menlo were "tied up".

"Yeah, well you know how it is, when you're into each other," Bose replied, still mixing the dough for the cookies with the decomposed chicken pulp mixed in.

"Well, we hit several female Treemounts in Dallas/Fort Worth tonight. We're closing in on Childress and should reach her soon."

Bose felt his eyes turn red as he broke the handle of the wooden spoon he was using to mix the dough --- splintering it in all directions. Anyone mentioning harm to any of the Treemounts ignited his rage.

"Whoa, man, what's eating you?" Basrick asked, watching as Bose's right hand shook violently.

"Oh, nothing much, I guess I just need to feed," Bose lied, knowing he and Justice not long ago completed a feast. "It's been a long day."

"Really? How many darts did you deliver to females this evening?"

"Well, not many. You know Menlo and I were busy, and then she had to go to work; and then I was at the library most of the day."

"Oh, yeah right," Basrick confirmed. "Looks like

you've been doing some work by the looks of your shoes man," Basrick pointed to Bose's Italian leather loafers that were crusted with sewage that lay on the floor of the basement at the little farm house where he was earlier.

"Yeah, man looks like I ruined my shoes."

"Well, I think those are done for. Looks like you'll be getting some new steps for your feet," Basrick pointed out, as he headed into the living room.

Bose quickly set the oven to baking temperature as he placed formed cookie dough on the sheet and into the oven to bake.

"Did you find out anything new?" Basrick called from the living room couch.

"Uh, just bits and pieces about Estes Treemount."

"Yeah, so did I. It appears he lived in Louisiana and branded all of his slaves with an Oak Tree to mark them as his," Basrick stated.

"Wow that is interesting. That would definitely make them identifiable." Bose tensed as he ran his hand over his naval scar which confirmed his identity.

Basrick turned on the television, catching the morning newscast. Amongst all of the harrowing stories, misery seemed to make a special delivery to their home.

"...Tonight one of SA PD's detectives was gunned down while the other was involved in another fatal attack similar to others that continue to occur. It is believed ten year Police Department veteran Detective Menlo Kildare was in pursuit of whom authorities now believe to be a serial killer, Detective Kildare was gunned down..."

"Bose, Menlo's been shot."

Bose froze at what he heard. He rushed into the living room to find Basrick staring at the television screen as video footage of Detective Prestwick Tausch's body rolled past the camera.

"...Detective Prestwick Tausch was identified at the scene by next of kin. Detective Kildare received Air Life services to Brook Army Medical Center on life support in guarded condition...In other news the oil well leak continues to spew in the Gulf of Mexico. Geologists are not certain how to stop the spill..."

"Oh, Gracious," Bose said, pretending to be stunned rather than pissed. He couldn't believe with the many fatal shots fired at her, she was still alive. She must have worn a bulletproof vest. The wound to the head must be the one that has her on life support.

"Look, man, we have to get to the hospital," Basrick said. "I'm calling Nacio to meet us there."

"Oh, Menlo," Bose wailed. It was all he could do to keep from cursing aloud.

***

"We accomplished a lot tonight," Nacio said, as he kissed my fingers.

"Yes, we did, sweetheart. There will be fewer females reproducing and eventually none of them will be able to reproduce at all."

"Yes, and we can enjoy our lives together, Mistress."

The closer we came to the mansion I noticed the feeling of contentment seemed to leave me, as Nacio's cell phone rang.

He answered the call through the car's hands free system. I knew from his demeanor before he answered it was bad news.

"Talk to me."

"Nacio, Menlo's been shot," Basrick said. "Bose and I are on the way to Brook Army Medical Center."

"We're on our way," he said, ending the call and slamming his foot down on the accelerator.

"Menlo's been hurt," I said. "I wonder what happened tonight."

"From Basrick's tone, it doesn't sound good."

***

When we arrived at the medical center, Menlo was already in surgery. Basrick was a mess, but Bose seemed to be holding up remarkably well. He appeared to have nerves of steel. Unable to determine his emotions, Bose seemed stoic --- apathetic even. Armando and Patience soon joined us as well. Menlo's surgery took several hours, yet there still was no explanation as to what occurred.

"Authorities suspect she was on the trail of a serial killer, but we know that killer is Justice," Nacio said.

"You mean you think she found Justice?" I asked. "He must have ambushed her."

"Yeah, that's possible," Nacio said. "Did she call you at all today, Bose?"

Bose turned to Nacio and gave a straight-faced answer as best he could. Again, he remained cool and unaffected.

"No not at all. If she had called, I would have been able to fight him off. Damn the Treemounts. They have a lot to pay for."

The on-call surgeon whooshed through the double doors to give a post-operative status report on Menlo.

"She's stable, but it's touch and go for now. I was able to remove the bullet fragment from her left temporal lobe, but she is in a coma and on life support."

All the while, the surgeon could not help to notice how pale the concerned bystanders were except for Solis, who looked to have a healthy complexion. This was strange considering the blazing south Texas heat.

Basrick came unglued, and the meltdown was not pretty.

"I will crush his head with my hands as soon as I see him."

Perhaps a loud roar would have seemed less threatening. The way Basrick hung on every syllable and enunciated each one slowly, indicated lethality. Nacio had to grip Basrick, to keep him calm --- no reaction from Bose.

"Hold on there, guy," Nacio called. "Let's keep it together for your mom and dad's sake, alright."

The surgeon looked at Nacio as he held Basrick. Nacio was careful not to make any sudden moves that would cause any suspicion from the surgeon. Everyone was on edge.

"Listen there is nothing that can be done at the moment. It's best you go home and get some rest," the surgeon said. Bose was the first out the door with no questions asked. He did not look back.

"I'm staying," Basrick said. "I'd like to be here if she wakes up."

The surgeon nodded, biding us good day. So much

has happened, and yet there are still so many unanswered questions.

"Why would Justice shoot her?" I asked. "It just seems that if he wanted to he would have just bitten her and turned her. Something doesn't add up."

"No, it doesn't," Armando said. "Someone else was there at that scene, causing something to go terribly wrong."

"Justice isn't alone, that's for sure," Patience added. "We have to find him, sweetheart."

"Nacio, time is running out," Armando said. "We have to get to Justice before there are more youngling vampires, or worse he makes an attempt to kill Solis as he promised."

"Let's regroup at the mansion. Bose has already gone. If I know him, he needs some solitude. Menlo's shooting has hurt him deeply."

Basrick stood his ground and refused to budge.

"I'm staying here with her."

We all nodded in response to him, and headed back to the mansion.

***

Bose sat at the kitchen table waiting for our return. The mood was solemn, as we filed in one by one. I pitied Bose. One minute he and his new female partner are happy and the next she is fighting for her life. Through all of this, he is still his ever-loving and caring self. There next to him was a batch of freshly baked oatmeal and raisin cookies.

"Mistress, I took care to make certain you were stocked with your favorites."

"You are a wonderful man. You always think of others. That is why we love you," I said hugging him, and consoling him. I reached for one of the scrumptious cookies, and wolfed it down. It seemed like an eternity had passed since I last ate.

"How are you holding up my friend," Nacio asked Bose. "Your silence has given us a scare."

"I will be fine, just fine."

I didn't think anything of it. Only that Bose remained very cool and calm. There is no way I could have seen Nacio in the shape Menlo was in and remained that calm.

"I need some fresh air. I think I'll go for a walk," he said, as he left the mansion.

"You see," Nacio said to me. "I knew he would want to be alone for a while."

"I don't blame him," I said. "This is awful."

"Yes, it is. Let's retire for now. We'll be back out tonight looking for Justice. Armando, please keep in touch with Basrick to let us know of Menlo's progress."

"I will," he said. "You'll know the minute I know anything."

Nacio took me by the hand, as I grabbed two more cookies to take upstairs. Each time Bose makes them, they always have a little extra kick to them. He knows I really like vanilla, and he makes certain the dough is swimming in it. I finished my cookies just before lying down. Nacio was plucking away at the computer trying to pinpoint all of the recent John Does found all over town.

"I know I can triangulate his whereabouts if I just look close enough. I just know it won't be long now."

I began to drift in and out of consciousness. My arms

began to feel heavy, as all of my muscles began to feel like stone. Voices cluttered in my head, but I couldn't make out what any of them were saying. They weren't of anyone that I recognized, but I felt as though I was falling. This experience was not like any dreamscape I've had in the past with my mother or grandmother. This felt as if death was coming to claim me.

My lungs felt completely stretched, unable to relax and contract on their own. The cookies began to reflux from my stomach, yet I could not move. Trapped in a state of sleep paralysis, I felt as though I would strangle to death on my own emesis. None of my muscles worked.

I heard Nacio call my name, but I could not respond. What is wrong with me? Nothing like this has ever happened to me before. I can't move.

***

Basrick sat at Menlo's side the entire time while at the medical center. Looking at her helpless and lying in the hospital bed only fed his taste for revenge against Justice and his family even more. He noticed her beautiful features, and wanted to resent her but found he couldn't. Angry and on edge, Basrick started to go over the questions in his mind in search of answers.

"What the hell were you doing at that location, Menlo?" he asked, as she lay there motionless. "You have to pull through this," he said stroking her cheek and twirling a piece of her wavy hair. A thrill of attraction flashed through him leaving him confused in the middle of the horrible situation.

Perhaps his grief confused him, and made him feel drawn to Menlo. Whatever the reason for his feelings, he did not fight the attraction.

An intensive care nurse came in to check on Menlo and to summarize her status. Standing at the foot of her bed, the nurse straightened the blanket covering her legs. The clicks and wheezes of the machine that was sustaining Menlo's life sent vital readings directly to the nurse's hand held digital notebook. She looked over at Basrick, as he sat at her bedside holding her hand in his.

"You must love her very much," she said. "I know when a man loves a woman, and love is written all over your face."

Basrick looked confused, but let the nurse make her predictions.

"Well, yes, she is a very special person."

"I can tell," she smiled. "Well, I won't interrupt your visit anymore. I just need to log in her personal effects. Poor thing, I heard she had a rough night. Things are just awful now. Hers wasn't the only tragic incident. Did you hear about the nun that got killed at St. Bernard Fernando Cathedral? My understanding is that Detective Kildare is the lead detective on the serial killings here in town."

"A nun was murdered?"

"Yes, and it was just like all the other savage serial animal attacks, but the police believe it's a serial killer."

Basrick's mind jumped into overdrive stringing information together to find answers to his questions.

The nurse went to the closet in the room and removed a see-through plastic bag with the name Kildare room 310 written across the front. Opening the bag, the nurse pulled out Menlo's slacks and blazer she wore the night of the shooting. Blood stained the front of her shirt in a straight line. Cataloging the clothing, the nurse quickly moved on to the shoes, as Basrick noticed something odd on the slacks Menlo wore.

"May I see those slacks," he asked.

"Certainly."

Basrick took the slacks from the nurse as she continued rummaging through the bag, picking out Menlo's navy pumps. Chunks of awful smelling sludge hung from the ankles of the slacks. As the nurse pulled the pumps out of the bag, another huge chunk came crashing to the floor from the soles of the shoes.

"This is the same mud that Bose had crusted to his shoes," Basrick thought to himself. "What the hell is going on? Why would Bose have the same mud as Menlo? Surely he would have told us of about this, yet he said nothing."

Basrick's suspicions of Bose heightened when he recalled that Bose had not brought home any archival evidence he promised to obtain for the hunt the night before. Bose returned in his disheveled state --- completely out of character for him.

"I have to get to the library and find out what is going on," Basrick whispered. He turned and looked at the nurse's name badge and bid her farewell.

"Nurse Cook, I'll return later. Please take good care of her. I won't be long."

Nurse Cook returned to the nurse's station and commented to a fellow nurse how sad and lifeless the poor guy in the Detective's room appeared.

Basrick dashed out of the medical Center, and found a narrow alleyway in which he was able to teleport straight to the Central Library. He teleported directly to the fourth floor of the library and arrived right between two towering genealogical stacks.

Basrick slowly approached the gum-popping desk clerk. The blonde instantly sensed his presence, and her fluttering eyelashes began to vibrate with anticipation.

"Pardon me; I'm looking for a volume entitled *Manifesto de Marina.*"

The desk clerk didn't waste any time, attending his request. The perfectly manicured ruby red nails plucked away at the keyboard locating the checked out book.

"It seems someone beat you to it. In fact he was just here the other day --- male, tall, blondish hair, and sparkling green eyes."

Basrick became more apprehensive by the second. Instinct kicked in and finished his deductive reasoning for him. The desk clerk's last statement slammed him with reality so hard he shuddered.

"This can't be true," he thought. "I don't know why it didn't dawn on me before."

He took care to return to the towering stacks before he teleported out of the library, and back to the hospital alleyway, and then back to Menlo's room. Little had changed since he left earlier. The nurse made certain to put a fresh blanket on Menlo, and brush the sides of her long wavy hair back from her face. Sleeping beauty could not have been more beautiful than Menlo looked to him.

"That sorry bastard did this to you, I know he did," Basrick whispered in her ear, as she lay silently. He gently kissed her forehead and her lips.

"I will make sure he never harms you again. None of them ever will."

Basrick called Nacio's cell phone, but he didn't answer. This only made him more apprehensive. Without wasting more time, he teleported to the mansion hoping to put some of his worries to rest.

***

"Believa get us a rental car, baby," Justice hollered. "We are on our way to Louisiana. We are going to pay my pirate relatives a visit. I have a little score to settle with sister Childress. Yes, indeed."

Completely zombied out, Believa nodded her head, and went into the other room to make on-line reservations for a rental car to rendezvous in Dog water Swamp.

"I reckon my Aunt Bureau is waiting for us, but Childress isn't. Surprise, surprise."

"Childress is going to pay for making me kill Basira. She will give a life for a life, and I'm going to Louisiana to collect what she owes me."

Justice continued to entertain wicked thoughts of revenge against his sister. He shut his eyes for a moment only to be startled when he felt the presence of another vampire --- Bose was poised in a lounging chair opposite him.

"Damn, man, you can't do that kind of mess," he squeaked. "You are going to get throttled sneaking up on me."

Tickled by the pissant threat Justice made which stemmed from his false sense of well-being, Bose giggled.

"Always remember, nephew, mine are longer."

"Yeah, well, whatever. I've had Believa make arrangements for a rental car. I'm ready to go to Dog water Swamp tonight."

"I agree. Tonight is the night. I can feel it."

"Well, you might as well know," Justice hesitated. "Childress is pregnant and due any day now. Aunt Bureau said the child is a girl and her birth can strengthen our family."

"Is that right? Then we will be on our way to Dog water tonight after we hunt."

"Since that silver is out of my wounds, I feel strong as an ox."

"Silver in any form is lethal to our kind," Bose stated. "You need to keep away from it."

"You ready to head out, Unc? I'm thirsty."

"Lead the way, nephew. Once we get our fill, I'll need to go back to the mansion once more and tie up some loose ends. I'll call you when it's time to go."

"Cool. I can hardly wait.

Drunken with revenge, Justice eagerly awaited to see his sister face to face.

***

Chaos unraveled the peace in the mansion. I could hear Nacio screaming my name, but I couldn't move.

"Armando, please help me!" I heard Nacio cry. "Get me some water and a cool towel for her head, she's burning up.

Please stay with me, baby, please. I don't want to lose you."

Armando and Patience rushed about the house, and nearly knocked Basrick down as he came in.

"What's going on?" Basrick inquired.

"Solis took a nap and she stopped breathing," Nacio cried. "I can't get her to wake up. She hadn't eaten anything except some cookies on the table. I can't remember when she last ate, but now I can't get her to wake up."

Basrick knew he must consider the severity of the allegations he was about to make, but the situation called for desperate measures.

"Sire, I know the situation is critical, but I need you to hear me out," I heard Basrick plead. "Bose was there when Menlo was gunned down."

"What, Basrick?" Nacio asked. "What are you saying?"

"He was there, Sire. He claimed to have been at the library, which I confirmed, but when he came home, his shoes were covered in sludge. Just now at the hospital, I saw Menlo's personal effects, and her shoes and slacks had the same sludge. He never mentioned any shots fired, and if she were in trouble he would have known about it."

"I can't talk about this right now, Basrick. My bride dying, help me."

With time running out, Nacio did the only thing he knew would save me, which was make a deep cut in his left forearm and allow blood to drip into my dry parched lips. The paralysis kept me from responding to his blood. I felt him turn my head to the side to clear my airway. Blood slowly trickled down my throat. My lungs cautious regained elasticity, allowing me to take shallow breaths --- bringing me away from the brink of death. His blood is a powerful antidote that strengthened me with each drop as it restored my life. Vampire blood has proven its worth by heightening my senses and the ability to cheat death.

"Thank goodness," Nacio praised, kissing my forehead and rocking me in his arms.

Feeling the relief transfer from Nacio, I knew the situation had improved, but the worst was yet to come.

While regaining consciousness, I caught the tail end of Basrick's disclosure. I hoped what I heard was part of a bad dream, but knew it was wishful thinking.

"Please sire, hear me," Basrick pleaded. "For what I say impacts everyone in this room."

Nacio held me in his arms, as he allowed Basrick to speak. Braced with tension, he watched Basrick closely as he spoke.

"How can you fix your lips to accuse Bose of such betrayal?"

"When I came to assist him with researching the Treemounts, Bose was out of character. In the centuries we have known him, he has never done any normal routine out of character. The day I went to assist him, he seemed off kilter. His stacks of book volumes were in disarray; Bose has never allowed such inconsistency in his work.

"This is not enough to accuse him of such treachery."

"There is more, Sire," Basrick continued. "When I researched the information on Estes Treemount, it was discovered he branded all of his slaves after purchase. The information connected to Estes Treemount proved to be pertinent. Bose checked out the volumes of the *Manifesto De Marina*, the slave ship manifests, and they are missing. He has not brought any information to us to review.

"Basrick what you say is not enough to accuse Bose," Nacio shouted, but Basrick cut him off.

"He is a Treemount, Sire. I only figured it out for myself when I looked at him. He bares the same physical features to Childress and her brothers. You must believe it. You must believe me, Sire. I would not make false allegations against our beloved Bose, if they were not true."

"Son, are you sure?" Armando inquired. "These allegations are serious and life altering."

Nacio looked at Armando with uncertainty in his eyes and then he looked back at Basrick.

"Surely you have more than the unsupported statements," Nacio spoke.

"I have reason to believe it is he who made the attempt on the life of our Mistress."

Nacio flew across the room and slammed Basrick into the wall for his seething words. Armando jumped in to run interference.

"You will be punished for such betrayal," Nacio hissed.

"Forgive him, Nacio," Armando stated. "But I must ask you to allow him to speak. Surely, Basrick would not make such allegations if what he says is not true.

Basrick began his explanation of the allegations against Bose again.

"I believe Solis was poisoned. When I returned from hunting the other night, I saw Bose mixing the cookie dough. He hadn't been hunting at all and said that he had been with

Menlo, yet he did not respond with concern when he found out about her injuries. I no longer trust him and his whereabouts are unknown as we speak. I'll bet if you call the medical center, the nurses will tell you Menlo has not had any visitors in the last few hours, further proving his absence. He has completely abandoned Menlo. His behavior does not depict that of a grieving lover. Just think about it, Sire. If I am wrong, I will leave and never return to this home. If I am right, our time is running short, and he plans to rendezvous with Justice again tonight."

Nacio stood unable to move as he contemplated Basrick's allegations against Bose. Basrick stood firm in his beliefs.

"You must find a way to see if he has the mark of the Treemount slave owner. It is located on his stomach, near his navel," Basrick continued. Nacio's anger flared.

"If what you say is true, our lives will never be the same and that means death must come to my kindred brother. He has attempted to kill my mate. His punishment will be death."

"All I ask is that you follow him yourself, Sire, and heed to my words," Basrick asked. "Keep him under surveillance and make your own determination. When he returns ask what he has accomplished in his hunt. You will know if he tells the truth."

Nacio had to consider the things Basrick said, but never thought his would be the hand to put his brother to death.

***

"I need to make certain that Solis is dead, and then we will take off to the east. The Botulism should have infected her pretty quickly and we can all move on," Bose thought to himself.

The entire household appeared to be in an uproar as Bose stood outside on the south lawn listening to the conversation between household members.

"What are we going to do?" he heard Patience cry. "This is so tragic."

"I don't know, sweetheart," Armando said. "I just don't know."

Bose smiled and confidently strolled into the kitchen. Satisfied his diabolical plan had been successful he boldly kept up appearances as if nothing happened. Sorely disappointed, he stood dumbfounded at what he saw.

"What's up, Bose?" Nacio called. "You good, man?"

"Yes Hefe, things are well."

"Solis sends her gratitude for the cookies," Nacio continued, and then attempted to bait Bose.

Tension thickened as Nacio asked Bose about his emotional state and Menlo's prognosis.

"Where you been, man, we've been waiting on you?"

"Oh, you know I just needed a walk to get some fresh air."

"Really? Anything you need me to do? I know how devastating this thing is with Menlo being in the hospital and all."

"No, not really, I'm good. I think I'm go up to my suite now."

Trying not to seem too evasive, Bose went upstairs to

his suite. As soon as he walked into the room, he could pick up the scent of the lovemaking on the bed sheets he and Menlo had slept on. Agony tried to creep in on him again, only to be chased away.

Bose reached for his cell phone, and dialed Justice.

"Neither one of these bitches died, which means we still have problems needing to be solved."

"What do you want me to do?" Justice asked.

"Meet me in Mission Park in 20 minutes."

Unbeknownst to Bose, Nacio heard every word of the conversation between the two traitors, as he listened through the walls of the suite. Broken hearted, he tried to come to grips with the fact that this was the end of his relationship with his oldest family member. Accepting this meant he would have to see the betrayal with his own eyes.

"I have to see this for myself. I'll meet you both in Mission Park in 10 minutes. This is the beginning of the end."

14

The Course

Circulating as a misty fog bank through an open field in the middle of Mission Park, Nacio surveyed Bose and Justice collaborating another strike against them all --Solis, the Caraways and him. Pain sliced through the lifetime of memories he had shared with Bose. The vision before him ended their kinship forever. Together, Nacio and Bose were each other's support while re-establishing a life amongst the living society. Protection of the other was a solemn vow that each had sworn. He listened in as Bose schooled Justice on his family history, and more plans to harm Solis.

"She is an obstacle. Once she is out of the way my mother will be free to rise once more."

"What's in this for me? I mean, if I do all the dirty work, what will I have to show for it?"

"Don't question what I'm offering you fool!" Bose bellowed. "Be glad I'm including you, because without me, you wouldn't have a chance. Look at what your dumbass has already done. You've attracted attention to our existence, which is a huge mistake. Once we start having paranormal investigators on our trail, we have to go on the run. I haven't been on the run in nearly a century and I'm not about to start again."

Justice stood before his uncle and looked awestruck, but held strong to his own desires.

"Look, Unc, I need money. All I can get. I have needs of my own that need to be met."

"Don't worry about dollars and cents, nephew. Your hands will be filled to the brim. Just make sure you get to Louisiana. I won't have Nacio and those wretched houseguests of his stopping my mother's return. You deal with your other affairs your own way."

"Ouch, damn that hurt, Unc."

"I'm headed back to the Masonry to get you the cash you need to do what you will."

With that said, Bose teleported out of the park leaving Justice to finish the slow drag he had going on a cigarette. For Nacio, seeing the truth makes a hell of a difference when it is seen with your own eyes.

Standing alone in the shadows of the trees, as misty tears seeped from his eyes, Nacio came to terms with what he saw. Betrayal pierced his chest deeper than any mortal wound could have after what he had just witnessed. As long as Bose remained alive, Solis would be in danger forever more. Hatred for his brother grew in his heart with every passing minute.

Nothing could have turned Nacio against Bose other than the fact that he was willing to put Solis in harm's way --- for that threat of harm, tonight is his kindred brother's last night on earth.

***

All was quiet as Bose disarmed the proximity of the security system once he was inside Puente Masonry. All machine operations had ceased, and the evening production was complete. A shipment of bricks and cement was due to go out for the completion of the southern Riverwalk expansion.

He looked up at the ceiling in the seven-story building and spoke a triumphant promise to himself.

"Once she has risen, I will serve Priestess Auldicia, my Goddess mother for all time. I will assume my rightful place at her side as she fulfills her reign on earth.

Unaware that he was in the presence of another, Nacio put a pin in Bose's inflated delusions of grandeur --- putting the vampire on alert.

"Your bitch dog of a mother will never rise to see the sun in this millennium." Nacio made sure his threat was a promise as it was deadly.

"Oh brother, my brother, you can't stop what is to come to pass. Why don't you join me in bringing my mother back to this life? Would you not do the same if it were your mother? Events have already been set in motion for her to rise. You are too late Nacio…too late. A legacy will be born on this night and the Treemount blood will continue to run free."

Taking his nails and running them along the steel wall, blood slowly ran down Nacio's fingertips as he gouged and peeled the metal back --- perforating the structure.

"You will be put down like the dog you are as well… just like your mother. She will not rise… I trusted you Bose as my brother and friend. We have been each other's rock for decades. This is how you would end that lifetime? So be it."

"So be it," Bose sneered.

Moving preternaturally, Nacio and Bose launched themselves at each other in mid air, like the sound of a massive vehicular collision --- slamming into the north concrete wall of the masonry, as crumbs of concrete fell to the floor. Nacio held Bose in a crushing vice headlock with the pressure of two tons.

Bose held his own as the Titan vampires waltzed around the main production floor of the masonry. Taking his left leg, he flipped Nacio over, flooring him on his back, leaving a crater sized dent in the floor, vibrating the building's frame. Bose raised his leg to bring the heel of his new black loafer down onto the center of Nacio's chest. Falling short of success, Nacio struck with the speed of a pit viper, catching the descending heel and throwing Bose off balance.

The two vampires wrestled fiercely in a joint death match, as they crashed into the concrete walls. Each impact carried enough force to bend the steel beams and girders, making the metals seem as flimsy as tin foil. Nacio's wrath against Bose had festered and intensified each time he thought of the attempt he made to kill Solis. The time had come for the height of his fury to be unleashed.

"What gives you the right to harm the person I love the most…who has loved you as a brother in return as well? For that you must die!"

"She is nothing. A no one," Bose heaved as he squeezed Nacio's shoulder, dislocating his collarbone from its shoulder joint. "I have been with you for centuries, yet you place her ahead of me?"

Without a moment to spare, Nacio released a war cry that rattled the glass fixtures in their settings. Tightening his grip on the rogue vampire, he quickly slid his fingers between the sharp fangs in the upper cavity of Bose's mouth. Pulling upward with one hand, and then pushing downward, Nacio stretched Bose's jaw open until the elasticity gave way --- shattering the joint just in front of his ears. Shattered bones echoed throughout the air ducts inside the building.

Blood leaked slowly from Bose's ear, as his jawbone speared his face. Flesh tore from his body, causing a ripple in his equilibrium --- falling to his knees in agony from embarrassment. The fractured jaw distorted his speech; nonetheless, he was still able to send out a deadly warning to his once brother, now adversary.

"Fool! The day will come soon enough and my mother, my true mother will rise and rule once more. You can't stop me. She has a power beyond reasoning, that will give me all of what I need…what I've missed, what I've always wanted. You will never be able to stop me… or her once she walks the earth again."

Watching Bose convey his message of doom only further fueled Nacio's hatred. He drew back his arm and aimed his knuckles for the tiny spot right between Bose's eyes. Punching with the force of a semi-truck and cutting Bose across his face, Nacio threw him head first over a railing, sending him into a vat full of clay that was online for morning shipment. Locating a spigot and turning on the hot water, he hoped mixing the clay would slow Bose from his pursuit.

Blood slowly coalesced with the nutmeg colored mortar as it stained the surface of the liquid. Bose sank, the more he struggled to get free of his sludge entombment. As soon as Nacio thought that was the end of the war with Bose, a huge air bubble broke the surface of the liquid --- a brown blob flew out of the mixture grabbing Nacio.

Pinned against the wall in, Nacio pulled the detached jaw that barely tethered itself to Bose's distorted face. One tug and Bose growled, as he was relieved of his fractured jaw leaving behind a serpent like tongue as it flicked side to side.

Strength began to leave Bose as he teleported out of the masonry in an attempt to flee the rage that stood before him. Nacio matched Bose with each move he made. Just before the final stage of teleportation took place, putting Bose out of the masonry vicinity and on the move, Nacio grabbed hold of his foot.

Dragging along through mid air during teleportation, Nacio's weight proved to be a hindrance for both vampires. Looking below as the battle continued, Nacio realized they were jetting towards the Tower of the Americas --- set to make contact with the south wall of the tower in three…two…one…

On contact at 689 feet, the impact of the two vampires hitting the south wall just underneath the tower's canopy was a type of sonic boom that popped the eardrums of those citizens who leisurely strolled through Hemisfair Plaza below.

Continuing the destruction, Nacio and Bose crashed through the veneer that encases the tower's elevator shafts. Fueled with rage, Nacio extended his fingernails on command. Head-locking Bose, he drove his nails one inch below the surface of Bose's scalp and ripped grooves from the beginning of his hairline to the nape of his neck. The disfigured vampire looked as if a grizzly bear had taken its time mauling its prey prior to consuming it; punishing Bose and making him suffer is the main goal.

"You dare harm Solis…you are the damn fool…and

have reached your days end in this life!"

Pain seared throughout his body from wounds that no human would survive. Communication from Bose was no longer coherent. One last futile attempt to defend himself came by laughing and heckling at Nacio that sounded like a raven cawing. This only pissed Nacio off, causing him to take a new fighting stance.

Bose received a forceful kick to his left thighbone---sending his mangled body flying across IH 37 and crashing into the 300-foot west glass of the Alamo Dome. Rattling glass shook the building, while cement debris showered down from the dome's rafters, sending the night duty custodians running for cover. A fallen comet to earth is the only other incident that could have caused more damage than the two vampires incurred.

Teleporting to finish what he started, Nacio traveled across the interstate to the dome's crash site just as Bose freed himself from the concrete rubble. Laughter from the dismembered vampire only continued Nacio's assault. Bose's tongue wagged as blood oozed from the jaw wounds.

"You cannot stop what is to come. You are too late and are no longer the Hefe!"

"Go to hell with your mother!" Nacio growled. He sank his fangs into Bose's exposed vulnerable area and ripped a section of flesh from his broken neck. Bose gave one last warning.

"No…my mother will come to you," Bose whispered an exhausted breath. "She will come for your tramp of a bride Solis and make her the lap dog she truly is."

No force could stop Nacio as his roar shook the ground

louder than the five o'clock locomotive as it rumbled down the railroad tracks at Iowa and Cherry Street. Crushing Bose under his left arm as he traveled in an upward cyclonic motion, he blew a hole in the roof of the dome to accompany the shattered west glass---then Nacio rebounded back across the interstate.

One last spine crushing press against Bose's neck, and Nacio made it to the top of the Tower of the Americas just as he ripped out all 33 vertebrae of his spine. The silver lightening rod that crowns the tower was in full view. With the betrayal playing continuously in his mind as the evil laughter filled his ears, Nacio reached the top of the tower and plunged Bose's broken body over the lightening rod --- staking Bose through his back, piercing his heart.

Death immediately fixed the eyes of the one being that was closer to him than any blood kinship for decades. Nacio looked into his brother's eyes one last time. Bose died with his broken body helplessly waving in the wind comparable to a sail hoisted high on a mast.

Teleporting down from the tower, he found a location between the shadows of two buildings standing in Hemisfair Park. Nacio watched in silence, as Bose rapidly began to decompose into silt. Showering the ground below and all that stood at the foot of the tower, the silt irritated the skin of the humans below.

He looked up toward heaven and screamed --- releasing the pain and anguish that festered in his soul from losing…his brother.

***

"Man, I wonder what is keeping Bose?" Justice wondered. "I'm sick of waiting. I'm going to hit the road. I don't have time for this. He left enough money to hideout for quite a while. I don't care about Priestess Auldicia, and all that other shit, and I don't need him. I just want to get paid, then I'm going to pay Childress back. I'm going to make things right for Basira's sake. I never should have killed her."

Justice planned to head to Dog water Swamp and carryout his vengeance.

15

Divinity Unbound

"I'm hungry, dammit," Childress barked. "Bureau come and get me something to eat."

Now with a full term swollen belly, things had settled down in the house in Dogwater Swamp. Urgata and Nayphous had completely broken up, thanks to Childress seducing him. It was pitiful how he struggled with the lust spell she seemed to put him under off and on. Nothing stopped her from being the tramp she was, not even pregnancy. The air began to thicken as she finished her last bit of steak tartar. She took one last bite of her food and called for Klein to retrieve her plate. Several extended family members came over and spent the weekend with them. There was plenty of food leftover for them to eat.

"Come and get this empty plate, Klein."

"You get up and get it yourself, tramp. You put this mouth pox on me, and I can't get no loving from any female for at least 10 miles from here, so go to hell."

Childress jumped to her swollen feet and threw the plate like a boomerang, narrowly missing the nape of Klein's exposed neck.

"Take that, damn fool," she hollered. "I bet you next time I tell you to come, you'll come," she stomped her foot, breaking her amniotic sac, and spilling the fluid in a puddle at her feet.

"Bureau," Childress called. "I think my water broke."

Klein jumped back as the amniotic fluid oozed onto the floor.

"Eeeoww, what the hell?" Klein hollered. "Auntie, come and get Childress, she's leaking."

Bureau rolled into the room with her Slim sitting in its usual place between her lips. "Klein, call your brother and tell him to get in here and help me get her situated."

"Now is not a good time for Erland, auntie. He believes dragon flies are chasing him. You can't interrupt him when he is like that."

Humidity and stifling heat turned the evening into an open-air sauna. Storm clouds rolled in as lightening scrawled across the night sky. Animals could feel evil veil itself over the land as a new female Treemount was about to be born. Priestess Auldicia's bloodline would lengthen, perpetuating the curse.

Sweating profusely onto a torn soaked sheet, Childress writhed in labor pain as her swollen torso hardened--preparing to bring forth the child she conceived. All of the extended family members spread about the house moaning and chanting at each other ---hearing Childress scream made things worse. Bureau was tense, well aware of the pending task.

"Klein and Erland. It's time to move her down by the water."

"For what?" Klein inquired, with his lips newly scabbed over from the healing fever blister sores from the hex Childress placed on him. "You mean you plan on her having the baby outside?"

"Do as I say, damn fool, and do it now."

Agitated and hallucinating, Erland began to swing at imaginary dragon flies he thought were pursuing him. He informed Klein, of the hallucinatory attack earlier that evening. Flinching and ducking to hide from the imaginary pestilence, Erland started the psychotic laughter that often followed when his altered state of reality settled in on him. Quickly losing touch with his surroundings, as the evening's tension took its toll on him---Bureau's tolerance of his psychosis began to wane.

"Heeheeheeheeeheehee, look, I caught one," Erland laughed.

Enraged at the lunacy of her nephew's mood swings, Bureau conjured a spell to silence Erland as easily as pushing the mute button on a television remote control. Straightening her stance from leaning over a laborious Childress, she spat these words to Erland's face.

"Lips be still and move no more." Bureau finished her spell with a wave of her left hand, dropping singed cigarette ashes on the wooden floor. What happened next brought Klein to a standstill.

Bureau's spoken words delivered a command that relaxed Erland's vocal chords, relieving his lips of all elasticity, forcefully turning them inward — silencing him. Hollowed cheeks and inverted lips gave him the look of an 80 year-old man without dentures. His hysterical antics ceased and he gave Bureau his full attention.

Touching his mouth, Klein looked on in fear. Afraid that his Aunt Bureau would cause his recently healed mouth pox to begin their oozing once more if he did not follow her instructions, he grabbed the end of the torn sheet.

A mute Erland took note of his brother's actions and grabbed the other end of the sheet. Miming was the only way he was able to respond to commands. Pointing to his mouth and waving his arms, confirmed Bureau's spell was in full effect. Both brothers began to hoist Childress onto a gurney made of two six feet bamboo poles and firmly stretched cotton cloth.

Making their way out of the room and through the house, the cousins and extended family members wailed as Childress continued in her pain. With each scream, she let out a ghastly yellow film that filled the air in the home. Stench accompanied the film, making the cousins cover their mouths and noses. Childress was carried to the water for labor and delivery.

Fierce wind gusts made the moss covered trees sway as leaves blew past a howling Childress. Dressed in a black ceremonial dress, perspiration plastered the garment to her aching body.

Terror stricken from the awful wailing, Urgata looked on as her mother Bureau sprinkled white protection powder around the area while Klein and Erland carried Childress to the water's edge. Although the residue from the protection powder was white, it turned their clothing black with smudges --- demonstrating the kind of power Bureau possessed being a descendant of Priestess Auldicia. As the mambo of Dogwater swamp, she had the power to summon the Loas for the birthing ceremony to commence.

"Haaayo...Ahhheelee...Mefeddo!"

Other swamp dwellers lined the shore armed with bongo drums, dressed in black garments. Drumbeats echoed far enough to vibrate off the tin roofs in the distance. Klein and Erland reached their destination at the water's edge with their sister in tow. Slowly, they lowered her laboring body onto a wooden raft docked at the pier.

Bureau chanted on above the whistling wind and the offbeat cadence of the swamp dwellers as they looked on in amazement. The birth of a new female Treemount was a sacred family tradition, one in which Bureau knew would please her long since deceased ancestor Priestess Auldicia.

In the practice of voodoo the gods or Loas are active participants. Although troubled at the fact that Childress had intended to sacrifice this child to the Loas, Agwe and Guede to solidify her power as the new mambo, Bureau had no choice but to continue in her niece's sinister plan. She knew that if she did not honor her wishes, her niece would bring sadness and grief upon her immediate family. Childress had already proven that she was far more powerful than she was, leaving her no alternative.

Bureau stood at the pier, as Childress seized in pain. She sprinkled more protection powder over her as she writhed in agony. Bureau mumbled a spell to set the raft a float out into the middle of the deepest part of the swamp. Legend had it that if anyone were to swim to the middle, the lily pads and vines in the undercurrent would pull them to their death as a sacrifice to the Loa Agwe. As the raft set out on its course, Bureau picked up a Conch shell that was one of many that lay at the water's edge from past ceremonies. Taking a deep breath that distended her belly and lungs, she blew into the Conch shell summoning the Loas, Agwe and Guede.

"Vooroo, toonde, ahoo Agwe, Vooroo toonde Guede. Hear me Agwe, Loa of water and Swamp. Come forth and receive this child. Hear me Guede, keeper of the cemetery and evil spirits. Send word to Priestess Auldicia that a female child is to be born to continue our namesake and crush all those who would stand against us!"

Marking its intended course in the middle of the swamp, the raft came to a halt. Wind continued to whip the raging swamp water against the raft, but the vessel was unaffected by its attempts to capsize it. Screams of misery escalated as thunder rolled across the sky followed by lightening comparable to the Northern Lights in outer space. Smelling unprotected flesh, the sound of alligator tails splashing and submerging into the murky water let Childress know she and her unborn child were about to become lunch for some hungry visitors. Bureau implored the gods.

"Give transfer of power to her now!"

Tremors began to move underneath the on-lookers feet, as violent waves continued to crash against the raft. Childress increased her volume with each wave of labor. Making an effort to escape her misery, she crawled to the edge of the raft with one last exerted effort screaming for mercy.

"Help me!" she cried out as she threw herself over the edge of the raft into the black water. Upon contact, water began to bubble rapidly as if the entire swamp was boiling. Green lights illuminated the water as it continued its effervescence. Submerged in murky water, there was no doubt Childress had met her inevitable death.

Astonished yet still unaffected the spellbound on-lookers continued their offbeat drumming in celebration of what their eyes witnessed. Bureau stood still and held her breath at the next thing she saw. Evil cloaked itself above the water, as rumbling underneath the swamp shook the feet of the bystanders.

With pressurized hell like heat in the midst of the swamp, a geyser erupted in the center, sending it 50 feet into the air. Cascading like Niagara Falls with the force of a Tsunami, the 50-foot geyser aimed for the swamps edge.

The on-lookers were mesmerized at the sight before them—no one blinked. Continuing their celebration, several of the cousins began to dance and shout. With one last crack of thunder from the sky above, Priestess Childress Treemount stepped out from the geyser's green glow --- evil reborn.

Evil had bestowed beauty upon her once more. Minus the midnight black highlights, her hair returned to its original blonde-red hue, as it hung past her shoulders. Jade green eyes looked out upon the many curious gazes that stared back at her. Supple skin covered her goddess like body, yet her womb still had not given birth. With a voice like that of a fallen angel, she announced her arrival.

"Know this. Let there be no mistake. I am the Queen Mother. Bow down!"

With one foot in front of the other, she hypnotically began to do her highly erotic dance. Known in the world of voodoo as the Banda Dance, Childress began gyrating to fast-paced drumbeats that seemed to entice her every movement.

Nayphous had just arrived at the swamp's edge. Missing Urgata, he tried reconciliation, but his thwarted efforts went unnoticed. He stood mortified at what he saw by the water. Captivated, he watched Childress erotically coax a physical response from his loins. He fought is desire to join her while his arousal began to run away with him. Rhythmic movement from her hips reminded him of the night they'd spent together. Holding his eyes shut, he remembered Childress slapping his face as he shuddered to ecstasy. Although he hated her, he also realized that he was madly in love with the most dangerous woman he had ever known.

Childress continued with her body-wave movements until she felt another stream of water run down her legs. Labor had finally reached its peak as her placenta membrane had finally released the child from its clutches after already going through several hours of painful contractions. Bureau sprang into action. She herself was a doula, better known as a mid-wife and had delivered all of her own children by herself.

Crashing to her knees in pain once more, Childress found her bearing on a rock and squatted. Not quite able to catch her breath in between contractions she labored on making the crowning of the baby's head difficult. Bureau coached while assisting her to push.

"You have to breathe, Childress, breathe!"

"I am breathing, dammit!"

With two huge grunts and one excruciating scream, Childress pushed the baby's body out into the world. Newborn cries of life let the on-lookers know the birth was a success, as they celebrated. At the edge of the shore, Childress lay in a puddle of mud with minnows and toads nearby to welcome the new legacy into the family. Overjoyed and gasping for breath herself, Bureau cheered.

"She's beautiful! She's so beautiful!"

With tears streaming down her face, the death of her sister Frances was the only other time that she had shed a tear. Bureau tied and cut the umbilical cord with a long pair of sewing scissors, freeing the little one into the world. Childress refused to look at the perfect little girl that her aunt held in her arms. Still punch drunk with power and hell bent on being immortal, Childress stubbornly refused to respond.

"She looks just like us. You can't give her up," Bureau whispered. "I won't let you do this, Childress. You can't sacrifice her."

"Look you can't tell me what…" Childress tried to finish just as her newborn baby girls hand grazed her cheek as Bureau stretched her arms to hand her to Childress. The newborn's loving touch wilted her mother into seeing her for the first time. Speechless at the sight of new life, Childress looked at her baby in awe. As the natural bond of mother and child unfolded, a black blur of a shadow blew across Childress--leaving her feeling cold and without her newborn in her embrace.

Shocked and dismayed, both Bureau and Childress looked up to see a staggeringly handsome Justice holding the tender naked newborn. With a set of long, nail sharp fangs dangling from his mouth, Justice proudly slid his tongue over his oral weapons and flashed a sinister smile.

"Hey there, sis, you sure did give birth to a beautiful baby girl. Man she is beautiful. Bet you love her too. Don't you?"

Pissed at the fact Justice stood amongst them as an uninvited guest, Childress tried to assume a defensive stance as her maternal instincts surfaced.

"What are you doing here now, Justice? Why did you wait to show up now? I see you didn't do what I told you to do before you let that vamp tramp bite the hell out you again."

"Oh, but you see that's where you're wrong you stupid two-dollar hoe."

Irritated, he snapped back with fangs in full view as he cuddled the baby girl. "You see, it's a new day. I loved Basira, but you wanted me to kill her. Now, sister dear, it is your turn to suffer."

Moving a wet piece of hair from the side of her face to the back of her head, Childress tried to stand but was unable to. With little agility, she positioned herself to sit on the rock as she continued to have words with Justice.

"Well, dumb bastard, you killed her. Don't blame me for everything."

"Yeah, you're right. Guess it was dumb, but not as dumb as having a baby by a damn dead man who shot his brains out because you hexed him into doing it. Isn't that right, Aunt Bureau?"

Oooh, that struck a raw nerve with Childress. With the little strength she had just after giving birth, she tried to conjure up a spell to make Justice harm himself in some way, but found she couldn't. Bureau had summoned Agwe and Guede --- their patience thinning from waiting for their human sacrifice. With an incomplete ritual, Childress remained in a weakened state. Justice held a hidden agenda of his own, one that included punishing Childress.

"Don't worry little one," Justice cooed to his newborn niece. "Uncle Justice is going to make sure you are well taken care of."

Taking one huge leap and disappearing into the night, Justice sped off into the darkness with the beautiful little blonde female Treemount in tow. Screams filled the night air once more.

"Justice, bring me back my baby! Give me my baby!"

Squeezing her core muscles and straining her vocal cords, Childress shouted as the last breath of exertion brought the placenta after birth from her womb falling to the ground. A leaky stream of blood and plasma from the life sustaining afterbirth seeped into the earth. Toads, a size smaller than flat cobblestones sat near Childress at the water's edge. The amphibian creatures got a whiff of the freshly delivered afterbirth and carried it on their backs down to the murky depths of Dog water Swamp. No one missed disposing of the afterbirth, and no one noticed as the blood disappeared leaving no trace of existence.

Childress went into hysterics as Justice faded into the night just as quickly as he had come. The on-lookers stood silently at the evenings events. No one said a word as wails of sorrow filled the air. Urgata and Bureau helped Childress get to her feet. Unsteady and weak, she allowed the mother and daughter to help her.

"Come on, Childress, let's get you inside before you get sick out here in the open," Bureau said.

"I'm not going anywhere until I get my baby back."

"For what? You didn't want her anyway. You were going to sacrifice her so you could take over everything."

Caught off guard, and fed up with Bureau, vicious resentment washed over Childress, as she let go of her impulses. For one, Justice confirmed that he had actually been in contact with Bureau while they were in exile here in Dog water Swamp. Secondly, it is true. Childress did want to be the only other mambo in the family.

In the distance of less than a foot between them, fury caused the infant less mother to pick up the sewing scissors used to cut the baby's umbilical cord, and jab them straight through her Aunt Bureau's right jugular vein. The butchered wound crossed Bureau's windpipe as the scissors entered underneath her left shoulder bone---severing the artery. Due to the difference in their height, this was a messy wound for Childress, spraying blood over all that stood nearby.

Shocked yet not surprised at her niece's actions, Bureau met a painful death. Childress watched as her aunt dropped to her knees, and she proceeded to step over her dying body. Laying eyes on Bureau for the last time, Childress quickly eulogized her fading aunt and bid her passage into the afterlife.

"I told you when I first got here, Cher. Nobody curses me, Bureau. You think I don't know you didn't want me to become the new Priestess? Like I'm that damn stupid? Now, look at you. You've been running your mouth to Justice telling him things that don't concern you or him. You're a dead floozy now aren't you, Aunt Bureau?"

Looking up and around out in the open Childress shouted --- mocking the Loas. "There's your damn sacrifice, now leave me alone!"

Bureau's blood spilled on the ground --- quickly seeping into the earth as she bled out. This blood streamed into the swamp --- causing bystanders to move out of its path as it ran past bare feet. The blood of the fallen mambo only partially satisfied the invoked gods. Blood caught the undercurrent of the swamp and was soon on its way out to Lake Pontchartrain, which would soon flow to the Mississippi River. Bureau's life sustaining blood and plasma found the flow of blood from the afterbirth expelled from Childress and carried by the toads to the body of water. A brisk current washed everything out to the Gulf of Mexico, emptying into the ocean.

***

Justice had made it back to San Antonio just before dawn in no time flat. He drove all night, only stopping for gas as the baby slept peacefully. He watched her little lips quiver while she slumbered. Watching her reminded him of what he could have had with Basira.

"You are so precious. It's too bad you were born to a bitch dog. Hopefully, you will have a better life unlike that tramp of a mother you have."

Without a clue of what to do now, he called his Uncle Bose on the phone in hopes of getting some support on what to do next. There was no answer, which was strange. Heading to the only place he knew, he started towards the Puente mansion in search of Bose. Making it to the long glamour spelled driveway, Justice figured he would take the baby to Bose and together they would figure out what to do next.

***

My illness had subsided, and I felt better. Basrick explained to me the details of how Bose betrayed us all. I grieved for our little family, but most of all for Nacio. Centuries of a friendship all destroyed over power and greed. We are afraid of losing Menlo, since her prognosis has not changed any.

Feeling well enough to go downstairs I sat on the couch a short while as I waited for Nacio to return. I didn't have to wait long --- my beloved teleported right in the middle of the living room. The wounds he sustained from battle are still fresh. He embraced me as we mourned together.

I stood comforting Nacio while he hung his head in grief. Killing Bose had broken his soul. Wearing the pain of ending his caretaker's existence in his eyes and on his heart, he sat silently before me, as his wounds healed right before my eyes. Bose had been involved in the ultimate deception --- betraying Nacio. It was even too unthinkable to speak of. I don't know how we are to recover from such a tragedy. I too loved Bose. I feel as though everyone close to me seems to end up dead.

Before I could speak another word, Nacio jumped from his seat sensing danger.

"Baby, what is it?"

"One of the Treemounts is near. It's Justice. He's come to find Bose."

Looking outside, a black Tahoe pulled up near the water fountain out front. Sure enough, I could see Justice Treemount, taking surveillance of the premises.

He parked the truck and got out. Walking around to the passenger side, he opened the door to retrieve something. He reached in and released the passenger seatbelt, holding a baby in his arms. His cautious demeanor indicated he could feel the presence of other vampires watching him, but was not sure how near or far they were from him. Nacio was already outside when Justice made it to the front porch of the mansion. Moving with preternatural agility, he made his presence known when he growled a warning to Justice.

"You are awfully bold to come here, Treemount, awfully bold," a monstrous looking Nacio stated, stepping out of the shadows 50 feet from Justice and the baby.

"Where's Bose? I just want to talk to Bose. I just want to talk, that's all. I didn't come here for trouble."

"Bose is uh…in the middle of a cleanup detail at the moment," Nacio smiled a sinister grin, just as Armando revealed himself from the shadows two feet from the intruder --- fangs drawn.

"You didn't come for trouble, but it's what you've found."

Patience followed suit behind her husband taking note of the baby Justice held in his arms.

"Look, I didn't come for more warfare. I just need to---."

Without further warning, Armando lunged for Justice grabbing him by the throat causing the baby to tumble out of his embrace. Patience was there with the speed of light to catch the little one before she completed a painful fall. Armando tightened his grip on Justice, feeling his windpipe starting to give and collapse into his spinal cord.

"My daughter is dead, and so shall you be as well."

"I loved Basira," Justice tried to speak, as the air was squeezed out of him. "Please take the baby, and raise her as your own. She is Childress's daughter, please don't let

Childress have her."

"Let him go, Armando! Please!" Patience pleaded with her husband. "Let him speak!"

Holding his ferocious stance, Armando loosened his grip that had Justice gasping. Nacio stood looking on --- ready to kill and implement punishment against anyone that posed a threat.

"Please, I could never be forgiven for taking Basira from you. However, I can try to save another life. Please, I didn't come to fight."

Nacio stood in shock with a loss for words. A gentle breeze blew softly as the last Caraway materialized next to his mother. Basrick looked back and forth between his mother and father confused at what he saw. Swaddled and slumbering peacefully, the newest Treemount female lie still as Patience cooed --- kissing her tiny hands.

"Mom, what is this? Why is he here?"

"This is Childress's daughter, Basrick. Justice is trying to make amends by giving her to us."

"Please accept my apology. I have to save her from Childress."

All of the vampires stood silent as Justice kneeled before the Caraways in full surrender asking for forgiveness. Nacio stood in doubt, circling Justice---waiting to attack on cue.

"How do we know that this is not some trick that you and your family have continued to perpetuate?"

"I don't want this child to be like her mother, Childress."

Remarkably, Patience came to his defense.

"I believe him, Nacio. Armando sweetheart, I believe that he is sincere."

"My sister is dead," Basrick shouted. "Have you all forgotten that?" Basrick stepped away from his parents as they continued to look on at the Treemount child. He found their affections for the child sickening and traitorous to the memory of his deceased twin Basira.

"He is telling the truth Basrick, for if he were lying we would surely know," Nacio stated. Never had Nacio witnessed such surrender from a creature coming from a bloodline as tainted as the Treemounts.

Armando and Patience wouldn't stop looking at the child. He stretched forth his cool hand and touched the baby girl's forehead. Although she had been born from an evil mother, he did not sense that true evil had overtaken her.

"Who fathered this child?"

"He was a detective that Childress seduced. His name was Mathis Bouvier."

"Was? How did he die?" Nacio inquired.

"Childress hexed him and according to my Aunt Bureau, he took a gun to his head. Childress was going to sacrifice this baby to the Loas Agwe and Guede to finalize her position as the new Priestess. I showed up just in time to save her."

Armando weighed in with reasoning to shed light on the situation.

"Her father was of some use in this world then. Perhaps his blood might save this child, but we can't keep her."

Patience felt her heartbreak the instant the last words were spoken.

"What are you saying? If Childress gets her, she will surely sacrifice this child. We can't let that happen."

Remembering what Grandma Olvignia and my mother warned me of while I slept. Providing some insight would surely impact the decision that seemed to already be made.

"Patience is right. If Childress were to get a hold of this child, who is a new life and ultimately a virgin, she will be unstoppable." A shouting Armando was still not convinced --- only acknowledging the danger to befall them.

"We cannot keep her."

"I won't let you take her. Please, don't make me give her up."

With newfound sorrow in her eyes, there was no way that Armando could refuse his beautiful wife. He looked at Nacio as he and I stood in each other's arms. It was as if Armando knew what Nacio would say.

"My friend, make your decision wisely. For there will be no peace with this child in our midst. Childress will surely be drawn out to pursue this child, even if it's nothing more than to make a claim."

"You can't let her have this baby," Justice roared. Patience didn't back down---maternal instincts so strong, with the impenetrable strength of a force field.

"Let the bitch come and take her best shot. It will be the last damned thing she does." Patience surrendered her newly mending heart.

"We will call you, Blessing. You are now Blessing Caraway."

I couldn't help but shed a tear at the scene of the little family. After months of misery, Patience almost looked like her old self. Basrick continued looking at the baby in disgust. Justice spoke breaking his gaze.

"Where's Bose?"

Tension settled in the air as Basrick's blood red eyes went unnoticed---we were so caught up in watching the joy little Blessing had brought to Patience. Hatred ran hot and deep through his veins as Basrick picked up the hedge cutters that lie in the yard. Holding them up high, he opened them snipped the baldhead of Justice Treemount from his shoulders. Blood oscillated through the air as the head hit the ground with a thick and heavy thud.

Fueled by grief and driven by sorrow, Basrick brought the twin blades back across each other to shear the rest of Justice's limbs from his torso, as they fell in a pile below his legs. Finishing his work by opening a vile of Colloidal Silver and dumping it over the remains, Basrick sneered with his fangs in full view.

The rest of us stood shocked, as the remains of Justice Treemount began to decompose in a pile of what looked to be red taffy as his flesh melted right before our eyes. He did not turn to silt as Basira had, as she fell from the night sky. More than likely Justice decomposed in this manner due to him being a newly turned vampire.

"Now you're dead and gone to hell just like your damned uncle, you illiterate murderous bastard," Basrick howled.

We all looked over at Basrick who stood before us now with a look of total satisfaction on his face. He had just avenged his twin's death and the attempt on Menlo's life. As he turned to walk away, the pool of remains that once were

Justice Treemount, began to sink into the ground. All the blood that spilled in the yard sank into the earth as well.

***

Rain began to fall softly---sending the residents of the Puente mansion inside. Closing the door on the nightmare and opening the chapter of a new one. Rain sent the decomposed remnants of flesh and blood down a nearby storm drain. Emptying out into the far reaches of the San Antonio River, the Treemount blood that once belonged to Justice flowed out into the Rio Grande deep in south Texas. Soon the cursed blood made a voyage deep into the Gulf of Mexico.

A strong current coalesced with the bloody remains --- finding its home in the worst manmade disaster in the United States history. An oil slick from a broken pipe 5,000 feet below the surface of the ocean appeared as just another disaster to be cleaned up, but the gateway to Satan's den had just rolled out the welcome carpet.

There was no way of knowing what the preceding chain of events indicated --- but there would surely be hell to pay.

Spilling Treemount blood in the act of murder perpetuates the curse that is the source of the family's evil. The city's storm drains flowed into rivers leading to the Gulf of Mexico, which currently had hurricane watches in effect. Two tornadoes formed in the gulf, each funnel half a mile wide, spinning out on the ocean surface. Wailing wind blew, as the air circulated thrashing all the sea life within its wall of water. Two waterspouts danced across the water headed for the

Corpus Christi shoreline.

Moving quickly, the storms traveled west --- destroying all that remained in their path. Catastrophic events would soon change the world.

***

We had finally gotten some peace during the aftermath of Nacio killing Bose and Basrick killing Justice, but dark storm clouds seemed to make the hours that followed dreary. Rain poured over San Antonio, flooding the entire Bexar County area. That was the outside world. Inside the Puente mansion, Patience was a sight to see with her new bundle of joy.

Little Blessing Caraway melted the skeptical heart of her new father Armando. Although her birth and existence in their hearts would never take the place of Basira, the Caraways were at least willing to allow their hearts to heal and their love to grow for the baby girl.

With the rain sealing me indoors, I caught a severe case of cabin fever. Even though he hated to be away from me, Nacio knew I needed some space so I decided to break out and head to Wal-mart. Shopping is a wonderful pastime for me, and I wanted to join in and spoil Blessing.

Arriving at the near empty store, I was able to find a parking spot in the front row. It didn't seem like the rain was going to end anytime soon. Making my way into the store, I went straight to the back to the infant section. I had plans to buy as many sweet little dresses as possible.

Filling the shopping basket with as many baby items

I could find for our new little house guest, I clumsily bumped baskets with someone I had met long ago. Our meeting had been at Affinity's wake. Believa Beaushanks shopped only a few feet from where I stood and was on her way to the checkout counter as well. I hadn't seen her in a while and yet, I remembered enough to know that she didn't look this bad the last time I saw her. Her sallow complexion explained she had been ill, with severely chapped lips and chewed fingernails.

"Oh, excuse me."

"No, excuse me."

"Hey, I know you. I met you at my friend's funeral."

"Yeah, I'm Believa. Believa Beaushanks."

"It's been a while since I last saw you."

"Yeah, I haven't been feeling well," she whispered. Believa's cart overflowed with feminine products and nausea medications. Just as I turned to leave, an early pregnancy test kit caught my eye.

My blood thickened as my heart raced. It dawned on me why her skin looked the way it did. Immediately, I took notice of the infected looking bite marks on her neck, and knew without doubt, that Believa was the vampire consort of none other than Justice Treemount.

Acknowledgement of who she is must have registered on my face, because Believa hissed loudly as fangs cut through the swollen gums in her mouth.

Gripped by fear and stumbling backward, I braced for battle. Reaching up to throw the first punch, I was interrupted by an alarm that roared through the store. She and I both turned toward the public announcement system overhead. I blinked once and Believa disappeared before I could attack her.

"Attention! Attention! The National Weather Service has just issued a tornado Watch for the Bexar County area. This is the first in the states weather history for the San Antonio area. The tornadoes are results from Hurricane Auldicia listed as a category five and will hit land in the next two hours. This is not a test...repeat this is not a test!"

The Embellish Saga continues…

…sneak a peek at

Auldicia Rises

1

The Hunt Is On

Childress mocked the Loas Agwe and Guede when she savagely killed her Aunt Bureau, thus placing more evil upon her family. Killing a blood related a mambo, was punishable with eternal flesh burning in Hell. Arrogance and conceit was enough for her to take her chances with her soul.

Urgata agonized over her mother's death --- stunned at the fact that Childress would kill her mother without any regard. Urgata knew that there was no way Childress could have possibly known the fate that was to come her way for doing such a thing. Nayphous ran to comfort Urgata. He threw a hateful glance at Childress. This proved to be a bad move on his part.

"Childress, how could you kill your aunt like this? You have damned yourself."

"What the hell are you looking at, Nayphous? I'm going to find my child. Then I'm coming back here for you."

"I won't be here, so don't waste your time."

"Either you are with me or against me. Make the right choice."

"Like I said…don't waste your time."

Clearing pasty mucous from her throat, Childress spit in his face, and then stormed off. With power rolling through her veins, she barked out orders to assemble her brothers.

"Klein and Erland, let's go."

Urgata finally found her tongue to speak to the cousin she hated fiercely.

"Childress the gods are going to come for you soon, and I'll be there to see to it that you suffer for what you've done. I promise you."

Reveling in her new power, Childress allowed the hatred she had for Solis, Justice, and now for Urgata to drive her motive. Raising her hands to the sky Childress whispered a hex that made all of the on-lookers fall to their knees in fear.

"I am the Queen Mother. As the wind blows and the rain washes the earth, I will destroy my enemies—starting with my brother Justice. He will be punished to death."

Childress turned and looked at Urgata and allowed her lips to turn in a wicked smile as she hexed her cousin.

"You have spoken your last words, my dear cousin, I hope you enjoyed them. You will speak no more."

Nayphous looked at Urgata as she stood before him terror stricken with no sound coming from her mouth. Childress had muted her voice, rendering her unable to speak.

Childress laughed as Mother Nature threw a lightning bolt across the sky hit a tree, causing in it to slam into the gothic looking house as it stood by the swamp. A fierce wind split the sky, peeling the clouds back that formed in the night horizon--- pouring torrential rains over the land. Black magic was the source of this storm and all that stood in it were in grave danger.

Knowing that she wanted her brother Justice and Solis dead and to reunite with her daughter, she set out on her new mission.

"Let's go fools. I want my baby back."

www.ingramcontent.com/pod-product-compliance
Ingram Content Group UK Ltd.
Pitfield, Milton Keynes, MK11 3LW, UK
UKHW041843190726
13854UKWH00002B/684

9 780578 063140